Broken Faith

James Green

Chapter One

A golden sun, a blue sky. A perfect summer day.

Wasted here of course.

This wasn't tourist Rome; it had no ancient glories like the Forum or the Coliseum, no wedding-cake grandeur like the Victor Emmanuel Monument, no film-fuelled romance like the Trevi fountain.

These towers of glass, concrete and steel weren't places of pilgrimage like St Peter's, unless, of course, you worshipped money.

This was where the business of Rome got done, and it could have been Canary Wharf, La Défense or Wall Street, except for the Roman sun bouncing off the concrete and glass.

A man was standing on the pavement, shading his eyes as he looked up.

He was middle-aged, of medium height, with a lived-in face and short grizzled hair. His casual summer clothes were well cared for and good quality, but he still managed to achieve a distinctly crumpled look. He carried no camera, map or guide book, so he wasn't a stray tourist, but nor did he look like someone who belonged in any of these offices.

But there he was, looking.

Jimmy Costello lowered his hand. The tall office block was like all the others and nothing, he thought, could look less like the home of a venerable institute of learning founded in the seventeenth century. But the top two floors of the block he was looking at was home to the small staff of the Collegio Principe. It was here that they lived and worked and had their being.

The Collegio Principe's life began as a bequest in the will of Cesare Borgia and had originally been housed in a minor Palazzo close to the Vatican. In those days it was a semi-religious institution staffed by Dominicans and Franciscans. Cesare had endowed the Collegio with farmland on the outskirts of Rome which would provide the income to support the friars and fund their work. That ancient farmland now was the site of this business suburb, home to bankers, brokers and financial wheeler-dealers of all types and sizes. And on the top of one of its towers of commerce were the offices of that one, small, ancient institute of learning and research.

The old Palazzo close to the Vatican still existed, now an exclusive hotel catering to the rich and discerning, but its lease remained the property of the Collegio and the annual rental reflected its enviable position. Whatever problems beset the Collegio's staff, lack of money was not one of them. The envy of many other academic institutions, they didn't have to worry about funding while they carried out their founder's wishes, to study the relationship between religion, politics and power.

Jimmy smiled to himself as he set off towards the entrance. The place suited Professor McBride, because what you saw with her was definitely not what you got either. He crossed the road, left the summer heat and went into the cool, air-conditioned reception.

'James Costello to see Professor McBride, Collegio Principe.'

The pretty girl behind the desk checked a screen then picked up a phone.

'Signor Costello to see you, Professore.' She put the phone down and made a visitor's badge for him while he signed in. Jimmy took the badge, slipped the cord over his head and put the plastic identification into his shirt pocket.

The pretty girl smiled at him. 'Please go up. You know the way?'

Jimmy nodded. He knew the way.

He went to the lift and pressed the button for the top floor where he got out and walked along the empty, carpeted corridor until he came to a door. He stopped and knocked.

'Come in.'

The voice was American.

The office was oddly furnished, a heavy, old-fashioned darkwood desk with brass-handled drawers down either side and an ink-stained, inlaid-leather top dominated the centre. Along one wall was a set of ultra-modern cabinets which might have contained anything from drinks to state secrets. On one wall hung a large abstract painting in a severe, chrome frame. On the opposite wall hung a small, dark oil-painting in an ornate gold frame. The carpet was pale blue and might to have been chosen to draw into the office the view from the big window, which looked south towards the distant, blue hills of Frascati. No phone, no computer, no paperwork, and no books: there was nothing to show that anything happened in this room. But the woman sitting behind the desk looked strangely at home there.

'Please sit down.'

She was like she always was, smart in a black office skirt and ice-white shirt that emphasized the blackness of her skin. Jimmy sat down.

'It is a small thing but it may be important. I want you to go to Santander in Spain and talk to an Englishman who lives there, a Mr Arthur Jarvis. You are to see if you think there is any truth in the information he passed on to Fr Perez, a local retired priest.'

She stopped. Jimmy waited. Nothing more came.

'And how am I supposed to do that?'

'By questioning him.'

5

'About what?'

'About –'

'I know, the information he gave to Fr Perez. What information?'

Jimmy waited. She was always like this. Getting a straight answer out of her was like trying to pull teeth with your fingers. You were lucky if you could get any kind of grip on what she was actually up to.

'It is very sensitive.'

'Like a bad tooth.'

She raised her eyebrows. For her that was a big response.

'I beg your pardon?'

'Granted.'

The eyebrows returned to ground level.

'I sometimes wonder if your help will really be worth having if I have to suffer your sense of humour alongside it. It makes me ask myself if it was a mistake to bring you out of Denmark.'

He accepted the rebuke. She was quite right, he owed her. Without her help he'd probably be dead or doing life in a Danish prison.

'All right, let's hear it.'

'As I said, it is a sensitive matter. Badly handled it could become serious.'

'And we wouldn't want that, would we?' She looked at him. 'Sorry, carry on.'

He listened in silence while Professor McBride told him why he was going to Santander to talk to a man named Arthur Jarvis. When she had finished he agreed with her that yes, it was sensitive, and that if he ballsed it up it could indeed become serious, very bloody serious. He left the office and went back down to Reception, handed over his visitor's pass, and was signed out.

Outside, the day seemed even hotter than when he had arrived, but that may have been because inside it was eternally set to American hotel comfort levels. He headed back to the nearest Metro station, half an hour's walk away with nowhere to rest or shelter from the sun.

He was hot and tired, with the beginnings of a headache, when he finally went down into the comparative cool of the Metro. He was out of the sun but with an hour's journey still ahead of him. It was days like this, he thought, when he regretted not owning a car. But as he cooled down, the headache left him and he felt better, and he knew that a car would be as useless to him in Rome as it would have been when he lived and worked in London. In London the traffic had been a nightmare; in Rome it was a horror story. The Metro wasn't crowded, the morning rush was well over and he was able to sit and relax as the train clattered its way to central Rome. He changed lines at Termini which was, as always, busy and noisy, and by the time he came out of the Metro at his home station, Lepanto, he didn't mind the sun and enjoyed the walk on the shady side of the quiet, tree-lined streets. Soon he would be back in his apartment and could get himself a cold beer.

Jimmy lived in a smart residential district north of the Vatican. His apartment was on the top floor of a four-storey building which looked just like all the other four-storey buildings that lined either side of the street, except that beside his main entrance there was a small restaurant, the Café Mozart.

He went up the stairs, let himself in, went to the kitchen and poured himself a cold beer. While he sat drinking he thought about Santander. He wondered if it would be as hot there as it was in Rome. Probably. But it was by the sea and that meant you got breezes. His mind slipped back to memories of another seaside town, Eastbourne on the south coast, where he, Bernie and the kids had gone on summer holidays. There had been brisk early morning walks, and evening strolls when they'd watched the sun setting over the sea. He remembered how evenings and mornings could be chilly even if the days were warm. He decided it would be a good idea to take along a light jacket. Santander wasn't Eastbourne, he knew that, but an ingrained English caution about seaside summer weather told him it was always best to be prepared.

Chapter Two

The heat came at you from everywhere: it was in the glare
off the sea, it bounced off the pavements and roads, it
wrapped itself round you, and pressed itself against you.

At least that's how it seemed to Jimmy.

He was sitting at a table drinking a cold beer. The table
was one of about a dozen beside a grove of palms which
stood on a rectangle of hard sandy ground between the
main road and the sea-front walkway.

Each table had its own bright parasol, but the shade
from the trees and the parasols made no difference to the
heat. Jimmy picked up his beer, more to feel the cold of
the glass than for any enjoyment of thecontents. To his
old-fashioned, north London palate, the beer was too cold
to have any discernable taste. He glanced through the
palms at the buildings on the other side of the main road
and toyed with the idea of crossing over into one of the
many air-conditioned bars for his next beer, but he quickly
gave up on the idea. He wanted to watch the big, white
ferry coming in. He'd seen it, or one like it, leaving when
he'd come into Santander from the airport. It had cruised
out into the open water like some kind of liner, and he'd
found it hard to believe when the taxi driver told him it
was just one of the routine ferries that shuttled between
Santander and the UK.

He put down his glass and looked out to sea. The ferry
was still far away, quite small but slowly growing in size.
While he watched he tried to tell himself that he was better
off outside. If he'd sat in one of the bars he would have

nothing to do but stare at his glass or the other customers or look out at the traffic. Out here he could look around, at the beach, the sky, the sea, the strollers on the walkway, and he would feel any breeze that might come in off the water. Except that when he looked at the sea he could see the heat-haze hovering over the sparkling blue that was almost a flat calm.

There was no breeze coming, not from the sea, not from anywhere.

He took out his handkerchief and wiped the sweat from his forehead, then gave his sunglasses a polish. He put them back on and looked at the crowded beach which lay just beyond the wide, paved walkway between the tables and the sand. All that bare flesh gently roasting.Thousands of otherwise sensible people paid good money to sit and lie in the burning Spanish sun and called it a holiday. He picked up his beer and took a drink. It wasn't quite so cold any more.

A young woman in sunglasses, wearing a white blouse and dark skirt, stepped off the walkway and came to his table, pulled out a chair and sat down.

'Good afternoon.'

Jimmy looked at his visitor.

'Do I know you?'

'No, but I know you. You are Mr James Cornelius Costello.'

A copper.

Only a copper would use his full name because only the police would have bothered to find out what it was.

'OK, so I'm James Costello. And you are?'

'Detective Inspector Suarez from the Santander police.'

She took out her ID and passed it to Jimmy who took it, looked and passed it back. She was a good-looking blonde and spoke English with only a slight Spanish accent.

'Is there something I can do for you, Inspector?'

'Yes, there is. I would like you to leave Santander. In

fact my superiors, who asked me to come and talk to you, would be happy if I could persuade you to leave Spain altogether.'

Jimmy took a drink of his beer. It reminded him of the bottled stuff he drank in Rome. It was OK, but it wasn't like a decent London pint. He missed London beer, especially Directors and London Pride.

'Any special reason, or does somebody not like the way I look?'

The Inspector took off her sunglasses and looked. A middle-aged man in a short-sleeved shirt, with a face which betrayed nothing of what he might be thinking. She'd been told it was supposed to be a dangerous face, but there was something almost gentle, or even sad, about his eyes.

No, she thought, it wasn't the way he looked.

'I'm sure you don't really have to ask, Mr Costello.'

'Yes, I really do have to ask because I really do want to know.'

The waiter came to the table through the trees from the bar beyond them. The Inspector ordered a beer. Apparently she wasn't in any hurry to go.

'You were a policeman in London. You left the police suddenly and disappeared. As far as we can gather it had to do with a gangland killing but it's hard to find out anything because nobody seems to want to talk about you, not even to another police force. After some years you returned to London, apparently doing some sort of work in a refuge. Two murders occurred, both connected with the place you were working. Again you disappeared and again no one wants to talk about it. Then, last year, you turned up in Copenhagen. More trouble and again you left, this time for Rome in the company of a Monsignor who –' the Inspector paused to give him what Jimmy's mum would have called an old-fashioned look, '– claimed you were carrying a Vatican diplomatic passport.'

11

Jimmy shrugged.

'I resigned, the hours didn't suit.'

'Just after you left Copenhagen an Englishwoman was arrested for the murder of her husband. When arrested she made the bizarre claim of self-defence, that he intended to kill her. When questioned your name cropped up in connection with an incident in Lübeck. That incident turned out to involve two dead bodies. That's a long list of dead people, Mr Costello.' The waiter arrived with her beer, put it down and left. 'By all means correct me if any of what I have said is wrong.'

'Even if what you say is right I'm not wanted by any police force that I know of.'

'No, Mr Costello, you're not wanted, certainly not by the Santander police. That's what I came to tell you, remember?'

'Very clever, but what I meant was, no warrants were ever issued against me.'

'No, that's correct. You're not on any list that we know of. We checked.'

'Then why the big interest? None of that stuff would be anything to do with the Spanish police, if any of it was true, of course.'

'It's true, Mr Costello, we both know that, so let's not play games. Bad things happen around you, people die. Now you've turned up in Santander and, like I said, my superiors want you to leave. Your name comes first on their not-wanted list. They sent me to tell you. Unfortunately, as you say, you have done nothing that I can use to make you leave, but I have given you the message and hope you'll have the sense to act on it My advice, my very strong advice, would be to leave and leave soon.'

'If your bosses want me to go, why not try asking me instead of threatening me?'

'And if I asked you, would you leave?'

12

'That would depend on how you asked.'

'How would you suggest I should ask?'

'With a gun in your hand, a finger on the trigger and in a voice which made me believe you'd use it.'

'And if I did it that way would you leave?'

'Oh, yes, I'd leave. Either that or, if I also had a gun, I'd blow your fucking brains out.'

She took a drink of her beer. If she was at all offended she didn't show it.

'Why are you here, Mr Costello? What brings you to Santander?'

'I'm taking a holiday. If all you say about me is true I think I must need one. Think of me as just another tourist bringing my much-needed euros into the local economy.'

'That's a lie, Mr Costello.'

'But you can't prove it's a lie, can you?' Jimmy finished what was left of his beer. It was almost warm now. His manner and tone changed. He wasn't here to get into trouble with the local police so why try to needle anybody? 'I'm here to collect some information.'

'Who for?'

'My boss.'

'And who is your boss?'

'Someone in Rome. A senior academic at a college.'

'Does he have a name?'

'Doesn't everybody?'

'If you are deliberately uncooperative, Mr Costello, I must assume you have something to hide from the police, that your reasons for being here are not ones that the police would approve of. They might perhaps even be criminal.'

'Assume what you like. If you want me to tell you anything about why I'm here you'll have to wait until I get clearance to talk to you.'

'I could arrest you, Mr Costello. We could talk at the police station.'

Jimmy tried a smile, it almost worked.

'No need to get tough, Inspector, it doesn't suit you.'

He got a smile back.

'Don't let appearances give you the wrong impression.'

Jimmy believed her. She wasn't big, but she was solid enough and looked to be in good shape. In fact, her shape looked very good. He wondered if she was trained in some sort of martial art. These days the muscle end of things was probably all scientific and factored into the training manual, it wouldn't be just using your fists and your boots in a cell any more.

'Arresting me would probably mean involving politicians. I'm not official but the information, if and when I get it, will be passed on and when it gets where it's going it will become official. If I get kicked out before I get my information then questions will get asked. Do you want to get the politicians involved?'

She took another drink.

'No, they are not usually helpful.'

'Then why don't you just sit back and drink your beer before it gets warm and let me make a call and then we'll see if I can co-operate?' She didn't answer, she put her sunglasses back on, picked up her beer and looked out to sea. Jimmy waited a moment. 'Make your call, Mr Costello.'

Jimmy pulled out his mobile. The woman carried on looking out to sea pretending she wasn't there and that she wasn't listening.

Jimmy put the number in then held the mobile to his ear.

'I need to speak to Professor McBride. Yes it's important, at least, it's important if my being here is important. Personally I don't give a shit one way or the other.' Somebody at the other end took offence. 'I know, I've been told before, I grieve over them at night. Look, just pass on the message. I'll give McBride half an hour to get back to me then I'll use my own judgement.'

14

He put the mobile down on the table. The woman returned to those present.

'I don't have half an hour.'

'If I'm right you won't need it. I'll get a call. Why not get me another beer while we're waiting?'

The suggestion got him another smile.

'I thought the man did the buying on a first date.'

Jimmy smiled back and he didn't have to make an effort this time. He liked her.

'No, you can't have it both ways. Either you're a tough guy in a bra and you buy the drinks, or you're a good-looking blonde chatting me up and I buy the drinks. It's your choice.'

She took off her sunglasses. This time Jimmy looked at her eyes. They were dark and she had a dark complexion so maybe her blonde hair came out of a bottle. It wasn't something he knew much about, but that was his guess. She raised a hand to a waiter who was clearing a nearby table. He came across and she ordered a beer. Then she put her sunglasses on again and looked out at the sea. It was still there. When the beer came the waiter put it down in front of her. She picked it up and passed it to Jimmy.

'You not having another?'

'No.'

Jimmy drank his beer and they both sat in silence. Then his phone rang.

'I'm sitting at a table outside a bar looking at the sea and having a beer with a local police Inspector who knows my life story and says her bosses want me tarred and feathered and run out of town and out of Spain. How should I know, maybe they object to my aftershave? There's been a lot of checking up on me and my friend here says they don't like what they know about my past, at least that's the reason they're telling me. Yes, I know it could be true, but then again, maybe it isn't. If they've checked as thoroughly as they seem to have done then either they've been taking a close look at me for a long time or someone's been feeding them information. It also means they knew I was coming. How should I know who told them?' He took the phone away from his ear. 'Who told you I was coming?' Suarez stayed silent so he put the phone back to his ear. 'No, she didn't. I didn't think she would. So, what do you want me to do? Leave, tell them why I'm here, what?.' Jimmy listened for a moment. 'OK, just as you say.' Then he put the mobile away. 'I'm here to talk to a Mr Arthur Jarvis. He's English and retired here about three years ago.'

The sunglasses came off again. He wasn't sure whether they annoyed her or she meant it to annoy him. Maybe it was just a habit. And when she spoke the tone of her voice changed, whatever she had been doing, she definitely wasn't chatting him up now.

'I'm sorry, Mr Costello, but you can't talk to Mr Jarvis.'

'It's a Church matter. A Catholic Church matter. As far as I know it is nothing to do with the Spanish authorities, certainly not the police.'

That was a black lie, of course, but she wouldn't know that.

'You're wrong. It is very much a matter for the authorities, especially the police. Mr Jarvis died two days ago.'

'Died? How?'

'A single shot to the head.'

That got all his attention. That, he had not expected.

'Suicide?'

'Suicides don't usually shoot themselves in the back of the head and then hide the gun so, no, I don't think suicide. Do you see now why we want you out of Spain? Your arrival coincides with a dead body, a resident Englishman. Like I said, bad thing keep happening around you, Mr Costello, and I'm Spanish which makes me a deeply

16

superstitious person. Also I don't believe in co-incidences.'

'When did he die?'

'The day before yesterday.'

'What time?'

'Shortly before eleven o'clock in the morning.'

Jimmy shrugged. That let him out.

'I flew in two days ago, but I didn't land until shortly after 10.45, so I don't see that I had time to have anything to do with it. Maybe I'm just a coincidence after all. They do happen.'

'No, Mr Costello, I cannot bring myself to believe you are a coincidence. Jarvis was killed for no obvious reason. There was no break-in. Nothing so far as we know was taken. There was quite a bit of money in a drawer of his bedside table. Nobody seems to have searched the house, nothing was disturbed. He lived quietly and there had been no trouble of any sort. If he had any enemies locally nobody knew about them. What we do have is that you come to Santander, and on the day you arrive Jarvis gets a bullet in the back of his head. Added to that, on being questioned, you admit to coming here to see him. You were once a policeman, a detective, wouldn't you say there was a connection?'

Jimmy shrugged. OK, he'd say there was a connection , but he certainly wouldn't say it out loud, especially not when he was being questioned by the police about a murder.

'I see now why my superiors were concerned at your presence.' Suarez continued.

'No, that won't work any more.'

'No?'

'Well, if you think I'm involved with a killing, shouldn't I be kept here and properly questioned, not kicked out? When I was a detective we followed up on things like that.'

17

'You are a foreign national with what I think are important friends in Rome, and I have my orders. Unless they change I will follow them. Santander is a nice town, Mr Costello, a resort, a place people come to enjoy themselves and have a good time. It's bad for us here when someone, a foreign national like yourself, gets brutally murdered. It upsets people. It upsets me. If the choice was mine I would indeed make you tell me what the connection was. Even if I had to beat it out of you in a police cell.'

Jimmy looked down at his glass. Maybe that side of things hadn't changed so much after all. He looked up at her again and guessed she would be good at it too. Certainly she looked as if that was what she wanted to do right at this minute. He understood the feeling. She'd just had a suspect for a fresh murder dropped into her lap and it looked like she might have to pass it by. But her difficulty was his as well. He didn't want to stay and maybe get put in the frame for a murder, but he didn't want to get kicked out either.

'But the point is, I *am* a foreign national. And, as you say, I have friends in Rome, so I'm afraid hammering the shit out of me might cause eyebrows to be raised. It might even get questions asked out of our Embassy, you know how they like things kept official and orderly. If you'd like to put me alongside anything that happened to Jarvis you'll have to do it the hard way, by police work.'

The Inspector stood up. The sunglasses were back on and there would be no more smiles.

'It cuts both ways. I can ask our Embassy people to make you persona-non-grata and then you'd have to leave. The information we already have on you even without Jarvis's death would be enough to get you kicked out in short order without any help from police work. What do you think of that, Mr Costello?'

'I think you speak very good English, Inspector.' She

18

began to leave. Jimmy called after her. 'Inspector.' She stopped and turned. 'Come back here at three this afternoon. If I can help you, I will, but you'll have to give me a couple of hours to make a few calls and check a few things.'

Inspector Suarez paused and thought about it. She still had her orders, but she was also a copper with a solid suspect.

'OK, Mr Costello. Make your calls and I'll be back at three. But be packed and ready to leave just in case.'

'I'll have a beer ready for you. I'll buy, it'll be our second date.'

The inspector turned and walked away through the trees to the road. A black SEAT pulled up. She got in beside the driver and the car drove off. Jimmy watched it go. He liked the inspector, they would be able to work together – if he got the OK from McBride, and if she could persuade her bosses to let him stay. He had a drink from his glass then took out his mobile and made his first call.

Chapter Three

Inspector Suarez was punctual to the minute. Jimmy watched the black SEAT pull up behind the palm trees where it had picked her up. She got out, said something to the driver, then closed the door and the car pulled away. Jimmy turned back and looked out to sea where the big white ferry was imperceptibly shrinking in size as it moved away from the shore and headed back towards the horizon, and England. England, almost a foreign country now, although he had once called it his own. Did he miss it? He wasn't sure. Would he ever go back? Probably not.

Suarez walked through the trees to his table and Jimmy pulled his attention away from the ferry. This meeting was business, the ferry-watching was just nostalgia. Suarez sat down, took off her sunglasses and put them into the neat, black handbag on a long strap which hung from her shoulder. Thank God, he thought, no more pissing around with sunglasses.

It was, if anything, hotter than when they had first met, but she still looked the same, the heat didn't seem to affect her. Crisp white shirt, black skirt, high heels, fresh as dew on a morning lawn. A cool blonde. Someone in control. She hung her handbag over the back of her chair, sat down and looked at the table, then at Jimmy.

'No drinks? I thought you were buying,' she gave him a false smile, 'to celebrate our second date, remember?'

It was a good beginning. Jimmy hoped it would last after what he was going to tell her.

'I told the waiter to bring them when you arrived. In

weather like this I thought you'd prefer your beer cold.'

The smile became genuine and she sat back.

'Weather like this isn't weather like this. When it gets really hot it's what we call weather like this.'

Better and better, thought Jimmy, or was she just a very clever copper? But he decided he didn't care. He liked her.

'You should have told me that before, it might have saved us both some time and effort. If I thought it could get any hotter than it is already I'd have been happy to leave.'

She was in no hurry, she was prepared to shoot the breeze for a time.

'What's the matter? Have you got something against sunshine?'

'Not in moderation, I'm a great believer in moderation.'

'Like not killing more than a couple of people at any one given time? That kind of moderation?'

The waiter came to the table with their beers. Jimmy let what she'd said pass. He'd made his calls, she was here to listen and it was time to get down to business, so he took a drink and began to talk.

'I was sent to see Jarvis about something he told a local priest, a Fr Xavier Perez. Fr Perez is retired now but it seems Jarvis had struck up an acquaintance with him when he first came out here looking at property and Fr Perez was still a local parish priest He used to go to Mass at Fr Perez's church. I was told that when Jarvis came out here to live, they became friends, and when the priest retired Jarvis used to visit him. On his last visit Jarvis said that he had stumbled across some information, information that was both serious and dangerous. A very senior Catholic cleric in the Basque region was an inner member of the ETA Army Council, actively involved in strategy and policy.' Jimmy could see from her eyes that he had her full attention. That would have popped your sunglasses off, he thought, pity you put them away. 'Jarvis told Perez he was frightened, said he didn't know what to do. For some reason he refused to go to the authorities, also he wouldn't tell Perez how he came by the information. Jarvis wanted Perez to arrange for him to talk to someone from the Catholic Church, someone who could advise him. The priest said he'd see what he could do. He wrote the whole thing down and sent it to the Bishop's secretary who must have passed the letter on to the Bishop who in turn sent it to Rome. Once there it was passed on to my boss, who was told to send someone reliable to talk to Jarvis and find out what, if anything, was going on.'

'They took it seriously?'

Jimmy gave a slight shrug.

'Seriously enough to follow it up. How seriously that is I couldn't say. I was told to come and check, see if it was anything more than an ageing, British ex-pat going gaga in the heat and imagining things.'

'I see.' Suarez took a slow drink and looked out to sea. Jimmy waited, he'd given her what he had and now it was up to her. She put down her glass, looked at him and gave a small shake of her head. 'No, it's crap, it doesn't work. No one would believe that some English nobody, an ex-pat, a newcomer, had really managed to find out anything about ETA, never mind that there was a senior Catholic cleric at the heart of a major terrorist organisation. How could he?' Jimmy could see her mind was made up. She took another drink but ignored the sea this time. 'No, it's all wrong, and you know it's all wrong.'

'That's right. It has to be baloney.'

'Which brings us back to why you are here.'

'Perez, in his letter to the Bishop, said there was something about Jarvis which made him almost believe what he was saying. In his opinion Jarvis was genuinely frightened, he wasn't putting on an act. The priest said he couldn't believe that Jarvis had indeed found what he claimed, but that the man obviously believed it himself. The priest said he thought someone ought to do something. It wasn't much, but it got the Bishop to send it to Rome and that was enough to get me sent here and make discreet enquiries. As things have turned out I don't have to be discreet because now it's a murder case.' Jimmy sat back. 'I arrived two days ago. I didn't try to contact Jarvis or Perez because I wanted to look around and get a bit of a feel for the place. Today you turned up and told me Jarvis was dead.' He took a drink. 'And that's it, all of it. At least all that I have.'

'Meaning?'

'In my experience my boss is about as straight as a spiral-staircase. If I had to make a guess I'd say I've been put in to see what I can make run out, like a ferret down a rabbit hole. You understand ferrets and rabbit holes?'

'Yes, I understand ferrets.'

'And when it comes to telling me what's going on I tend to get the facts in such a way that I go in the direction my boss wants instead of the way I should be going.'

'Meaning what exactly?'

'Meaning what I've told you is what I've been told. How much of it you believe has to be up to you.'

He waited while Suarez thought it over.

'OK, Mr Costello, if your boss might be twisting the facts why do *you* think you were sent to talk to Jarvis? What's your opinion?'

Jimmy sat back and spread his hands.

'Me? I don't have an opinion. I got told what I got told. I came to Santander, found a hotel, looked around and got my bearings. I was told to be discreet so I wasn't about to rush in anywhere. I would have made contact with Jarvis or Perez tomorrow or the next day, but you popped up and told me the news. I didn't know what to expect when I got here, but I certainly didn't expect Jarvis murdered. Nor did I expect to find out that your lot had been digging into my

23

past.'

'But now that you do know, what's your opinion?'

'My opinion is that somebody in Rome tipped you off that I was coming and that same person told you where to look to find out all about me, but I have no idea why anyone should have done that. And that's it, all of it, what I know and any guesses I might make and none of it makes any sense. As to what I was supposed to get from Jarvis and Perez, I don't have an opinion.'

'So what are your instructions now? I assume this boss of yours gave you some.'

'I was told to stay and assist you in your enquiries. Fullest co-operation etc., etc.'

'And what if we don't want your co-operation?'

Jimmy expected the question, he'd been told to expect it. This was where any budding friendship took a nasty beating.

'Then you won't get it. I'll fly back to Rome and report to my boss that you didn't want any help. My boss will talk to whoever placed the job and say you didn't want any help. That person, whoever they are, will talk to someone in the Church down here and you'll find you'll get exactly what you want, no help. Every door the Catholic Church can close round here will be slammed in your face. I guess you would know better than me how many doors that would be and how it would affect this enquiry or any other they chose to get involved in.' He'd made his point, he'd delivered the threat, now he had to hold out the carrot. 'When I came I thought I was on a wild-goose chase. But Jarvis is dead, so I'd say I was wrong and whatever's going on is wild all right, but nothing to do with geese.'

Jimmy took another drink and then sat back. OK, that was that. That was the game-plan he'd been given and he'd used it. Now Suarez, had the ball so he'd have to wait and see what she did with it.

It didn't take her long to come to a decision.

'Do you have a contact number for this Fr Perez?'

Jimmy took out his mobile.

'Ready?'

Suarez collected her handbag, took her mobile out then nodded. She keyed in the numbers as Jimmy gave them to her and the phone got answered as if the person on the other end was expecting a call.

'Hello, Fr Perez? This is Inspector Suarez of the Santander police –' She listened for a moment and then put away her mobile. 'He says he has been instructed to refer all contacts or enquiries from the authorities to the Bishop's office. Under no circumstances was he to talk to anyone from the police about anything. All contacts are to be reported to the Bishop's office and all enquiries directed there to be dealt with.'

Jimmy gave her a smile.

'Then I guess you'll have to phone the Bishop's office.'

'Do you think it would it do any good?'

'Not if somebody had already anticipated your unwillingness to let me join in on this.' The smile became a grin, 'although I suppose I shouldn't say that. Maybe I'm supposed to refer all questions from the authorities as well.'

'Very funny.'

Jimmy switched of the grin.

'Or perhaps it's just Perez for the moment, but as I said, you'd have to phone the Bishop's office to find out one way or the other.' He waited while Suarez thought some more about it, then decided play-time was over. He'd more than made his point. 'Look, I need to be on the inside on this, my boss was very clear about that when we spoke. I can't tell you why because I didn't get told, just what to say and I said it.'

'And you don't know why he wants you on the inside?'

'No.'

'You didn't ask?'

'No.'

'Could you make a guess?'

'No.'

Now it was Suarez's turn to smile, but it wasn't a nice one.

'And that's your idea of help?'

'Look, if there might be even a remote chance of a terrorist tie-in, and that would be a very big if, your lot can go one of two ways. You can hand over the killing and all the information I've given you to whatever outfit here deals with terrorists, whoever is your Special Branch.'

'Or?'

'Or you can let it stay as a straightforward killing for the time being. If I'm allowed to tag along I can help you handle the Church side and see that you get off-the-record co-operation which is probably the only way you'll get full co-operation.' He could see she wasn't impressed so he tried again. 'If my boss in Rome wants me in as badly as I think, then why not ask for something to get me alongside?' That got a response. Now he had her interest. 'You want to know what this is all about, so make being told a condition for letting me keep in touch with whatever develops.' He could see Suarez was interested. 'Why not at least talk to your people about it? If my side can close doors they can open them as well. You need information and co-operation, my boss can see that you get both.'

Suarez still wasn't convinced, but the way Jimmy looked at it, unless Spanish policing was very different from what he had known in London, neither she nor her local superiors would want whoever was their equivalent of Special Branch taking the murder away from them. He put his hand round his cold glass. He didn't take a drink because it still didn't taste of anything, he just held the glass and waited. He'd shot his bolt as far as persuasion went and sometimes silence was the best argument.

Suarez gave the sea the once over again. Jimmy joined

her and noticed the ferry was much smaller, before very long it would have disappeared over the horizon. He carried on waiting. Suarez gave up on the sea and shuffled her drink on the table but didn't pick it up. Jimmy could feel the heat getting to him. He'd nearly forgotten it, but now it came back. He put his cold hand to his cheeks and forehead. It helped, but not much. God, it was hot, and she said it could get hotter. Suarez finally surfaced.

'OK. I'll make a call and try to find out who I should contact to see if we can get you attached to whoever's running the investigation, but I wouldn't hold out too much hope. I doubt that I'll get anywhere; what we know about you won't exactly help.'

'Sure, I understand, but don't place too much faith in what you got told about me.'

'No?'

'Think about it. I get sent here and your lot get told I'm coming. They also get told all about my past. Jarvis gets a bullet in the head the day I arrive but I don't know that so when we meet I volunteer the information that I'd come to see him. Quite a connection, and neatly arranged so that my involvement with Jarvis came directly from me, no third party needed. To arrange for all of that to happen must have taken a whole lot of effort, so I'd say someone was setting me up for something, wouldn't you?'

She smiled again. A nice one this time.

'That thought had crossed my mind.'

Thank God, thought Jimmy, she's got a brain as well as looks, maybe we can be friends after all.

'Maybe I'm your best way into what this Jarvis thing is about. If your lot don't let me co-operate in some way then I'll go back to Rome and you'll lose what might be the best lead you've got. Unless I'm wrong and you've already got some good leads?'

But Suarez wasn't friendly enough to give away free information, not yet.

27

'I'll see what my boss says. You wait here.'

She got up, slung her handbag over her shoulder, and walked out onto the walkway between the tables and the beach. She took out her mobile and Jimmy watched her make her call. There was quite a bit of talking and she did her share. Was she going to bat for him or was she just talking? When she'd finished she put her mobile away and came back to the table. Before she could sit down Jimmy stood up.

'Listen, do you mind if we sit inside? This heat's too much for me.'

'Sure, I would have suggested it but I thought you preferred it out here. You were out here last time I came.'

'Then, I didn't have anybody to talk to, so I sat out here to watch the ferry. It's not much but it's better than staring at your beer. And it wasn't so hot.'

Jimmy went to pick up his beer.

'Leave it. I'll get cold ones inside.'

'Thanks.'

And they walked together through the palms. Jimmy's head hurt with the heat but he wasn't bothered. The friendship hadn't taken so very much of a beating after all, nothing more than a little slapping around. No, on the whole he was well satisfied, even though his head did hurt.

Chapter Four

Inside the bar it was pleasantly cool.

'Better?'

Jimmy nodded, the pain in his head had already eased.

'How do you stand that heat each day?'

'The truth is that we don't usually get it as hot as this. Even some of the locals are suffering. You just picked a bad time to come if you don't like the heat.'

She called the waiter over and asked for two beers.

'Not in a hurry to dash off somewhere?'

'No, I have some time. My boss will see what he can do and get back to me. Until he does I've been told to sit on you.' The way she looked at him made Jimmy feel that she had chosen her words carefully and expected some sort of a reply, but he couldn't think of one. Charm, wit, an easy manner with women: these were not something he'd been blessed with, and suddenly that annoyed him. Suarez got things going again. 'What do you do in Rome?'

'Not much. I went there after the Copenhagen thing. My boss offered me a job, I didn't have anywhere else I wanted to go and nothing I wanted to do, so I got myself a flat and settled in. This is the first job I've been sent on.' He tried a smile. 'It doesn't seem to have started, well does it?'

Suarez ignored the question and the smile.

'Did this boss of yours get you out of the Copenhagen thing?'

'Yes.'

'Is it the Monsignor who said you worked for the

Vatican?'

Jimmy gave a short laugh. The idea of the Monsignor as his boss tickled him.

'No, it's not the Monsignor.'

'So who is this mysterious, all-powerful boss?'

'Professor McBride of the Collegio Principe.'

'Part of the Vatican?'

'No, not the Vatican. It's an independent college. They study things.'

'Like?'

'The relationship between, religion, politics and power. Don't ask me how they study it, I've no idea. They just study it.'

The waiter brought their beers and a silence fell for a few moments. Then her mobile rang. She took it out and answered it. She pushed her chair sideways so she wasn't looking at him while she was on the phone and crossed her legs.

Jimmy watched her as she talked. He liked the way she looked; he also realised that what he liked about the way she looked had very little to do with getting into a good working relationship. He felt confused. She was young enough to be his daughter. Why would he feel attracted to a total stranger he had only met twice, and a copper at that? She was still talking, not paying any attention to him. Jimmy told himself it was rubbish, there was no attraction. He couldn't feel anything for her, he was too old for that sort of thing. Unfortunately he had a sneaking suspicion he wasn't telling himself the whole truth.

Suarez finished her call and said something in Spanish to nobody in particular. Jimmy didn't need to have it translated because she looked like someone who had just got bad news. She put her phone away.

'Apparently I was wrong. I didn't need to get in touch with anyone about you.'

'No?'

'No, someone has already had a call from Rome, from a monsignor who said he was acting on behalf of a very powerful name. He requested, on behalf of the name, that you be allowed to stay here as an observer and be informed of the progress of the investigation into Jarvis's death. As the present investigating officer speaks no English I have been told to take over and provide you with all the information you require.'

'That's good isn't it? It means –'

'Would this Monsignor be the same one who pulled you out of Denmark?'

'I suppose so.'

'Well he seems to deliver messages for some very influential people.'

The look on her face showed Jimmy she was not a happy bunny. In fact it made it clear she was a very unhappy bunny.

'What's the matter? Why is that not good? I thought it was what we wanted?'

'It was what you and your boss in Rome wanted.'

'OK, it was what *I* wanted, but I still don't see why you think it's bad news.'

'This morning I was nothing but a messenger boy in all this. I speak good English so I got sent to tell you that we wanted you gone. The Jarvis case wasn't mine, it was nothing to do with me. Now I'm pushed in as investigating officer and a colleague gets pushed out, which means his nose will be out of joint.' But Jimmy wasn't really paying attention. He was thinking that whatever she was this morning, it wasn't a boy, not a messenger boy, not any sort of boy. But he kept his opinion to himself and let her carry on. 'Your boss must throw a pretty powerful punch. Who did you say he is?'

Jimmy pulled his mind back to the job in hand. But it wasn't easy. She was still sitting with her legs crossed.

'Professor Pauline McBride, the original American

Superwoman.'

Suarez uncrossed her legs, pulled her chair to the table and took a drink. Any anger in her voice was gone.

'A woman?'

'In a manner of speaking.'

'I'm surprised. I would have thought ...well, not a woman, not in Rome.'

'That's because you haven't seen her in action. You wouldn't be surprised if you knew her. She eats broken bottles for breakfast and makes human sacrifices at the full-moon. She makes Attila the Hun look like Goldilocks. And she does it all without getting even so much as a crease in her neat, white blouse. And no one ever sees her hands move.' He tried to get some humour into his voice. 'Sometimes they call her the Shadow.' But Suarez wasn't amused. Why was he trying to amuse her? Why was he trying to get her interest? He gave up and went back to work. 'So, I'm in?'

'Oh you're in all right, but just as an observer.'

'And you, how do I stand with you?'

'You've just dropped me into the shit with a lot of the people I work with. How do you think you stand with me?'

'You know what I mean. Are we going to work together on this?'

Suarez looked at him for a second trying to make up her mind.

'You tell me what you really think about it all and then I'll tell you how we stand.'

'Fair enough.' Jimmy marshalled his thoughts. He'd been a detective once, now he had to think like one again. 'A retired English guy tells an old priest friend something that, if true, is dynamite. Other people get told but no one takes it too seriously because the source is Jarvis and how would he come by that sort of information? But now Jarvis is in the morgue with a bullet in the head and you say it wasn't a break-in that went wrong or anything like that which means it was a cold-blooded killing. So perhaps he really did know something after all, or was involved in something, something that made it worthwhile for him to be killed. Let's look at what we've got, what we've been told by the priest, Perez.'

'That he knew something about ETA.'

'Yes.'

'But that has to be –'

'I know and I agree but let's look at it anyway. First, why tell the priest? Not because he was frightened. If he really was frightened, very frightened, he'd be more likely to tell nobody, to keep whatever it was to himself. But if for some reason he had to tell somebody then he would go to someone who could protect him, like the police. But what he actually did was go and tell an old priest. Why tell Perez? How could Perez help him if it was to do with ETA? And Perez certainly couldn't protect him if the terrorists got to hear about it.'

'OK, why do you think he told Perez?'

'The only reason I can think of is that Jarvis wanted what he knew passed on.'

'It makes some sort of sense, not much, but some.'

'And what is it that he wants passed on? I mean, so far as we know, what did he actually say, "I have this big secret about ETA, about their inner-council, and what I want you to do, Fr Perez, is tell somebody else that I have this really dangerous secret." It's madness. Once he's done it, Perez knows, plus whoever he decides to tell. Perez writes to the Bishop's secretary so now he knows, and so does anyone he might tell. Then the secretary tells the Bishop so he knows plus –'

'Yes, yes, I get the picture. By the time it gets to Rome a lot of people either know or could know. Not the best way to handle a secret that's dangerous enough to have you really scared and maybe killed.'

'Correct. At least three people at this end know the secret as well as Jarvis. These people have all been told that there's the possibility of a high-up Catholic cleric at the heart of the terrorist organisation ETA. Question one, how did it stay a secret and not get leaked to the media? Next, your lot get told that I'm coming here to look into something but you don't get told what it is I'm looking into. All you get told is where to go so you can put together a picture of me that will make you send me packing almost as soon as I arrive. You knew all about me this morning but you didn't know why I was here, I had to tell you that. So question two is, why were you told I was coming and that you should dig into my background? Next question, why was Jarvis killed on the day of my arrival? I'm like you, I don't believe in coincidences, so there has to be a connection. If there is then we ask the last question, what connects me to Jarvis?' Jimmy took a drink. 'OK so far?'

Suarez picked up her glass, took a slow drink, studied the glass for a moment then put it back down.

'So far, keep going.'

'Either somebody at this end is up to something, or somebody in Rome is, or both. Jarvis was part of it and it frightened him, if he really was scared like the priest says, which he probably was because, as it turns out, he was right to be frightened.'

'Because now he's dead.'

'Exactly, and it's been very carefully arranged to make it look like I'm part of whatever it is. So should I start being frightened? Is whoever topped Jarvis now going to come looking for me?'.

Suarez shrugged.

'Don't ask me, I only got given the case ten minutes ago.'

'I tell you one thing we do know for sure, the one thing this can't be about is a frightened bloke asking to talk to someone from the Catholic Church about ETA terrorist information he'd somehow picked up.'

'Agreed, so what is it you're saying? That Jarvis and Perez and all the rest didn't happen the way you were told?'

'No, I didn't say that. It may have happened that way. Remember, I told you that when my boss gives you the facts she makes them point the way she wants you to go. I know, she's done it before and believe me she's good at it.'

'So what about your boss as the one who's organising it, whatever it is?'

'Because she doesn't arrange for people to get killed.'

'Sure?'

Jimmy nodded.

'Yes, sure. She's on the side of the angels, she's just a bit rough in her methods sometimes. Which leaves us with, Jarvis was killed because he was involved in something going on here, and the way he died makes it something criminal. But that stymies any connection with me because I have no connection with Jarvis or Santander, criminal or otherwise. And that leaves us with just one option, that Jarvis's death and my arrival were one hell of a coincidence. And that won't work because neither of us likes coincidences.'

Suarez looked at Jimmy's glass. It was empty.

'Another?'

'Why not, I'm doing most of the talking.'

Suarez summoned a waiter and ordered another beer.

'You worked all that out since we last met this morning?'

'It wasn't hard. It was all there, you just had to think about it.'

Suarez took a slow drink of her beer. Then put it down and looked at it for a second. The glass was almost empty. She looked like she was deciding whether to have another.

Jimmy waited, he didn't think it wasn't such a big decision, but it was her decision so he waited. Then Suarez looked up at him.

'OK, Mr Costello, we'll work together, not just make it look like we're working together.'

'Good, and it's Jimmy if we're working together.'

'I'm Seraphina.'

She leaned across the table and they shook hands.

'Nice to meet you, Seraphina.'

'And you, Jimmy, nice to meet you.'

The beer came, Suarez didn't ask for another.

'So, Jimmy, if we're going to work together tell me a little about yourself.'

'You know plenty already.'

'True, but tell me something I don't know.'

'I was born and raised in London, was a copper, retired, thought about becoming a priest, changed my mind, and now I work for Attila the Hun's big sister.'

'Brief but not very helpful. What rank did you make?'

'Detective Sergeant.'

'Never married?'

'Yes, but she died.'

'I'm sorry.'

'Why? You didn't kill her, cancer did.'

'I'm still sorry. Family?'

'A son, he died as well, in Africa, some nasty local bug. There's a daughter and two grandchildren in Australia. One day I might even see them.'

Suarez waited a moment to give Jimmy time to put away what she could see were old, painful thoughts. It explained the sad eyes, she thought.

'Do you want to know anything about me?'

'No.'

That got a smile. He liked her smile.

'OK, Jimmy, when you've finished your drink we'll take a walk and I'll bring you up to date as far as I can which won't be very far. I only know what I read in papers, saw on TV and what I got told. You know, police gossip.'

'Fine. It'll be somewhere to start.'

So they sat in silence while Jimmy drank his beer, each thinking their own private thoughts. Suarez was thinking about Jimmy and Jimmy was thinking about Jimmy. It had turned into one of those afternoons for thinking about Jimmy.

Chapter Five

Today it was a lemon yellow shirt and fawn slacks but the same black handbag. Suarez had worn a different outfit each day and she'd looked good in all of them.

'What do you think?'

For a moment Jimmy thought she was asking him about her outfit. Then he realised she was asking him about the house they were in. He dragged his mind away from the way she looked to the room they were sitting in, a small living room.

'It's great. Thanks for getting it for me.'

'No problem. Your own place is better than a hotel room if you're going to be here for a while and it was empty for a fortnight, the next let isn't for two weeks. After that we'll sort something else out. And don't worry about the money, my cousin will give you a good price.'

'Tell your cousin he can charge the full rental. I won't be the one paying.'

'In that case I'm doing you both a favour, he lets the house, you get somewhere comfortable to stay, and everybody's happy.'

'I'm surprised it's not occupied at this time of year. The town looks busy, plenty of tourists.'

'Not as busy as it used to be. Maybe the best days are over. People want exotic, to go to places like Thailand. Money's tight all round. It's hard to find anything that pays well these days.'

'There's always crime.'

Suarez laughed.

'Too true, Jimmy, there's always money in crime.'

The neat little house was in a quiet street a short walk from the sea front, one of a terrace of identical fronts differentiated by the bright colours they were painted. The front door opened onto the street but it had a small back yard where there was a table with a parasol, chairs and, of course, the inevitable barbecue. Suarez had suggested it and then arranged things with her cousin. As it was a holiday property he'd been able to move straight in. Now, after twenty-four hours of residence he felt at home.

Jimmy threw the folder he'd been reading on to the coffee table between them. It was an English translation of the Jarvis autopsy made for the files of the British Embassy, a small courtesy when one of your nationals has part of his head blown off. Suarez had dropped it off on her way to work and said she'd be back to go through it with him in an hour. He'd gone through it carefully twice, once after she had left and again now before just before she came back.

He wanted to let her see what a thorough job he could do. He wanted to impress her. She was sitting opposite waiting to be impressed.

'You want a coffee or anything?' Suarez shook her head. Jimmy picked up the last piece of bread and apricot preserve from his plate and ate it, then finished his coffee. Breakfast was over. Now it was time to go to work. 'As far as I can see, apart from a bullet in the head there's nothing. It went in at the back at the base of the skull and exited through his forehead and blew off most of the top part of the front of his head. What calibre, it doesn't say in the file?'

'Nine millimetre. Ordinary parabellum bullet.'

'How tall was Jarvis?'

'One metre eighty-two, just under six feet. Like you say, the bullet went in at the back low and came out at about the hair line and hit the kitchen wall at two metres twenty-seven.'

'So the killer was shorter than Jarvis?'

'Possibly, or held the gun to make it look like he or she was shorter, or knew how to make sure the bullet did the maximum damage.'

'Well it all looks very professional, burn marks round the entry point so up close and certain. There's nothing else from the scene of crime report?'

'If you mean forensic, no, nothing worthwhile. It wasn't any kind of robbery, just clean and certain. There was plenty of money in a drawer in the bedside table together with a passport and an airline ticket to Paris for the day after he was killed. Nothing was touched or taken so far as we can see.'

'Was there a return ticket?'

'No and no sign of any hotel reservations.'

'What do you think the trip to Paris was about?'

Suarez gave a slight shrug.

'Could be anything, a break, meeting somebody, how could we tell? All we have is the ticket, the passport and the money.'

She was right, unless there was a good reason it wasn't worth following and he couldn't come up with any good reason. Jarvis was going to Paris. Lots of people went to Paris. He left it alone.

'He was found in the kitchen and there was no sign of any struggle?'

'In the kitchen and no struggle.'

'Then he must have known whoever it was. He went into the kitchen to make coffee or something, the killer followed and did what he did. Was there any sign of a clean up?'

'No, and no evidence of a visitor but that doesn't mean there wasn't one. According to the case notes nobody saw anything or heard anything.'

Jimmy stood up and picked up his breakfast things. He

continued talking as he headed for the only other downstairs room, the small dining kitchen.

'Mid-morning, is that a quiet time where Jarvis lived?'

Suarez had followed him. She stood in the doorway with her arms crossed, leaning against the woodwork while Jimmy took his mug and plate to the sink.

'It's residential, out of town, it's always quiet but at mid-morning I guess anyone who was going out, to work, to shop, to go to the beach, would have already gone. I'd say it would be a quiet time.'

Jimmy put his things down beside the sink and turned round.

'But the killer couldn't be sure there'd be no one around to hear a shot. A gun makes a big noise, the sort of noise that gets noticed. Or maybe there was a silencer?'

Suarez shook her head.

'No, you wouldn't get those kind of burn marks with a silencer.'

'That's right.'

'It's a pity though. A silencer would make it definitely professional. As it is we have clean but noisy, which could make it a lucky amateur.' Jimmy walked away from the sink. Suarez looked past him 'You not going to wash up?'

'Later.'

'Men, always put things off.'

He gave her outfit a look.

'And women, always putting things on.' She gave a small laugh and made way as Jimmy walked past her. She smelled as nice as she looked if you got up close. Jimmy thought it would be nice to get up even closer. But that wasn't why she was there, so he went back to the coffee table, sat down and pulled his shoes towards him. 'So there's nothing for us to go on at the scene. Nothing in the house and no witnesses who heard anything or saw anything.'

Suarez came and stood beside his chair. She shook her

41

head.

'Except anything we get out of his computer.'

Jimmy finished pulling on his shoes.

'How's that going? Got into it yet?'

'We'll soon be there. The boys we've got on it think they'll find porn. The security is good, but, like the killing, not quite professional. If it is porn that gives us something to work with.'

'It's possible. If it's nasty enough and there's others involved it might lead to a killing.' He sat back. 'What I still don't understand is, why bring in ETA? Jarvis couldn't have any ETA connection. It doesn't make any sense.'

Suarez sat down.

'I've been going over that and I think it was because of you.'

'Me!'

'Think about it. You arrived and we were waiting. There had to be a reason for that and one reason could be that when you told us there was a possible terrorist tie-in, no matter how unlikely, we couldn't ignore it. We would have to get involved and check it all out. That would mean that somebody wanted the police to get involved in what you were here for.'

Jimmy did as she'd asked, he thought about it. It made some sense, not a lot, but more than anything else they had.

'Did you find out who gave you the tip about me?'

'Your boss, Professor McBride.' Now why am I not surprised, thought Jimmy, as Suarez went on. 'If I'm right, then McBride knew Jarvis was going to die, which means she had it done or knew who was going to have it done.'

What she was saying sounded right, and with anyone else in the frame he would have agreed, but he was still sure McBride didn't kill people or have them killed. He tried it out his way.

'Maybe she knew someone was going to gun Jarvis but couldn't stop it so she sent me and tipped you off and then –'

'Stop it, Jimmy. You're going up a blind alley. If she knew anything, either about the ETA thing or that Jarvis was a target, why play complicated games? Why not just tell us direct?'

'Good question, I wish I had a good answer.'

'Then ask her. Now you know it was her, just ask her.'

Jimmy didn't like it. It was the right thing to do, the obvious thing, he could see that, but he still didn't like it so he stalled.

'Where does that get us?'

'It gets us the answer.'

'No. It gets us *an* answer.'

'I see, she'd just lie. I thought you said she was on the side of the angels.'

'She wouldn't see it as a lie. It would be true in a way – '

Suarez said something in Spanish and got up.

'This is ridiculous. This isn't police work, it's a party game.' She looked down at Jimmy. 'Except it's not a game. A man has been murdered and my job is to find out why he's dead and who killed him.' Jimmy lowered his eyes to the table and let Suarez work through her frustration. 'You were a detective so if you can help, fine, but if you and your boss want to piss about with this investigation you can –'

It was Spanish again but Jimmy felt he had got the gist of it. He looked up.

'Finished?' Suarez sat down. She was finished but she still wasn't a happy copper and he couldn't blame her. 'Nobody's trying to piss you about,' he lied, then tried to get back to the business in hand. 'Who have the police questioned?'

Suarez look at him and then grudgingly answered. She

also wanted to get back to the business in hand but she still wasn't happy.

'Some of the other UK ex-pats who live here and knew Jarvis. Neighbours, places he was known to visit.'

'What about the priest, Fr Perez.'

'I went round yesterday afternoon.'

'What did he say?'

'That they weren't really friends, they just liked to talk. They'd first met when Jarvis had come over here looking for properties, they saw each other a few times after Jarvis moved here permanently, met in the street, had a coffee together a couple of times. When Fr Perez retired he asked Jarvis to drop by and visit him. He enjoyed keeping his English in good shape and Jarvis liked to talk religion so they met and talked. Then he told me pretty much what you told me, about Jarvis being frightened and talking about a Catholic big-wig on the inside of Eta. He didn't give me anything we didn't know already but I don't think he was holding anything back. If he's lying or hiding something he's good at it.'

Priests were good at it, thought Jimmy, they showed you the priest you wanted to see, the smiling, cheerful priest at weddings and christenings, the sombre priest at funerals. Priests who had been at it long enough could be anyone you wanted on the outside. But, if Perez wasn't going to tell any more than he already had, there was no way, at the moment, he could be pressured so Jimmy left it alone and moved on.

'What about the ex-pat community?'

'Jarvis wasn't much of a mixer, he was known, had the odd meal or drink with some of the British residents, used the same bars and restaurants sometimes. Mostly he seems to have kept himself to himself.'

'Did he have any kind of sex-life?'

'There was no evidence of a girlfriend. There was an unopened packet of condoms in the bedside drawer but nothing else.'

Jimmy's mind circled what they had and let a small link develop in his head.

'How many of the ex-pats are Catholics?'

'How should I know?'

'Can you find out?'

'I suppose so, the hard work got done when we collated the list to interview them about Jarvis. If they registered their religious affiliation when they applied for residence we can access it easily enough. Why?'

'Let's say you arrive as a stranger here and you want to fit in quickly. You want people to know you've arrived and then forget about you. One way would be to make contact with somebody already here and get them to introduce you around but do it without any fuss. If there was a couple of Catholics already here you could go to their church, pretend to be a Catholic and there you are. And if the priest speaks English you cosy up to him and that makes it look even better. To the ex-pat community you're a Catholic who likes to talk religion with the local priest, keep yourself to yourself and pretty soon you get ignored, chalked down as somebody not worth bothering about. You don't speak Spanish so the locals don't give a toss about you either. Bingo, you're in, accepted, pigeonholed and invisible. Just like Jarvis.'

Suarez liked it. Jimmy was pleased she liked it. He was even more pleased when she followed up on it.

'Or better still, if you wanted to make contact with someone who was already here because of a shared interest in the internet, then through a church would be a good way, it would look natural, innocent. Catholics? It's a good thought. The list of ex-pats is in the car. I'll call in, find out if any of them are on file from their applications as Catholics then I'll check –'

'No.'

'No?'

'No, *we'll* check. We're working together on this, remember?'

Suarez remembered.

'Sure. You ready?' Jimmy nodded and got up. 'What about your washing up?'

She didn't mean it seriously.

'That's OK, you can come back and do it later.'

She laughed. But Jimmy noticed she didn't say no. He felt pleased with himself, like a shy teen kid again.

He picked up the folder and handed it to her. He liked the way things were progressing. The only trouble was, hedidn't mean with the investigation …

Chapter Six

The black SEAT stopped on the drive of a large bungalow, obviously the home of someone who had done well before coming to live in Spain.

'Who is it this time?'

Suarez looked at her list.

'Mr and Mrs Henderson. Both retired. He used to be an accountant, she was a teacher.'

'He must have been a good accountant, there was never much in teaching.'

It was Mr Henderson who came to the door, a short, chubby man, balding and in his middle to late fifties. When Suarez showed him her warrant card he seemed to become nervous and tried to edge back behind the door which he pushed a bit more closed.

'What is it?'

'It concerns a Mr Jarvis.'

'Really, Inspector I have spoken to the police already, we both have. My wife and I knew Mr Jarvis very slightly. We can tell you nothing more about him, absolutely nothing.'

'I understand that, Mr Henderson. I have only a couple of questions. Are you or your wife Catholics?'

Henderson's surprise at the question overcame his nervousness for a second. The door inched open and a little more of Henderson emerged.

'Catholics?'

'Yes.'

There was a pause before he answered and when he did

his voice was no longer nervous so much as cautious.

'My wife is a Catholic. Why do you ask?'

'It appears that when Mr Jarvis first started coming to Santander he went to Sunday Mass at Sancta Maria Mater Dei church. Is that the church your wife uses?'

The answer was still cautious.

'It was.'

'Perhaps we could come in, Mr Henderson. Is your wife at home?

Henderson had got a grip on himself, he was more in control now. He even managed a weak and insincere smile as he stood back, opened the door and they went in. He lead them through the house onto a patio which looked out over a large, well-kept garden. Unless they were both fanatical gardeners Jimmy assumed they employed someone to look after it, or maybe two, given the size of the place. He must have been a very good accountant, thought Jimmy. On the patio by a table and in the shade of a large umbrella a woman was sitting reading a book. She turned and looked at the trio as they came out of the house. She was also in her fifties, with her iron-grey hair pulled back giving her sharp features a severe look. She was thin, which did nothing to soften her appearance. She reminded Jimmy of a character in a book he'd read at primary school who had frightened him, a wicked school-mistress who did something nasty to her pupils. He couldn't remember what it was.

'It's the police again, Dorothy, something about going to Mass. This is,' he turned to Suarez, 'I'm sorry I didn't catch the name on your identification.'

'Suarez, Inspector Suarez, Mrs Henderson, and this is Mr Costello, he is acting as a liaison in the investigation.'

Mrs Henderson didn't get up. The way she was looking at them, Jimmy felt as if she suspected them of walking mud or something worse across her best carpet. He almost looked down at his shoes.

'Costello, it's not a Spanish name.'

'No, it isn't.'

Jimmy had taken a rapid dislike to the woman. He didn't like her manner, the way she looked or the way she spoke. He glanced at Henderson, soft and ...what? Sly maybe? Then he looked back at Mrs Henderson. She was angular and hard and he instinctively felt there had never been much chance of any little Hendersons. Mrs Henderson waited but when she realised he didn't intend to offer her any further information she transferred her attention to Suarez. Jimmy got the feeling she would like to smack his leg and then tell him to stand him in a corner with his face to the wall.

'What is it you want, Inspector?'

'You husband says you are a Catholic, Mrs Henderson. Do you attend Mass on Sundays?'

'I don't know what that has to do with the police but, yes, I am a Catholic and I do go to Mass on Sundays.'

'Do you go to Sancta Maria Mater Dei church?'

'No. We used to go there some years ago but then we moved house, the area was going down. The wrong type was moving in.'

'The wrong type?'

'Loud and common. Plenty of money but precious little of anything else. I now go to the Jesuit church.'

'When you went to Mater Dei was Fr Perez the parish priest?'

She thought for a moment.

'Yes he was.'

'And did you first meet Mr Jarvis there?'

'No, I never met him there. The police have already been told that we hardly knew Mr Jarvis other than to say hello if our paths crossed, which wasn't often. What very little I saw of him didn't give me the impression that he was our sort of person.'

'Loud and common with money and precious little

49

else? The wrong type.'

She gave Jimmy a look, but as she didn't have a ruler handy he felt safe with his hands out of his pockets.

'I'm sure I couldn't say what type sort of person he might have proved to be if we had known him, Mr Costello. But, as I said, we didn't know him so I couldn't comment.'

Suarez intervened, she didn't want things turning too nasty.

'I see, thank you, Mrs Henderson.'

Mrs Henderson went back to her book. They were dismissed, they could go out to play now.Mr Henderson took his cue.

'I'll see you out.'

Henderson led the way back through the house and closed the front door behind them. They got back in the car.

'Well, Jimmy, I'm not sure it's any use but we've got our first point of contact. Jarvis used the same church as she did when he came here.'

'But she says they didn't know him. Of course she could be lying.'

It was more wishful thinking than anything else.

'I doubt it. It would be too easy for us to check. Still, it's a connection, not that I see it takes us anywhere.'

They were standing by the car. Jimmy looked back suddenly at the bungalow. A face disappeared behind a curtain. It was just a glimpse, but enough to that see it was a chubby face.

'Maybe it does. She said, "we".'

'We?'

'She said, "we used to", that means they both went to Perez's church. She might not have met Jarvis but that doesn't mean he didn't.'

Suarez face lit up with a grin.

'I like it.' They got into the car but Suarez didn't start

the engine. Jimmy watched the window. The curtain moved slightly. Chubby was still watching. 'So, we have Henderson maybe alongside Jarvis but if so, keeping it to himself. What did you think of him?'

'I don't know. Retired early and with plenty of money. There's something about him, nervous, sly. But with a wife like his that may not mean much. And he's been watching us since we left.'

Jimmy pointed to the window and Suarez looked but the curtain didn't move.

'Doesn't mean much.'

'No.'

'And her?'

'Poison. Self-centred, bossy poison. He's probably shit-scared of her and if they ever had a fulfilling sex life I'll eat your handbag.'

'Nothing doing, it's an expensive one, but I see where you're going. Timid, bullied husband with no sex-life to speak of. What does he do for thrills?'

'I wonder if he has a computer?'

'Oh, he'll have one, everyone has one these days. But unless we turn up a lot more than we've got I doubt we'll get to have a look at what he's got on it.'

Jimmy agreed.

'So who's left for this morning?'

'Just one, Harold Mercer. I kept him till last.'

'Why's that?'

'Because he's the only one on the list who might count as a bit of a celebrity. I wanted to surprise you'

'A celebrity? How come I haven't heard of him then?'

'Are you a big reader, Jimmy?'

'I read a book once. It didn't take.'

'I thought so. I'm told Harold Mercer is a writer of crime fiction. I thought you might enjoy meeting someone who makes a living out of crime.'

'We'll see.'

Chapter Seven

'Fuck me, it can't be!'

He was a big man, wearing a gaudy shirt and the accent was London, definitely north of the river. He stepped out of the doorway with his hand out. Jimmy took it.

'Hello, Harry, when did they let you out?'

'Jimmy fucking Costello, as I live and breathe. Where did you spring from?'

'Here and there. I move about.'

The man who had answered the door laughed.

'Still the great communicator, I see.'

'That's right, Harry, still no such thing as free information.'

Suarez stood by the door and looked from one to the other. Harold Mercer was maybe five to ten years older than Jimmy, well-tanned, over six foot tall with a shaved head. The neck of his brightly-patterned, short-sleeved shirt hung open and around his neck were assorted gold chains. He wore tailored shorts and flip-flops and there was more gold on his wrists, with faded tattoos on both arms. Suarez took the same dislike to him as Jimmy had taken to Mrs Henderson. She didn't like his looks, his manner or his language and what she didn't like most was that he knew Jimmy and Jimmy obviously knew him.

'You know Mr Mercer?'

Jimmy shook his head.

'No, I don't know any Mr Harold Mercer. I knew a Harry Mercer once, but he didn't write. He was a blagger, a thief, an all-round low-life and muscle for some of the nastiest villains ever to walk north London.' He turned back to Mr Mercer. 'How you doing, Harry? Nice to see you again.'

Mercer grinned.

'And you, Jimmy boy, and you. Come in, come in both of you. This calls for champagne.' And he led them through the imposing villa into the living room where he stopped, turned, and looked at Jimmy again. 'As I fucking live and breathe, Jimmy Costello. Hasn't anybody killed you yet, you bastard?'

'Not yet, Harry, I'm still around.'

Harry looked at Suarez. He didn't need to see any ID. He still knew a copper when he saw one, even a good-looking one like her. He looked back at Jimmy.

'Still playing copper? You're a bit long in the tooth aren't you? And if you are, you're well off your patch. What's brought you out from under your stone into the sunshine?'

'I thought we were going to get champagne. Or has the mood changed?'

'Sorry, I never could get any kind of stranglehold on the social graces. Sit down both of you. I'll be right back.'

They sat down and Harry went out of the room. Suarez gave Jimmy a look and Jimmy gave a Suarez a shrug. It was nothing he'd planned. He was as surprised as she was. Harry came back with a tray. There was a bottle of champagne and three glasses. Suarez refused the glass Mercer offered her.

'Not for me, thank you.'

'Not while on duty?'

'Not while driving.'

'Very sensible. Here you are, Jimmy, you're not driving.'

Jimmy took his glass. The cork popped, and Harry poured the wine, then sat down and held up his glass.

'To old times.'

53

Jimmy held up his.

'And fair shares for all.'

Harry laughed.

'Bugger that. Now I'm making legit money I don't share it with any fucker, not even the tax man.'

They both drank. Suarez stood up. Mercer looked at her but didn't get up.

'Not going already, dear?'

'Oh, I think so, Mr Mercer, I can see you two have some catching up to do. Mr Costello will deal with what I came to ask you. Please don't get up, I'll make my own way to the door.' Harry hadn't looked like getting up. She turned to Jimmy. 'You'll get a taxi?'

'Yeah. I'll catch you later.'

'Good day, Mr Mercer.'

'So long, love.' Suarez left. 'Who's the fancy copper?'

'Local inspector, name of Suarez. I like her, she's OK. Got me somewhere to stay.' Jimmy looked round. 'Not like this though. It looks like you're doing well for yourself.'

'Better than when you last saw me. Remember that? The security-van set-up when you thought you were going to get Denny Morris. Last time we talked was in an interview room with you asking me what I'd stand for to help clear the back-log.'

'As I remember you all walked on that one.'

'Yeah, we walked. It was a neat piece of work, like everything you ever did. It was down to you, wasn't it? You got the fix put in?'

'No, Harry. I was just a Detective Sergeant. I couldn't put that kind of fix in.'

'OK, some high-up actually did the business, but it was clever, it had Jimmy Costello written all over it. We knew your work when we saw it. Still, who cares? It's all ancient history now. I still make a living from crime, but now only by writing about it. Another?'

54

Jimmy held out his glass.

'Why not?'

Mercer refilled their glasses.

'It was something you said to me in that interview room got me started on all this. Remember what you said?'

'I said a lot of things.'

'You said I was getting too old, I should learn a proper trade next time I was inside. Well I took your advice.'

'You got sent down again? I never heard.'

'It was a fuck-up not so long after the security-van thing. Me and Sid, you remember Sid Temple, little bloke, good with a knife?' Jimmy shook his head. 'Anyway me and Sid joined an out-of-town geezer who told us he had a walkover. We checked him out and he was kosher so we went off our own turf with him and tried to knock over a bookies in Birmingham. A shooter went off and – well, like I say, it was a fuck-up. I wasn't inside when the gun went off, I was the wheel-man. No one actually got hurt so I only drew a ten stretch. You know what I did when I was inside?'

'Tell me what you did when you were inside, Harry.'

'I studied with the Open University. I got a degree in English Literature. We were all mugs taking to crime. If I'd done some proper schooling instead of setting out to be Jack-the-Lad I could have done this writing lark years ago and not spent my time with hooligans, wasting any money I made on booze, tarts and gambling. We were all just a bunch of fucking mugs really, especially the clever ones who could have made it going straight. Remember Nat?' Jimmy nodded, he remembered Nat. 'He was a clever bugger, he had the brains to be anything and look what happened to him?' Jimmy knew what had happened to Nat but he let Harry go on. 'Somebody car-bombed the fucker. I was inside but I heard about it.'

Mercer poured himself another drink. Jimmy watched him. Was he getting maudlin on two glasses of champagne? Or had he been drinking before they had arrived? Jimmy looked at his watch. Ten-past eleven. He'd started early, then, but he hadn't looked like he'd been hitting the bottle when he'd answered the door.

'Help yourself, Jimmy.'

Jimmy reached to the bottle and poured himself half a glass.

'I never had you down as a literary type, Harry, more the violent type as I remember.'

'I was then, when we knew each other. Like you, nasty and vicious, not a nice bloke to have around. In stir I decided it was time to use what I knew in a way that didn't hurt people any more. I didn't think I'd end up a writer but once I started studying I thought, why not? What about you, Jimmy, you still hurting people?'

'Not intentionally, I gave it up a long time ago.'

'But not the money, don't tell me there's no money in this for you, whatever it is. There always had to be something in it for Jimmy. That hasn't changed has it? Whatever you're up to over here, you'll get your share out of it.'

'That's right, Harry, I'll get what I want out of this.'

'I thought so, still the same old fucker.'

And he finished his glass and poured another.

'So how did you get started as a writer? Just put it all down in words, what you'd got up to with Denny and your mates, turn it all into a story?'

'If it was that simple every villain in London would be at it. No, it's like anything else. You learn your trade, you practise and practise until you get it right. Then you need to get lucky. I got lucky, a real London villain turned writer made enough of a story to get my first book taken on by a publisher. Once it did OK I decided I could make a living out of it. Writing the second one turned out to be a real bastard, I had to graft at that but I managed it and it did better than the first so I came over here to get away

56

from everything and get on with writing. An ex-villain turned writer sounds all right in a newspaper or magazine but there were too many old connections in London for me to have stayed on.'

'You put the lads in your books, then?'

'Yeah, most of the boys were in there one way or another.'

'And they didn't mind?'

'I didn't have much to do with them after I came out and my first book got published. The ones I met who knew what I was up to seemed more pleased than anything to think they were getting written about.'

'What about me? Was I there?'

'A really bent, bastard of a copper? Well, I couldn't leave you out, could I?'

'Just as well you didn't ask what I thought about putting me in a book.'

Mercer laughed.

'What? Tell you I was putting you in a book and have you putting me in hospital? You were never one for the limelight were you? Besides, our paths never crossed after we walked from that set-up. But don't worry, you only had a small part and I didn't say what you really got up to. You got killed in chapter four of the first book. A character based on Denny Morris killed you and you remember what Denny was like, it wasn't a nice way to go. See, writing isn't like what really happened. Some people in my books have to get what they deserve. The really bad guys like you don't get to walk away like they did in real life. The public like happy endings where people get what's coming to them.'

Harry poured the last of the champagne into his glass and took a drink. Jimmy smiled.

'What was it, wishful thinking on your part, Harry? Knocking me off the way you would have liked to see me go?'

Harry paused.

'Maybe, most of us wanted you to go, that way or any other way. You were a toxic bastard, Jimmy. It would have been nice to see you getting what you deserved.'

There was genuine regret in his voice.

'Sorry you and the boys all got disappointed.'

Mercer took another drink that emptied his glass.

'What the hell? I say fuck it. It was all long ago and now it's all just stories in books, smoothed out and tarted up to please the punters. A little peep into the cess-pit. You were there, you were one of us, you remember what it was like. Stupid fuckers making stupid talk in shit-house pubs and backstreet clip-joints. Hurting people, doing jobs, doing time. It was all shit, but it was the only shit you knew so you rolled about in it and put on that you didn't notice the smell. When I went inside that last time I guess I must have developed a sense of smell. That, and knowing I didn't want to go back inside for another stretch once I got out. Do you know how many years I've done in stir? Sixteen, not counting young offenders' time. With my record if I'd have gone down again – well, I decided I wouldn't go down again and, like I say, I got lucky with the writing. So here I am in the sun with money in the bank and no coppers breathing down my neck.' He looked across at Jimmy. There was no friendliness in the look but there was a lot of something else. 'Except you. Now you've turned up. What you up to here in Spain?'

'Know a bloke called Arthur Jarvis?'

'Heard of him, saw it in the papers and on the telly, didn't know him. He got croaked a few days back didn't he?'

'That's right. You didn't know him, never came across him anywhere?'

'No, I don't mix with the local Brits. Like I say, somehow I never got round to getting any manners and my language is still fucking awful. And this isn't the Costa del

58

Crime, this is the Costa del Retired Middle-Class Suburbia, so I keep myself to myself, walk a bit, eat out, have a few drinks and write. If I get any urges I have a girl sent round, but I don't get many urges these days. I know what you're thinking. It doesn't fit with the me you knew in London in the old days. Well, maybe it doesn't but I like it, it suits me.'

'No rough stuff?'

Mercer put his glass down and held up his hands so Jimmy could look at the back of them. There were no rings and Jimmy could see why. The joints were noticeably swollen. Harry put his hands down.

'I can hold a glass and still use two fingers on a keyboard to do my writing but if I hit you with one of these I would be the one that you'd hear screaming. I take stuff for it, but it doesn't do much good. Give it another couple of years and they'll look like fucking claws.' He put his hands down and looked at them. Then he looked up again. 'So, what's Jarvis got to do with anything, what's your interest? And why the visit here from you and your sexy inspector?'

'It's nothing, at least nothing that applies to you. She's got you on the list as a Catholic. You were never a Catholic, Harry. How come you're on the list as one? As I remember it you were never the religious type.'

That got a laugh.

'Too fucking true. It was when I wanted to come over. I had a record, didn't I?. I wasn't what you might call a desirable candidate so I put down anything I thought might help.'

'How did you think that would help?'

'They were all supposed to be RC over here, at least that's what I was told. Anyway, I wasn't exactly familiar with abroad was I? I mean look what happened when I went to fucking Birmingham. I wanted to blend in, being an ex-villain was OK back in London but it was no good to me over here. I came here to get away from all that so on the forms I put down RC.'

'Ever go to church?'

'A few times, just for appearances.'

'Where about?'

'Here and there, there's plenty to choose from. I can't remember which ones, like I said, it was only for appearances.' Jimmy stood up. 'What you doing? Not going already? Stay and have a chat, I'll open another bottle.'

'Got things to do, Harry. We can't all be successful writers, can we?'

'Go on, stay and have another drink.'

'Harry, you didn't like me in London and I didn't like you. Now I'm out of it and you're out of it so I'll stick to what I'm doing and you stick to what you're doing and we'll leave it at that. We met again by accident but we still wouldn't like each other. Thanks for the drink. I'll see myself out.'

Jimmy turned and left. Mercer watched him go. When he heard the front door slam he pulled out a mobile and made a call. Suddenly he wasn't maudlin any more, he was stone-cold sober and serious.

'Hello. Some woman inspector's just been to see me and she had a bloke called Costello in tow. Oh, they did, did they? Well after you, they came to me. Never mind who he is, he's going to be trouble. Why? Because the bastard was always trouble. We'll need to talk.' He listened for a moment. 'OK, three, at the usual place.'

Mercer put the mobile away. Outside the living room door Jimmy moved quietly away and silently let himself out of the front door. He walked quickly down the drive noting the number plate of the silver Mercedes parked there as he passed it. Once out onto the road he phoned Suarez.

'I think we've got a live one. He's set up a meet with

someone at three, sounds like Henderson, he phoned as soon as he thought I'd left. He drives a silver Mercedes, licence plate –' and he gave her the number. 'Where are you now? Thanks, I don't have the number for any taxis. I'll wait on Mercer's road. I'll walk down from his place and wait.'

Jimmy put his phone away and walked down the road the way he and Suarez had come. After a few minutes when he was well away from Mercer's villa he stopped and waited for the black SEAT to arrive.

So, Harry, you're still at it are you? Writing not enough for you after all. Well, why not? Why change the habits of a life-time?

And Jimmy waited, remembering Harry Mercer and the old days when, like Harry had said, Jimmy had been one of them.

Chapter Eight

Harry's silver Mercedes was parked outside a bar-restaurant in an unlovely street of assorted commercial buildings. The bar-restaurant overlooked the parking area for the ferry terminal and the sign above the entrance showed a bull's head with big horns, a ring in its nose and a grin on its face. Next to the bull, in large red letters was *El Toro Restaurant Bar*. Inside it was big, clean, and functional, with plastic-topped tables and plain wooden chairs. In the UK it would have been a fish and chip restaurant on a sea-front promenade set out to deal quickly and efficiently with a sudden rush of customers when the summer rain pelted down at lunchtime. Here it wasn't the weather that produced the crowds, it was the ferries. The café got busy as the cars rolled up to await a ferry, and when a ferry unloaded there were always plenty of people who wanted to eat before setting off to wherever they were headed. The local British ex-pats were scrupulous in avoiding places like El Toro, always careful to guard their status as residents not visitors. The loss was theirs because, in spite of the façade, the interior décor and inevitable burger and chips on the menu, the food was mostly well-cooked dishes using local produce and gave excellent value for money.

Mercer and Henderson sat at a table well inside the café away from the main window and the entrance. There was no ferry due in or out and only two other tables were in use by what looked like port workers. Mercer was sitting facing Henderson and had his back to the bar where a solitary barman was reading a paper. Had he been facing the other way he certainly would have noticed when a man slipped out of the staff door behind the bar and joined the barman. The new arrival spoke quietly to the barman then picked up a towel and began to wipe a glass that was already clean. Henderson was too preoccupied to notice anything except Harry, what he was saying and the way he was saying it. There was a bottle of red wine on the table between them. Henderson's glass was half-full, Mercer's was empty and hadn't been used. While Harry did the talking Henderson did the drinking, his role limited to listening, looking worried and fiddling with his glass between drinks.

'I'm not a happy person, Henderson, and the way things are going I'm getting unhappier by the day. Do you know what I do when I feel unhappy? I hurt people. I used to use these,' he held his hands out and turned them over, looking at them, 'but they're not up to it any more. Now I have to use something else, an iron bar maybe, or a chisel.' Henderson looked more worried and fiddled harder. 'I know it's irrational, deviant even, but what can you do? You see, with me, old habits don't die hard, they don't fucking die at all so if I get much more bad news someone is sure to get hurt and it's usually whoever comes to hand. How about you cheer me up and tell me why Jimmy Costello is here?'

Henderson's voice was a nice blend of fear and panic but he managed to keep it low.

'I don't know, how would I know?'

'Because you said Costello and that woman Inspector came to see you before they came to me. I knew Costello from London, years back, so I started chatting about old times and she pissed off without saying what the visit was all about. I got nothing out of Costello except, did I know Jarvis? I told him no, so I never got to find out *what* about Jarvis. That means I'll have to ask you what has them

63

doing a second round of visits, won't I? What was it they wanted?'

Henderson took a drink.

'It was something to do with Dorothy being a Catholic and which church she went to.'

'What else?'

'Nothing else. Just Dorothy being a Catholic and which church she went to.'

Harry sat and thought for a moment and then spoke quietly, more to himself than to Henderson.

'No, there's nothing for them to find. We've been careful, Jarvis didn't use the same church to meet me as the one he used for you. Nobody knows anything, nobody except us and we're not likely to talk, are we?'

But Henderson had finished his wine and was pouring another glass so he missed Harry's question and after a drink asked one of his own.

'What's going on, Mercer? Why was Jarvis killed? Is it anything to do with us, did you do it?'

Mercer almost laughed.

'No, you stupid bastard, I didn't do it and I didn't have it done. Why would I do it? I needed Jarvis alive, he's no good to me dead is he?'

'Then who? Somebody shot him.'

But this time it was Mercer who wasn't listening. Something was niggling him. They'd been careful but –

'Which church does your old woman use?'

'What?'

'If the cops asked the question it must mean something. Which church?'

'The Jesuits' one. It's that big old one down by the –'

'I know where it is. What did they say when she told them?'

'Nothing. They didn't seem interested.' Then he remembered. 'I think they were more interested in the other one.'

'What other one?'

'You know which one, Mater Dei, where Jarvis and I used to meet.' Something clicked in Henderson's brain. He reached across the table and took hold of Mercer's arm. 'Do you think they've connected me with Jarvis?' His worried look moved up a gear and he began to sweat. Mercer brushed off his hand and looked at him. He would need to be sorted or he'd fall apart. Luckily he wasn't just weak he was also stupid.

'No. They probably want to trace Jarvis's movements since he arrived, background stuff. Nothing to worry about.' The simple lie seemed to calm Henderson. He emptied his glass and poured himself another and drank half of it at one go. Mercer watched him. 'Are you driving?'

'No, I came by taxi. I knew after your call I'd need a drink and I'm not stupid.'

Mercer didn't bother to disagree.

'What else did they ask?'

'Nothing.'

Mercer reached across and pulled Henderson's arm back to the table as he was about to take another drink. The glass hit the surface and some of the wine bounced out.

'Think, you stupid bastard. What else did they ask?'

The menace in Mercer's voice brought on more sweat but Henderson did as he had been told and thought.

'The priest. They asked if the priest was there.'

'What priest? Where?'

'The priest at Mater Dei. They asked if he was there when Dorothy used the church.'

'Which priest?'

Henderson thought hard again but this time drew a blank.

'I can't remember. I never knew him. I only went with Dorothy enough times so it would look natural when Jarvis and I met up. I'm not interested in her damn mumbo-jumbo. Once Jarvis and I had made contact and set things up I stopped going. How do you expect me to remember a name? It was three years ago for God's sake.'

Henderson picked up the bottle and poured, but the wine stopped almost straight away. Henderson put the bottle down and motioned to the bar. The new arrival was still busy but with a different clean glass. He watched as the barman went across to the table. Henderson pushed the empty towards him.

'Another bottle.'

'Certainly, sir.'

The barman picked up the empty bottle, gave the spilt wine a wipe with the cloth he was carrying and left. Henderson waited until he was back at the bar before he spoke again.

'Why did the woman policeman have that Costello with her? What's a policeman from England doing here?'

But Mercer wasn't listening. He was slightly turned looking over his shoulder at the bar. He turned round and his attention went back to Henderson.

'Did you tell anyone we were going to meet?'

'No, of course not.'

'Not that witch of a wife of yours?'

'Certainly not. I don't want her to know about you. It's bad enough that I have to know you.'

'Well someone knew we were going to meet because we've got company. There was only one barman when we came in, now there's two. Look around the place, it's not exactly rush-hour is it? Why the second barman?'

The original barman came out from behind the bar and brought the new bottle of wine to the table. Mercer nodded towards the bar.

'A bit quiet for extra staff isn't it?'

'He's new, a trainee, I show him what to do when it's quiet.'

'I see.'

The barman left.

'See, Mercer, he's no one, just a trainee.'

'Trainee my arse, he's a copper.'

Henderson looked at the bar. The spare barman was intently studying the glass he was cleaning making it abundantly clear he was not at all interested in what was happening in the bar.

Henderson looked around. Mercer was right, the place didn't need a second barman and he didn't look like he was being trained except at cleaning glasses. But Henderson didn't want Mercer to be right.

'Maybe a ferry is due.'

'No it isn't, that's why we came here. If number two isn't a copper I'll eat my –' But if Henderson wanted to know what Mercer would eat he was disappointed because now something had clicked in Mercer's brain. 'Fuck. It's Costello. The bastard must have had me followed and that means he knows something. All the drinking together and talking about old times was just pissing about. His turning up was no accident, he's here to stick his nose in. Well, I think we can make sure Jimmy fucking Costello gets fixed all right.' He sat back and smiled at Henderson. 'Maybe there should be an accident, and I think I know how to arrange one.'

Henderson's alarm grew.

'No. No violence, Mercer. You always said there would be no violence, but now Jarvis is dead and you're talking about accidents.'

'I lied.'

Henderson's hand shook as he refilled his glass from the fresh bottle. His sweat glands were now on double-time. After he had taken a drink he took out his handkerchief and wiped his forehead.

'But if that man is really from the police then they know we've met and they –'

'Shut up. All they know is that we met. And that's all they know for certain. If they knew more we'd both be sitting in an interrogation room or a cell by now.'

'But –'

'Shut it and keep it shut.' Henderson shut it quickly and kept it shut while Mercer thought. 'I called you, I asked to meet you. I wanted to ask you if you might do a bit of accountant work for me. We met here because we knew it would be quiet and a bar made it friendly. We talked about it but you decided you couldn't help so we drank some wine and you asked me about my books. After we'd had a few drinks I left. You decided to have another bottle and stayed on. All right, you got it?'

Henderson had got it but he didn't like it.

'It sounds a bit thin to me.'

'I don't give a Chinese shit what it sounds like to you, it's what we'll both say when they ask. If we both stick to it and say nothing else we're clear. There's fuck-all they can do. Understand?'

Henderson nodded. His was not a violent nature, but it had been patently obvious ever since they had first met that Mercer's was. Besides which he couldn't think of anything better.

Mercer poured a tiny amount of wine into his glass, swilled it around then stood up with a big smile on his face, big enough for the new barman to see from across the room. When he spoke it was loud enough for the barman to hear, for everyone to hear.

'Well, thanks anyway, Mr Henderson, sorry we can't do business together. It was nice to meet you, goodbye.'

Henderson smiled weakly and it took him a moment to realise Mercer was holding out his hand. He took the hand but said nothing. Mercer took his glass to the bar and put it in front of the new barman.

'Good luck with the training, mate.'

The barman didn't reply. Mercer turned and walked out

of the bar. Henderson watched him get into his car and drive away. The place where the Mercedes had been parked was immediately filled by a black SEAT. A man and a woman got out and headed into the bar. Henderson recognised them as the woman Inspector and the man Costello. He quickly poured himself a glass of wine and drank it at one go, desperately rehearsing the story Mercer had given him. Jimmy and Suarez came to his table and sat down. Suarez asked the questions.

'How do you do, Mr Henderson. We seem to have just missed your friend, Mr Mercer. Please, could you tell us why you two met? What was your business together?'

Henderson clumsily poured another glass, drank some, consigned his soul to God and began to tell her the story Mercer had given him. As he spoke he knew he had been right. It sounded thin.

Chapter Nine

They left Henderson sweating and drinking in the bar. He was in a bad way and would soon be worse but he'd told his story and managed to stick to it so they left him to his fear and his wine. Suarez suggested they park the car and walk while they talked. Jimmy agreed and they drove to the sea-front, parked and began to walk. Suarez didn't seem to notice the heat. Jimmy did, but he liked the idea of their walking together like a couple of tourists on holiday together so he was prepared to put up with it.

'So, what did you make of Henderson's little performance?'

'Mercer has him scared witless, his wife has him scared spineless, I don't see that we'll get anywhere by joining in and frightening the stupid bastard shitless as well.'

Suarez laughed.

'Not how I'd have phrased it for my report but I agree. Still, we need him to talk to us, unless you think we would be better off having a go at Mercer.'

'No, Harry'll be no help, not unless he's sure we can send him away for a long time, then he'd deal, but we're not even close to anything like that.' They walked on each with their own thoughts. With Suarez it was the case, with Jimmy it was Suarez and, unfortunately, the heat. The sky was clear blue and Jimmy felt as if he could simply reach up and touch it. He took out his handkerchief and wiped his forehead. It came away damp. I must look like bloody Henderson, he thought, and the thought didn't sit well. He stopped. 'I'm sorry, I thought it might be OK but do we have to be out here? This bloody heat is frying me.'

Suarez looked at him.

'Yes, you do look a bit well-done. I should have remembered the heat bothered you. You should have said.'

'The heat bothers me.'

'OK, let's go to the bar and get a cold drink.'

'Yes, let's.'

And they turned back towards the car.

They drove to the bar where they had first met. Suarez stopped by the grove of trees and Jimmy got out.

'Get us some beers. I'll park up and be back in a minute.'

Suarez drove off and Jimmy looked through the trees at the tables with the parasols and the sea beyond. Very holiday brochure: in a magazine he would have liked the look of it. He turned his back on the holiday postcard scene and walked into the welcoming cool of the bar's shady, air-conditioned interior. Inside the bar it wasn't busy and the waiter came straight to the table.

'Welcome back, sir.'

Either he remembered Jimmy as a previous customer or as someone who got visited by the police.

'Two beers.'

The waiter left and Jimmy set about trying to get his mind into gear. Henderson had been very frightened when they turned up but they weren't the reason. That had been Harry's work. Whatever Henderson and Harry were mixed up in was serious enough to get Henderson sweating, drinking and clamming up behind a weak story. That might make it even murder serious. The beers came and a couple of minutes later Suarez walked in.

'What are you doing back here? Why not sit outside? There's plenty of shade. You don't have to be in the sun.'

'We could, couldn't we? And you know what, we could look at the sea again. That would make a nice change. Maybe the ferry will put in an appearance and make our day.'

Suarez grinned and pulled out her chair.

'I guess the heat can be hard work if you're not used to it.' She sat down while Jimmy took a long pull at his cold beer. 'OK, now you're out of the sun, what did you make of Henderson's story?'

He put down his glass.

'It sounded thin to me, like something you'd make up on the spur of the moment if you'd suddenly realised you were being watched. But I doubt Henderson has the imagination or guts to do it, so I suppose Mercer spotted your man behind the bar and told Henderson what to say when the police turned up.'

'Yes. But if they both tell the same story it will do the job. We can't fault it so I can't pull either of them in for questioning.'

'What about Mercer? He's got heavy form, sixteen years he told me, and the last time it was for armed robbery. Couldn't you pull him and question him on the strength of that?'

'And how do I explain pulling him in? Why should his form bother us now if it hasn't before? Anyway, what's the point? If it's like you say then he's been round the ring often enough to know all the moves. He'd just admit his record and say, so what? He's done his time, there's nothing currently against him and now he makes his living as a respectable writer so where would it get us?'

She was right. Harry was bomb-proof as things stood.

Funny, thought Jimmy, he'd never marked Harry down as a clever one, yet here he was in Spain, obviously doing well and, according to the story, an established writer of crime fiction. But Jimmy didn't buy into it. It was fiction all right and somewhere there was crime, but it wasn't happening in any books that Harry wrote. Arthritic hands or not, Harry the villain was still for real and he was still violent.

'No, it doesn't hold together. Harry's wrong, he's up to something and it isn't writing about crime, it's crime pure and simple. Did you unlock Jarvis's computer yet?'

'Yes, apart from his own stuff there was hard porn, children, rape, lots of it, and like I say very, very nasty. If he was alive, Vice could have put him away for a stiff stretch according to the boys who saw the stuff.'

'Porn means money, and the nastier the porn the more the money. Jarvis obviously had a source. The question is, was it for his own use, or to distribute to other like-minded individuals?'

'Mercer as the supplier, Jarvis as distributor?'

'It's a thought, and I don't have any others. Mercer's in the frame, so is Jarvis, so is the porn. Jarvis's money had to come from somewhere and if he had access to plenty of the real nasty kind of porn it could mean he didn't buy it, he sold it.'

Suarez took a drink and thought about it.

'With Mercer's background he'd probably have no trouble in making contacts with people who could make what was wanted.'

'Henderson was an accountant so he could look after the financial side. Mercer sees to supply, Henderson fixes the money and Jarvis is the delivery boy. A neat and profitable little business if true.'

'It would certainly tie them all together and if they fell out, if Jarvis got greedy or wanted out, then pop, Mercer puts a bullet in his head.'

'It's possible. Harry's got bad hands but he could still pull a trigger without any difficulty.'

'It makes a line of enquiry.'

'What do we know about Jarvis before he came to Spain?'

'He was a teacher. That's what he put down on the forms.'

'How old was he?'

'Fifty-one, and he'd been here for just over three years.'

'And from the autopsy no health problems except being dead. A fit teacher under fifty who can afford to pack it in and retire to Spain. Nice going. Did he do any work here?'

'Not officially, none that we could turn up.'

'So how was he fixed for money?'

'The bills we found at his house seem to have been paid on time and he had statements showing just over two thousand euros in the current account of his bank, and a pass book for a deposit account where he had a balance of over twenty thousand.'

'Fixed up OK then, and it wasn't from any teachers' pension fund.'

'From his bank statements there was a regular monthly payment of three thousand euros into the current account from the deposit account.'

'So how did the deposit account keep up with that?'

'Cash deposits. Various sums, nothing regular and nothing so big questions might get asked.'

'A teacher leaves his job in the UK and comes to Spain. He's not taken on a pension so he's not taken early retirement, has no job that anyone knows of, but he's comfortably off with a steady but erratic income. What was his house like?'

'Neat, clean –'

'No, I mean what sort of house was it, big, small, in a good area?'

'Comfortable, two bedrooms, all the fixings and it's in a nice enough area, residential, quiet, handy for town and the beaches if you don't drive.'

'So not at the cheap end of the market?'

'No, not the cheap end.'

'Did he own it?'

'No, he rented it.'

'From?'

74

'From a company that has properties in different parts of Spain, Iberian Property Holdings. It operates out of Gibraltar and only deals on-line. We didn't look at it closely but it looks genuine.'

'Gibraltar?'

'Probably a tax thing. Also it means they can bypass a lot of UK and European regulations. It doesn't mean anything, lots of small companies do the same.'

'An ex-teacher who moves to Spain, rents a nice house and lives comfortably with a decent supply of money which comes from nowhere at all.'

'Who ends up dead in his own kitchen with a bullet in the back of his head.'

Jimmy finished his beer. 'Another one for you?' he asked Suarez.

'No thanks.'

He beckoned the waiter. 'One more beer, please.' The waiter left. A group of four elderly people speaking English loudly came in and sat at a table by the window, obviously relieved to be out of the Spanish sun. Having paid to get it they were now busy avoiding it. They must have liked the look of the pictures in the holiday magazine as well. Jimmy pulled his mind back to the business in hand.

'What about Henderson?'

'Fifty-four, owns an accountancy business in the UK, Coventry. Semi-retired and came over here five years ago with his wife. He goes back to England about six times a year to keep an eye on things. They had a house in town when they arrived, then two years ago they moved out and bought the place where they live now.'

'Did they sell the other house?'

'Nobody checked, why?'

'When I was a copper you checked everything. Times must have changed.'

'OK, I'll check. And before you ask, I checked to see if

Mercer really does write crime thrillers. I went on Amazon and there are four under his name. He is a writer OK?' The beer came and Jimmy took a drink. Suarez waited until he had put his glass down. 'If we're right about these three and they're together in some porn thing, I think the connection won't surface here, I think it will be in England. They've been very careful to make sure there was nothing to tie them together since they arrived but maybe they weren't so careful before they came. If we could turn up something in the UK we might get a line on how the business was set up. If we can get reasonable grounds that they're in it together we'll have something here to turn the screw with, especially on Henderson.'

'If the porn is as nasty as you say, why not stay with that? If you get something and try to use it as leverage on Jarvis's killing you just make work for yourself. Why not bang them up for the porn if you can and settle for that.'

But Suarez wasn't interested in the suggestion.

'If we can fix the porn on them, fine, but the murder comes first, Jarvis's killing is what this is all about.'

Suddenly Jimmy felt angry. What was he doing? He wasn't a copper any more. He'd been sent here to do a job. How the hell had he got mixed up in a police investigation?

'It might be what it's all about for you but I didn't come here to sort out any murder or uncover a porn ring. I was sent to look into whether a senior Catholic cleric was mixed up with terrorists, remember?'

Suarez look a little surprised.

'I thought we were working together on this?'

'Maybe we are, but not for the same reasons.' Suarez pushed her chair back, crossed her legs and looked at him in an odd sort of way. Jimmy didn't like the way she was looking at him, it disturbed his thinking. In fact, his thinking wasn't the only thing it disturbed …

'Look, I'm going for a walk. I need to think about a

few things.'

Suarez nodded.

'Sure.'

But she kept on looking.

Jimmy didn't get up. He didn't want to go back into the sun but he couldn't think properly with Suarez there. That was why he'd got angry. She bothered him, got in amongst him somehow. She was becoming too much of a distraction. It was her legs mostly, he kept wondering where they ended.

'Sorry. I don't know why I blew up like that.'

'That's OK. Everyone blows up now and then.'

'And this bloody heat bothers me.'

She got up.

'OK, Jimmy, you stay here. If you want to think you won't do it so well in the sun, not if it bothers you. You sure it's just the heat?'

Jimmy looked up. Was she laughing at him?

She was still looking at him in that odd way and it still disturbed him but, no, she wasn't laughing at him.

'Just the heat.'

'Fine. You sit tight and drink your beer, I'll go and set things in motion to find out if there was any special reason why Jarvis left his teaching job and if the Hendersons sold their first house.'

'Thanks, I wasn't looking forward to the sun again.'

'No, I could see that.'

Suarez left the bar heading for her car and Jimmy began to think. First he thought about her legs, then her figure, then –

No, he wasn't looking forward to going out in the sun again. But he was looking forward to something. What? He wasn't sure he knew the answer to that. Or maybe he wasn't ready just yet to admit that he knew the answer all too well.

ChapterTen

Jarvis. He had been the start of all this, and now he was dead. But why was he dead? He'd told the priest, Perez, about the ETA thing. But if killing Jarvis was to stop that information getting passed on, if it ever existed, then Perez would have to be killed as well. And if ETA knew about Jarvis, if they knew he had told …

Jimmy stopped. This was no good. He tried to clear his mind. It wasn't easy but he tried. If any ETA information did exist the only reason Jimmy could see for Jarvis to die was to protect the source, whoever had given Jarvis the information. But that didn't make sense either. Why wait to kill him until he had passed on the information? No, that side of it all had to be rubbish. It had to be. So he left it alone and moved on.

Jarvis was connected to Henderson and Mercer, that had to be why he was dead, with Mercer or Henderson as the trigger and Jimmy's money was firmly on Mercer. So, what should he do? Suarez thought there was a better chance of turning up a connection in the UK. That made sense. If –

His phone rang and, when he answered it, he recognised the voice. It was a monsignor from Rome, the one McBride had sent to pull him out of Copenhagen.

'Professor McBride wonders why you have not been in contact.'

Jimmy was glad of the distraction, and he decided to make the most of it.

'Because I've become romantically involved with a

stunning blonde who desires my body. It keeps you busy that sort of thing, cuts into your time.'

'I see you don't change, Mr Costello, you still have the same sense of humour.'

'That's me, always the same.'

'Can you give me some idea of what progress, if any, you are making?'

'Well, soon I hope we'll be holding hands – '

'Please, Mr Costello. Spare me any more of your low comedy. A small amount goes very far I assure you.'

'Yes, but will she go very far … all right, all right. I haven't been in touch because there's nothing to report, nothing concrete. I was sent to talk to Jarvis but he's dead, no one knows why or who did it. I'm working with a local Inspector who thinks Jarvis may have been involved with a local porn ring. Also there's an ex-con named Mercer living here who could be into something –'

The Monsignor's voice cut across Jimmy's flow.

'Mr Costello, you were sent to Santander to do a very simple task. You were certainly not sent to look into any porn ring or discover ex-criminals. Have you spoken yet to Fr Perez?'

'No.'

'Why not?'

'I'm not sure yet what to ask him.'

'Ask him about the information Jarvis gave him. Surely that's simple enough.'

'That's the problem, it's too simple. I don't see that just asking him about that gets me anywhere.'

'It gets you finished, Mr Costello, and it gets you back to Rome and that is what Professor McBride now wants. She has decided, and I agree with her, that the whole business is becoming too involved, so just go and talk to Fr Perez then come back here. Is that understood?'

'But my stunning blonde looks at me shyly from downcast eyes, surely that means something. Dare I hope,

79

do you think?'

But the phone had gone dead so he put it away.

He liked the monsignor, he didn't change either, he still had no sense of humour. But Jimmy wasn't really convinced that his clowning had been just a joke at the monsignor's expense. He had a sneaking suspicion there might actually be a bit more to the stunning blonde than that. He pulled out his phone again and made a call.

'It's me. I've had a think and what I think is that it's time to talk to Fr Perez. I'll be in touch.' Jimmy rang off and then dialled the number Professor McBride had given him for Fr Perez. 'Fr Perez? My name is Costello, James Costello. I would like to meet with you and discuss a letter which you sent to the Bishop via his secretary and which the Bishop forwarded to Rome. No, I am nothing to do with the police. I was asked to make enquiries into the matter unofficially on behalf of someone in Rome. No, I quite understand that you would want to confirm who I was and why I want to talk to you. Have you a pen? Then if you phone this number you will get all the confirmation you require.' Jimmy gave him the contact number for Professor McBride. 'My number is,' Jimmy gave him his mobile number, 'I look forward to hearing from you.'

He put away the mobile, finished his beer, went to the bar, paid then left. He crossed the road, went through the trees, past the tables and on to the walkway above the beach. A slight breeze had started coming in from the sea and it didn't seem so hot any more. He started to walk, finally his brain was back in gear and a small idea was beginning to form in his mind.

It would be a real help if Jarvis had taught English and been caught with his trousers down. Yes, that would be a real help.

Chapter Eleven

'Another coffee, Señor Costello?'

'No thank you, Father.'

The old priest leaned forward and refilled his own cup and then sat back.

'I spoke to Professor McBride yesterday. She was most encouraging, yes, most encouraging, and she spoke highly of you, as a man in whom I could place full trust.' Jimmy tried to look encouraging, like a man in whom you could place full trust. He wasn't sure how it should go, but he tried his best to look the part and let the old priest carry on. 'I'm afraid eleven was the earliest convenient time. The sisters are busy until then and it would be inconvenient for me to have visitors. But after eleven things calm down …'

Fr Perez had begun to talk as soon as the nun who showed Jimmy into the old priest's room had closed the door behind her. Jimmy wasn't sure whether he was nervous or garrulous or both. Now he seemed to be settling.

Fr Perez's room was on an upper floor of a local convent, where he and another retired priest were cared for by the sisters and in return said daily Mass for them. From the open window you looked over tree-tops and red-pantiled roofs to distant hills.

'Forgive me if I talk so much. I like to speak English and it is not like riding a bike. If you don't use it, it slips away. I don't get out much now and I have few visitors. The sisters who look after us all speak nothing but Spanish as does Fr Fernandez.'

'You talked English with Mr Jarvis?'

'That is so. He visited and we talked.' The priest made a gesture to the open window. 'I have a lovely view but it is not the same as conversation.'

'What did you and Jarvis talk about?'

'Religion mostly. Sin and forgiveness, God's mercy, how Confession worked, was there a heaven and did there have to be a hell? He was an intelligent man, educated. It seemed to fascinate him that the destructive power of sin was equally balanced by its attraction. The nature of sin is an interesting –'

'Sorry, Father, you've lost me. What was it exactly that Jarvis was interested in?'

Fr Perez thought about the question for a moment.

'I think his main interest was sin and its consequences. Yes, I'd say that whatever we talked about it somehow returned to that theme one way or another.'

'Could you be a little clearer, Father? What about sin?'

'Let me see. It's a big subject, I dare say we covered a lot of ground and I didn't always pay too much attention. It was the company and the conversation I enjoyed. I would have been just as happy to talk about football, although I must say …'

Jimmy quickly dragged him back before he could get started on football.

'Maybe a simple example?'

'An example?'

'Something to show me the sort of thing you discussed with Mr Jarvis.

The old priest thought for a moment.

'An example, yes, I think I have one. If sin could only destroy then no one would sin, and if sin gave pleasure or reward without retribution everyone would very quickly become sinners. Although as I see things today it seems that for most people –'

But the example hadn't helped and Jimmy decided he

wanted to move on.

'Did you get the impression he was or ever had been a Catholic?'

'Oh no, he was definitely not a Catholic nor ever had been. Catholics aren't interested in how sin works, or about the tension between its attractive and destructive powers. In fact most Catholics don't think about sin or religion at all. They go to Mass on Sunday, if that, and are the same as everyone else for the rest of the week. I sometimes think that –'

'But Jarvis came to Mass at your church when he first came to Santander.'

Fr Perez, reluctantly it seemed to Jimmy, finally accepted that Jarvis, rather than the state of world, or the Catholic Church, or football, was the subject of this visit.

'Yes, I remember him when he first came to Santander. He made a point of making himself known to the few English people who came to Mass and when he found I spoke English he seemed to want to strike up a friendship.'

Fr Perez paused.

'Yes, Father, you've remembered something?'

'No, not remembered. It was something I found odd. His attempt at friendship was forced, it was an act. At the time I wondered what it was about, what it was he wanted from me, but he persisted and as it enabled me to talk English I co-operated. I was a parish priest and busy so we didn't meet often or for long and then he stopped.'

'Stopped?'

'Yes. He stopped coming to see me.'

'Was this before or after he had moved here?'

'Before. He'd turn up at Mass, we'd arrange to meet and talk and then he'd go back to England. It happened four or five times, then it stopped.'

'Did you ask anyone about him, any of the English who came to your church?'

'No, why should I? He came, he went, people do. It

83

was none of my business.'

'But he came back. He came to see you here.'

'Yes, when I retired. He came to see me and then began to visit. As I say, I have very few visitors so I let him come and we talked.'

'His friendship had become real, not an act any more?'

'No, I don't think so. My part was more that of some sort of informal confessor. No, not confessor, guide perhaps.'

'Guide?'

'Through the world of sin and guilt, forgiveness and redemption. I told you, he seemed fascinated by the consequences of evil and its attraction. I didn't mind. We spoke English and I have plenty of time so I let him talk about anything that suited him. He was never a parishioner, nor even a Catholic, so the state of his soul was his own business. I never enquired as to his private life which was, I presume, the source of his interest. That again was his own affair.'

'Didn't it strike you as odd that someone who wasn't a Catholic should have come to Mass at your church?'

'No, not particularly, not at the time. When he had come to Mass he received communion so I assumed he was a Catholic. It was only later, when he came here and we talked, it became clear he was not and never had been a Catholic.'

'Could it have been an academic interest, something he thought about, studied, a sort of hobby?'

'Oh no, it was firmly rooted in reality. I have talked to too many troubled people not to recognise the difference between academic interest and lived experience. But whatever it was that troubled him we merely talked, he never asked me for my advice or help. If he had I would have told him that he was playing a dangerous game. A very dangerous game.'

'Sorry, I don't understand, what sort of game?'

84

'There are two kinds of evil, Señor Costello, rational evil and spiritual evil. Rational evil seeks personal gain or advantage without regard for the good or ill of others. You can see it every day all round you, greed, pride, lust. These are all very human failings, very rational sins. Spiritual evil is quite different, it is a form of worship, a form of religion. It is the desire for evil to prevail for its own sake. It is Christianity in reverse. Señor Jarvis was close to something evil and I think close to worshipping it, wishing it to prevail.' The priest seemed to come out of a reverie, as if he had been talking to himself, not Jimmy. His manner changed and he gave a dismissive wave of his thin, bony hand. 'I cannot be sure, you understand, it is no more than a speculation. It is only one explanation out of what, I am sure, are many others for the sort of man he was, or more accurately, the sort of man I thought he was.'

'But you never tried to help him?'

'He didn't want help.'

'And you never thought he might convert? You didn't try to convert him?'

Fr Perez laughed.

'Good heavens, no. No-one should become a Catholic unless they cannot possibly avoid it. It is like it says on your cigarette packets, it can seriously damage your health.'

'I know what you mean, Father.'

'I was sorry when I heard he had been murdered, sorry but not surprised.'

'No?'

'As I said, he was playing a dangerous game. Evil never exists in the purely abstract. Like good, it expresses its existence in actions, and its consequences are always, in the end, destructive. In my opinion it destroyed Mr Jarvis.' The old priest gave Jimmy a smile and sat back. 'And that, I'm afraid, is absolutely all I can tell you about Señor Jarvis. All we did was make a convenience of each other.

He needed someone who could talk about sin and evil and I needed someone who spoke English. Concerning the ETA matter, everything I know I put in my letter to the Bishop's secretary. I can add nothing more, except that I find it highly unlikely that Mr Jarvis could actually have come by such information. The only explanation I could offer is that he was mistaken or it was some sort of delusion. Perhaps he sought a brief moment of celebrity, to be in the spotlight and be noticed. I understand some people do that sort of thing. I made the same point to the lady inspector who came to see me but she seemed unconvinced and I have to say I cannot blame her.' Jimmy sat silent for a moment. 'Tell me, Señor Costello, what exactly is it that you do for the Vatican?'

'I don't do anything for the Vatican,'

'But I was given the impression –'

'I know, Professor McBride is good at impressions. You should see her do Attila the Hun's big sister.'

'I'm sorry, I don't follow –'

'I work for Professor McBride who in turn works for a college in Rome. I go on errands for her when her friends in Rome want something done.'

'And this errand?'

'I was to talk to Jarvis but when I got here he was dead, murdered.'

'I see. So now you talk to me.'

'So now I talk to you. It's taken me a bit more time than I expected to get round to you because I found I had to talk to the police first.'

'Then, Mr Costello, I fear your journey has not prospered. As I said, I wrote down all I knew and passed it on. I can add nothing to what I have already told you, not about the late Mr Jarvis and certainly not about terrorists.'

'You have no idea who this senior cleric might be, if there was such a cleric?' Perez shook his head. 'Nor how Jarvis could have come by the information if it's true.'

86

Again Perez shook his head. 'You know nothing more than you wrote?'

Perez gave a shrug.

'It is as I told you. It didn't make sense then and it doesn't make sense now. How could Mr Jarvis get information about the inner councils of ETA? It has to be nonsense. He barely spoke Spanish, never mind Basque.'

'Did you like him?'

Perez had to think about it.

'No, I don't think so. He was too self-centred, too inward looking. I would say that if I had known him he would not have been a nice man.'

'But you let him visit you?'

'Why not? As I said, he was an educated man, he spoke well and was widely read. I enjoyed talking to him. I didn't have to like him.'

'Did he ever tell you what he did before he came to live in Spain?'

'Yes. He was a lecturer in English Literature at a university. Also he wrote books, novels. He said he had given up education and turned to a life of crime. He said education was the higher calling but that crime paid better.'

'I see. Well, thank you, Fr Perez. In so far as you could, you've been most helpful.'

Jimmy stood up. The priest stayed seated.

'I have enjoyed our talk, Mr Costello, I hope we can do it again.'

'No, Father, you've told me all you can. I'm not educated or widely read and I'm not interested in spiritual evil. I stick to the rational sort.'

He held out his hand. Fr Perez shook it and Jimmy left the old priest in his nice room with its pleasant view. The sister who had answered the door when he came let him out and he walked out of the convent gardens onto the quiet street and headed back towards town and his little terraced house. What had Perez told him, too much or not enough? How much was true and how much lies? That was always the problem with priests, one minute they were marrying you, then baptising your kids, then burying your wife, and they always knew exactly what to say and how to look while they were saying it. Perez was no different. He'd put on the manner he thought the occasion needed, it was all an act. Still, thought Jimmy, it was a bloody good act, so it must have been an important occasion and that tells me something. Perhaps that tells me quite a lot.

Walking back to his house he thought about Jarvis. Maybe he had been an English teacher after all, although certainly not at any university. That was handy. The novel writing thing was probably to explain where his money came from. Perez didn't look like the crime-thriller type so there wasn't much chance of him asking awkward questions. The priest had just accepted the story and forgotten it. Now, next question, was Jarvis caught with his trousers down and, if so, did he get sent down for it and if he did, where did he serve his time? And the last question, was Harry Mercer doing time there as well? That would make a neat fit. That would explain a lot, a hell of a lot.

Chapter Twelve

As Jimmy walked through the streets he looked back over what had happened. He'd been sent to find out about Jarvis. Then he'd been told to cosy up to the police investigation on Jarvis's death. Then he'd been told to drop it all and hurry back to Rome, but only after he'd spoken to Perez. McBride was jiggling him about like she had him on a string, why?

He'd told Suarez she was on the side of the angels and didn't have people killed and he'd believed it when he said it. But when you came right down to it, what did he know about McBride? That she'd used him like a cat's paw to do her dirty work in Rome and people had died. She hadn't had them killed, but they still died.

Yes, all true, but against that she'd protected him and tried to hide him when the shit hit the fan ...

Also true, but only after her dirty work was done.

OK, but she'd saved his life in Denmark and got him safely out.

True again. But did that mean she was on the side of the angels or did it mean that she saved him to use in some other piece of dirty work? *This* piece of dirty work.

Jimmy thought about the old priest sitting in his chair in his room with a view. He'd looked as if he couldn't hurt anyone. In fact he'd looked as if he'd find it hard to get to the window and enjoy the view. And those small, bony hands. Could he kill anyone with those? Then he thought of Harry. Harry had duff hands but not so duff he couldn't pull a trigger. The priest was old and small but just because he hadn't got up and walked around didn't mean he couldn't if he wanted to. And Jarvis knew him. Jarvis would have gone into the kitchen with the old priest behind him without any worries at all. But a priest? Could a priest …? Of course he could. Udo Mundt, the man McBride had used to save his life in Denmark, was a priest and he was definitely somebody who knew how to get people killed. Christ, how could you know about people?

And on that question Jimmy decided he'd had enough. He couldn't do people, not the ordinary sort. Professional villains he could do, professional villains were simple, they were what he'd grown up with. They were just bad guys who did bad things. But this? This was all different. This was too mixed up. Harry was an out-and-out villain. Harry was at it. That bit he understood. Henderson was almost certainly mixed up in it and now looked more like a victim than a perpetrator. What about Mrs Henderson? He didn't like her but then he didn't like most people. It didn't make them all criminal. Was Perez a bad guy just because he was connected to Jarvis? Jimmy thought about what he was doing, what he had spent so much of his life doing when he was with the Met. He was helping Suarez build up a little world and making people fit into it.But what if the people didn't fit into their little world. How hard would he push, how much would he bend the truth to get the result he wanted? And who did he want it for, himself, McBride or Suarez?

He turned onto the sea-front walkway, about fifteen minutes from his street. His mind came back to where he'd started, McBride. On the side of the angels or not? And assuming he could answer that or any of the other questions, where did it leave him?

McBride had got her tame Monsignor to tell him he wasn't here to get involved in a murder or a porn ring, that he should stick to Perez and then come back. Well, he'd seen Perez and that looked like – like what? He thought about his talk with the old priest again and decided he didn't know. Maybe he'd stay on for a bit anyway. He didn't feel like walking away from things just yet. Maybe he'd try to help the police nail Harry. Just for something to do, for old time's sake. But niggling away at the back of his mind in a small room marked *Conscience*, a voice kept asking a question – would he be staying to get Harry or to get Suarez? And if it was Suarez it wouldn't be for old times' sake. But Jimmy closed the door of that room. He didn't want to think about Suarez so he walked on thinking about other things, but very soon found that what he was thinking about was Suarez again. Still, if the choice was her or Harry, well – so he left his thoughts alone to sort themselves out and headed for home.

Back in his house he made a cup of tea then made a call. Suarez answered.

'Hello, it's me. If you check with the UK you may find Jarvis did time in England. No, I don't know for sure, it's something that the old priest told me. Jarvis said he was a university lecturer teaching English Literature before he gave it up and came over here to write crime novels. We know he was a teacher, not a lecturer, and he stopped teaching very early for some reason. One reason would be if he got sent down because he played footsie with a student or two. We also know that Jarvis isn't the crime writer, Harry Mercer is. I think that might be how the connection got made, in the nick. If I'm right I think we'll find that Harry Mercer was doing time in the same prison as Jarvis. Why? Because it fits the facts, that's why. Harry's a villain who only associated with other villains and, apart from an error of judgement in Birmingham, never worked outside of London. Where would a teacher or even an ex-teacher meet up with the likes of Harry Mercer except inside? It won't be too hard to check where Harry did his time and if it clicks with any time Jarvis did then we're off and running, we'll have a solid connection and if we're lucky you might even be able to follow it through and rope in Henderson along the way.' Jimmy listened for a second. 'Yeah, I was lucky, I don't think the old priest meant to be helpful, in fact I think he was trying to make sure he told me nothing that was of any real use at all.' Jimmy listened. 'I agree. Put Henderson alongside Mercer and Jarvis on a porn charge and you'll have enough to ask him if he'll please come down to the station and help with your enquiries. From what I've seen he'll spill his guts once you can get him into an interview room with anything that looks remotely like evidence.' He listened again. 'OK, let me know when you've got anything.'

Jimmy put away his phone and looked at his watch. Time for lunch. A couple of cold beers first and then some fish. They did good fish here, he'd tried a couple of places and they had impressed him. He liked fish, if it was good-quality and fresh. Jimmy left his little house and went to yet another place to try the fish. He sat down and ordered a beer and looked at the menu. It wasn't a tourist place so it was all in Spanish but that didn't deter him, most places you could get by with English and a smile. The waiter brought his beer.

'I'd like the fish. Can you tell me what fish you've got?' The waiter looked at him, spread his hands, shrugged and said something in Spanish. Jimmy tried again. 'Fish. I'd like a meal, lunch, fish.' The waiter shrugged again and looked around as if appealing to the other diners none of whom took any notice. Jimmy realised he'd found somewhere or someone who, for whatever reason, chose not to do English. He stood up. 'Sorry, mate, I don't speak Spanish and you don't seem to speak English. I'll go somewhere else.' Jimmy began to leave the table and the waiter caught his arm and began to speak rapidly. Jimmy stopped and looked down at the hand on his arm then spoke quietly. 'Let go sunshine or I'll break your fucking arm.' The waiter's hand dropped from Jimmy's arm and he stood back. He turned and called out across the room. A man came from behind the bar to the table. They spoke in Spanish.

'He says you ordered beer and now are leaving without paying. If you order a drink you must pay for it.'

'I ordered beer in English and I got beer. I asked him for fish in English but he seems to have forgotten how to understand. I asked him to take his hand off my arm in English and he suddenly remembered he could understand again.' Jimmy looked at the waiter. 'It sort of comes and goes doesn't it, pal?' The waiter said nothing. 'Still, if he decides he can't understand my order I'll leave and eat somewhere else. Is that a problem?'

The man from the bar thought about it. He wasn't big but he looked useful, competent. The man spoke to the waiter who turned and left.

'I will take your order. What do you want?'

Jimmy found he wasn't in a good mood any more and he didn't want the fish even if it did come in English. If he stayed, there would be trouble and he found trouble was exactly what he wanted.

'I want to leave. I want to leave peacefully without any trouble but I want to leave. I've lost my appetite for food or beer.'

The man looked at him. Jimmy noticed that the other diners were now taking notice.

'Then if you pay for your drink you are free to go.'

The man didn't move and there was no easy way round him between the tables.

Jimmy looked at the bottle on the table then back at the man.

'I'll toss you for it.' The man frowned. Jimmy took a coin from his pocket and held it up. 'Heads I pay, tails I don't?' Jimmy didn't wait, he spun the coin, caught it and slapped it onto the back of his hand. He didn't look at it.

'Tails. I don't pay. Now I'm leaving, sunshine, either past you or through you and I don't give a shit which it will be.'

The man stood for a second then moved to one side. Jimmy went past him, through the room and out into the street where he turned and walked. He didn't care which way he was going.

Now what the fuck was that all about, he thought. But he knew what it was about. It was about a frustration and anger that sometimes, from nowhere, built up in him. He decided to give lunch a miss, he'd lost his appetite. He'd walk. It was hot and the heat would tire him and when he was tired enough he'd stop somewhere for that cold beer.

Would he have hurt the bloke?

Yes, he decided, he would, and he would have enjoyed it.

Jimmy began to walk in the heat, to try and get tired and let the anger die down and drain out of his system. Where did it come from, that pointless hate? But he knew where it came from, it came from who he was and who he'd been, and it was who he'd always be so long as he let it boil up and take over.

About twenty minutes later he was sitting in a bar, tired and feeling nothing except that he needed to sit down out of the heat for a while and drink a couple of cold beers.

He forced his mind back to the meeting with the old priest. He knew he should be satisfied. He'd got everything he expected and a bit that he hadn't expected.

But he wasn't satisfied.

Something wasn't right. Did it matter? He'd done what he had been sent to do and it was what everyone said it would be, a dead end. He'd done all he could. His mind moved on to the murder. It was probably no more than thieves falling out. Should he just wrap it up and go back to Rome.

Why was he fucking about pretending to be a

detective? Why wasn't he wrapping it up and going home? What was the point of hanging on? Was it because he was looking at something and not seeing it? Was something staring him in the face and he just couldn't see it?

The picture of Suarez sitting opposite him with that look which disturbed him, looking at him with her legs crossed came to him. Was it Suarez?

It couldn't be Suarez. He hadn't looked at another woman since he had started going with Bernie when he was sixteen, a lifetime ago. He still didn't want to look at another woman.

So why did he look at Suarez and why did he think it might be her that was keeping him here?

Oh, well, beer and cool down, maybe even a snack to make up for the missed lunch. He'd give it two days and then fuck it, whatever it was. It could stay in Spain and he'd go back and report that there was nothing to report. He smiled to himself. At least I can squeeze two more days' expenses out of McBride and, considering she gets nothing in return, that's something. Maybe that's what's staring me in the face.

But it wasn't and he knew it.

That night Jimmy lay in bed, naked with a single sheet thrown over his thighs and legs and the bedroom window open. He couldn't sleep. His mind wouldn't switch off and it was too hot. Outside the cicadas chirruped endlessly. He lay in the dark, sweating. Then, from downstairs, there was a noise, muffled but like the breaking of glass. Jimmy threw off the sheet, got up and went to the door which he'd left open in the vain hope of creating a breeze through the room.

He stood and listened. Somebody was definitely down there, in the kitchen. He heard a click as the kitchen door opened, then he heard the bottom stair creak. Whoever was there was coming up. He padded quickly across the room, arranged two pillows to look like a body and threw the sheet over it. The room was dark but there was just enough light coming in through the window to make it do the job. He went back and stood ready behind the door which he'd eased half closed. After a minute the door began to be pushed back. Jimmy stood, made a hard left fist, raised it and drew back his elbow. Someone was in the bedroom. As he passed the window going to the bed Jimmy had enough of a target. He stepped out, the figure turned and Jimmy hit it hard.

The knuckles landed on the side of the face but it gave Jimmy a better sense of his target and he hit again hard. This time it landed square. The figure staggered towards the window, Jimmy moved in and felt a sharp pain under his left ribs. He ignored it. He moved slightly and hit again, this time with his right fist into the middle of the body. Something fell to the floor as the figure gasped and fell to its knees. Jimmy stepped behind, bent down, grabbed the head, slipped his hands round the neck then rammed his knee into the figure's back as he pulled and twisted. Something cracked and the body went limp.

He let it slip out of his hands and it slumped onto the floor. Jimmy stood back and breathed deeply for a moment, then went and switched on the light. It was a swarthy, youngish man in a light suit. Jimmy bent down and felt his pulse. There wasn't one.

'Shit.'

He was out of practice, he hadn't meant to break his bloody neck. Then he saw the knife beside the body with blood on the blade. He looked down at his side below his ribs. It was his blood and there was more coming out of the wound the knife had made. He pressed his hand onto the blood and went and sat on the bed. He picked up his mobile with his free hand from the bedside table and keyed in a number with his thumb.

'Hello, it's me. I know what fucking time it is. Listen, I think you'd better get over here, I just killed someone.

Yes, you heard right, I killed a bloke. I broke his neck. How would I know who he is? He broke in, came at me with a knife and I broke his neck. Look, can we hurry this up and leave explanations till later, only the knife got used and I'm bleeding.' He looked down, his hand over the wound wasn't doing much good. The blood was seeping from between his fingers and from under his palm and running down his side. There was already a stain on the bedclothes. 'I'm making a mess of your cousin's sheets. You better bring an ambulance with you.' He put the mobile down and looked under his bloody hand. He was bleeding all right. Then he looked at the corpse on the floor. 'And what the fuck were you playing at?'

He took another look at his wound and the blood that had run down his side. There seemed a lot of it and the pain was kicking in. He hoped the ambulance would get here soon. He pulled the sheet up and put it over the wound and pressed with his hand, then looked back at the body.

He was too old for rough-stuff, too old and too out of practice. He hadn't meant to kill him, killing people got you noticed. He'd got his hands in the wrong place on his neck, that's what it was, just got his hands in the wrong place. He lay back on the bed beside the pillows. That's all it was, when his knee hit and he pulled it just snapped his neck. His mind began to drift. Why hadn't the stupid bastard brought a knife with him and come in through the open bedroom window? Silly sod.

And with that considered judgement on the uninvited visitor, now dead on his bedroom floor, Jimmy slowly passed out.

Chapter Thirteen

When Jimmy came round he was in hospital with a bandage round his middle which showed a dark stain on the left side where the knife had gone in. Suarez was sitting on the edge of his bed. Standing behind her, leaning against the wall of the room, was a squat, sad-looking man of about Jimmy's age. He had greasy black hair, was wearing a badly-fitting suit, and looked as if he had always been there and could go on standing there for ever. The sad man looked on impassively as Suarez told Jimmy the knife had gone deep but hadn't done any serious damage. He'd been lucky, the doctor said. A bit more to the right and the world would have been short one James Cornelius Costello. It was a nasty wound and he had lost quite a bit of blood.

'So when can I get out of here?'

'No, you can't. You're all stitched up,' she smiled, 'but not in your London police sense. There'll be quite a bit of pain if you try to move and –'

'So when can I get out of here.'

'Yes, I thought you might be like that. The doctor has agreed, after considerable persuasion, that you can leave as soon as you genuinely feel up to it. But he insisted you should rest up and even when you can get about you should keep walking to a minimum until you've had the stitches out. The doctor says you should stay home and rest. So I guess you need a home.'

Jimmy looked past Suarez to the sad man.

'Is that what he's here for? Is he going to give me a

home? I can't very well go back to your cousin's place, it's a crime scene.'

'He's my boss. He's here because he wants to talk to you.'

'So why doesn't he say something?'

'Because he doesn't speak English.'

'Then he's fucked isn't he, because I don't speak Spanish.'

'No, Jimmy, he's not fucked, because I'll translate. Don't try and be a hard case, you're not up to it today and won't be for quite a few days more. Be good, co-operate.'

Jimmy tried to pull himself up in the bed so he could get into a sitting position but quickly gave it up. The doctor was right, it was very painful. Suarez saw what he wanted. She slipped off the bed, stood over him, put her arms under his and pulled him up gently so he was sitting. It was still painful but he didn't mind, he got the smell of her hair, it was nice, and while she was holding him he felt her breast press against him. She was strong, he thought, not that it mattered, but it stopped him thinking about other things she was.

Once he was sitting up Suarez arranged the pillows behind him then began to act as interpreter for her boss, who had suddenly come to life. He left the wall to hold itself up and started to ask his questions. They went through the events of the night before. All Jimmy knew was that he heard a noise, got up, did what he did and the guy's neck got broken by accident. He had only meant to hurt him enough to keep him quiet, to disable him. It was an accident. But Jimmy got the distinct impression that the detective found that hard to believe. He felt that way because telling it out loud made it sound hard to believe, even to himself, and he had been there. When the detective had finally finished, he told Suarez to tell Jimmy not to leave Santander and surrender his passport at the nearest police station, then he left.

Suarez began to follow him but at the door she stopped.

'Call me when you want to leave and I'll come and get you. But remember, don't be a hard case, co-operate and make sure you're sufficiently mended before you leave otherwise you'll be straight back in.'

Then she left and a nurse looked in so Jimmy asked for coffee.

He spent the rest of the morning sitting still and trying to let his mind be blank. He wanted to be out of hospital as soon as possible and knew that meant resting up the wound so that was what he did. While he was at it he tried to rest up his mind as well. He rested, dozed, woke up, drank some orange juice which had appeared by his bed, then rested some more. The doctor came and took off his bandage and examined his stitches, seemed satisfied and left the nurse to put on a new bandage, a nice white one with no dark stain. He ate some soup and drank coffee and the day slowly passed.

That night he dreamed, a confused dream in which he could never get to where he was going, partly because no one would tell him where it was that he was going and partly because of locked doors to which only McBride had the keys. She looked at him through windows that wouldn't open and he glimpsed her down corridors or across crowded rooms. But she was always gone when he got there and the door through which he could follow her was always locked. He woke twice and twice went back to sleep but the dream, changed but not really any different, persisted until he woke once more and it was morning.

The nurse eventually came in, opened the curtains and spoke to him in Spanish. He smiled, he was co-operating. He had orange juice and coffee for breakfast then he was left alone. He decided his mind had rested enough so he started going over things; Jarvis, Mercer, Henderson, his night-time attacker, but somehow the smell of Suarez's hair and the feel of her breasts against him kept on pushing themselves in and he had to keep pushing them out again. He forced himself to think of McBride's command delivered by her tame Monsignor and his talk to Perez. It all had to fit together somehow, but how? He thought about Jarvis being shot, Jarvis in prison and Harry in prison, he thought about it all until they brought him a light lunch. He tried to eat it but it was a tough struggle. It was fish, but it wasn't good fish. After lunch he slept again and this time there were no dreams, at least none that he could remember. Late in the afternoon he woke, thought some more, then slept again. After a while he woke again, ate another light meal, which wasn't fish this time, thought some more, then slept and dreamed another frustrating and confused dream in which he was looking for Suarez and McBride was always getting in the way.

Then, suddenly, a new day began.

He stuck it out until lunch. It was the lunch that had made him call Suarez. It was fish again. He could look at it, just, but there was no way he could eat it, and he was getting hungry. She came and helped him dress and then took him in a wheelchair down to her car where the nurse who was with them helped her get Jimmy in. The nurse and Suarez spoke then Suarez got in and they drove off.

'She was asking me if I had a wheelchair for you at the other end. I told her I did.'

'Do you?'

'No. You'll have to use the lift. Think you can manage it? If you die on me all hell will break loose.'

'Then I'll try not to die on you.'

Suarez stopped her car outside a block of apartments which stood among other blocks of apartments. She helped him out of the car and got him, slowly, to the lift. Then they went up to her apartment where she sat him down in the living room and put a small stool under his feet. Jimmy lay back in his chair and closed his eyes. It had been a short car ride, a few steps to a lift and then a few more into the apartment, but it had made him feel like shit and told him how weak he really was. Suarez peeled open his shirt and examined the bandage. It seemed all right, no blood stain had appeared.

'It seems ...'

But when she looked at him he was asleep. She pulled his shirt closed and left, closing the door quietly behind her. When she came back half an hour later Jimmy was still in the chair and still asleep, so she left him to recover from his premature exit from the hospital. He was asleep, not dead, so all hell hadn't broken loose. Not yet.

When Jimmy opened his eyes, on the table beside him was his jacket. On top of it was a bulging carrier bag from which hung a sock. Suarez came into the room from the kitchen and saw him looking at it.

'I got a few things from the house and brought them here. You'll have to stay here until you're fit to walk. The doctor said you shouldn't be on your own until the wound has knitted enough not to be a problem.'

'Then I'd better try walking.'

Jimmy began to get up.

Suarez hurried to him and gently pushed him back into his chair.

'No, not too soon, there's no hurry, there's nobody else here.'

Jimmy sat back.

'Where do I sleep?'

'There's a spare room. It's all fixed.'

'How did you swing it? I'm not fit to be out of hospital.'

'I told the doctor we were worried there would be another attempt on you. We needed you where we could look after you and we didn't want the world to know about it so he should make sure it wasn't made too well known among the staff. I guess I made it all sound a bit dramatic. Anyway, he let you go so here you are.'

'And was that your idea or your boss's?'

'God, not my boss, he knows nothing about it.'

'And if he finds out?'

'It would be better if he didn't until you can walk and talk, so my advice is get better soon, then neither of us need worry about my boss.'

Jimmy sat back and decided she was right, he should try and get better as soon as possible then her boss wouldn't be a problem. But there would be other problems if he was living in her apartment. He felt sure there would.

Chapter Fourteen

Two days later Jimmy walked slowly and gingerly to the balcony and carefully eased himself into a chair. The balcony had room for a small table and two chairs and a terracotta flowerpot with some sort of plant growing in it. Jimmy looked at the view. He liked it even if it was only other apartment blocks, all much like the one they were in. There was no sea anywhere, no beaches, and no bloody ferry. It was peaceful, domestic. An awning stretched out above the balcony but it wasn't necessary. Suarez's apartment was on the second floor and the sun in the late afternoon sky made the shadow of the block opposite fall across where he sat. It was still hot, but not punishingly so. On the table were two glasses. One held brandy, lemonade and ice; in the other was orange juice, also with ice. Jimmy picked up his orange juice, swirled the ice round, and took a drink.

Suarez came out with a plate of cooked meats and a bowl of salad sitting on two plates with knives and forks balanced on the edge of the plates. She laid everything out on the table and sat down. She picked up her drink and took a sip.

'I don't like it, Jimmy.'

He held out his orange juice.

'Then don't drink it, swap with me. I don't like orange juice.'

'Idiot,' she smiled, but the smile didn't last. 'I don't like how all this is shaping up. And my boss doesn't like it either. In fact I can't think of a single person who does like it.'

'What's there to like? I've been stuck with one of my own kitchen knives and the man who stuck me is in the morgue.'

'That's the problem, you. How long have you been here? Hardly any time at all and we've got two dead men that are connected to you. That's a high body count by our standards.'

'Jarvis was dead before I could have got near him and if some bloke breaks into my house and tries to stick a knife in me I don't see how I can be held responsible.'

'Oh, you can be held responsible all right, because you killed him. You broke his neck, remember?'

Jimmy remembered.

'Do you know anything yet?'

'He flew in from Madrid the morning of the day he broke in, didn't check into any hotel that we can find, and he appears to have had no luggage. He obviously came to do a job and expected to be gone as soon as it was done. You, it seems, were the job. He must have waited somewhere until two in the morning, broke into your kitchen to get a knife, and then went upstairs to finish you off.He had a return ticket to Madrid on a nine o'clock flight. If things had gone to plan he'd have probably been on his way before anybody found anything. He had his passport in his jacket. It says he's Romanian but it's a phoney, a good phoney, but still a phoney. We're checking the name in the passport on flights into and out of Madrid and we might turn up something but it's a hub airport, that means a lot of people passing through from all over. We might find where he came from but even if we do it probably won't get us anywhere.'

Jimmy carefully reached down and picked up his plate, put a couple of slices of meat and some salad onto it, then picked up his fork and ate a couple of mouthfuls.

'You've covered the ground but it sounds like you

haven't turned up much.'

'Jimmy, for God's sake, it was a contract. Somebody wants you dead and it seems that they can arrange for that to happen at short notice. I'd say that makes the connection between you and Jarvis quite a bit stronger. Jarvis dies on the day you arrive, you start asking questions and somebody sets it up for you to get killed. Yes, I think I could safely say there's quite a connection.'

Jimmy didn't waste time disagreeing. If the hit-man had come in by plane that would explain why he had to get a knife and came in through the kitchen instead of coming through the open bedroom window. It looked like a contract all right, but who the hell wanted him dead and was prepared to pay someone to do it? Even in Romania, if the bloke *was* from Romania, it couldn't have come cheap.

Suarez used her fingers to fill her plate and took a mouthful before speaking. 'So, Jimmy, who wants you dead?'

Jimmy shrugged and winced as the stitches stabbed him with pain. He carefully and slowly put his plate back onto the table. He suddenly found he wasn't that hungry.

'No-one that I can think of. Once, a while ago, there were people who might have organised something, a contract, a professional, but that all got straightened out in Copenhagen. At least I thought it had.'

'What people?'

'It's an old story, something that happened long ago?'

It wasn't so very long ago but Jimmy wanted to think of it that way, something in his past that he could forget about.

'Forget long ago, who was after you?'

'I told you, that got straightened out. If it had been them I'd be dead. They don't climb in through kitchen windows to get the murder weapon out of a kitchen drawer.'

Suarez picked up her glass and was silent for a while.

Then she took a drink and put the glass down and ate some more.

'Is it all true, what we were told about you?'

'I don't know, you were a bit vague on details.'

'Come on, Jimmy, you know what I mean. To me you seem an all right sort of guy, but we were told to expect someone who was anything but all right, probably a killer among other things. Just tell me it's not true.' Jimmy sat in silence. He didn't have the answer she wanted, but she still wanted an answer 'It's true?' Jimmy continued to sit in silence. Suarez took another drink. 'So, when was the last time you killed someone, Jimmy, apart from last night?'

'Why do you want to know?'

'If you're staying in my apartment I think that entitles me to ask, don't you?'

Well, thought Jimmy, if she wants to know she might as well know.

'The last time I killed anybody was a long time ago. He was a villain and I was a copper, a bent copper as it happened, on the take. When I wouldn't take his money he said he would go after my kids, they were just little then. So I killed him.'

Suarez thought about it.

'Just like that?'

'No, not just like that. I made it look like an accident. I did a good job and it got put down as an accident.'

'And that's the last time?'

'No, not really. I could say it was, but I'd be doing the same as McBride, telling you half the truth so you would see things the way I wanted you to.' He took a sip of his juice, it didn't help. He didn't expect it to, it was orange juice. 'Not so very long ago there were people who wanted me dead and they were the sort who could get it done. Like I said, they didn't climb in through kitchen windows to get knives. They brought their kit with them and they didn't miss. McBride arranged for me to disappear and I finished up in Denmark. But the past caught up with me and people got killed. Depending on how you look at it you could say I killed them. It wasn't my finger on the trigger but I was the reason they died.'

'How many?'

'Two that I know of?'

'The two in Lübeck?' Jimmy nodded. 'My God, Jimmy, what the hell are you?'

Jimmy didn't look at her. He looked straight ahead.

'I'm a bloke, I had a wife, a family and a job. I was a bad husband, a bad father and a bad copper and I have to live with that. Now I've got nothing except that I'm alive, though God knows why, and I mean that, God knows why and I don't. I work for Professor McBride because she saved my life. She screwed me up but she also saved my life. I try, that's what I do, I try, try to do the best I can but ...'

But the words ran out. Words didn't make it right or sensible or anything else so he stopped using them.

Suarez took a drink then finished what was on her plate. She stood up.

'I'll say this for you, Jimmy, you certainly have a past.'

'But do I have a future?'

It had come too quickly and it had come out wrong. Or had it?

Shit, he hadn't felt like this since he was a teenager and now he was old enough to be her fucking dad. What was happening to him? He looked at her. She was looking at him in that funny way again. Oh, Christ, he thought, just let her laugh. Let me see that she thinks it's all a load of bollocks. One good laugh at a stupid old bastard who's made a fool of himself.

But Suarez didn't laugh, she did worse.

She smiled.

Chapter Fifteen

Jimmy waited. Was he pleased or not? Did saying it out loud make any difference? Did her smile mean anything?

Suarez broke the silence that had suddenly come between them.

'You did it for money, these killings?'

It wasn't what he had expected.

'No.'

'Did people ever pay you to kill?'

Jimmy's thoughts were now thoroughly jerked back from what he'd said and how he felt.

'No, not really. I did a lot of things for money, but not killing, I was never a professional in that line.'

'Well, the way your visitor friend down at the morgue died could say different so let's stick with that for the time being. Let's stick with snapping his neck like a breadstick. Where did you learn that charming trick? Think about it and tell me when I come back.'

Suarez took her plate and her empty glass through the open sliding doors into the living room. Jimmy picked up his orange juice, swirled it, and put it down on the plate amongst what was left of his meal. He didn't want orange juice and he wasn't hungry. He sat looking out at the balconies of the other apartments. On some of them people, normal people with normal lives were sitting talking about normal things, or doing whatever normal people did on balconies in the late afternoon. After a few minutes Suarez came back out with a fresh drink and sat down.

'OK, I'm settled, tell me all about it.'

'I explained all about that at the hospital. It was an accident. I just meant to put him out of action. I got my hands in the wrong place and he just sort of snapped. It's been a long time since I rough-housed with anyone and you need to keep in practice. I was out of practice so I made a mistake.'

'Jimmy, you've killed someone. This investigation was already beginning to look like it could turn messy and now you could have turned it into a disaster.'

'How do you work that out?'

'Someone who is supposed to be liaising with the police while they are working on a murder uses excessive force against a burglar and breaks his neck. You wouldn't say it will be a disaster when the media gets hold of it?'

'He had a knife. I should have just lain in bed and let him stick me?'

'They'll say you put him out of action when you hit him. That you could have disarmed him. That you didn't have to finish him off. And the way you did it looked too professional.'

'I've told you –'

'Yes, I know. It was an accident. The problem is that it doesn't look like an accident.' She took a sip from her drink and looked into space for a moment. 'What exactly do you do in Rome, and who is this Professor McBride?'

'I told you, I'm just an errand boy. Jarvis came up with that cock-eyed story and I was asked to talk to him and report back. It's not my fault he took a bullet in the head the same day as I arrived.'

'Take some advice, don't keep saying it's not your fault. It damn well looks like your fault and you should be able to see that even if you don't like it and even if it's not true.'

'OK, maybe some of it is my fault, but only some of it. I had no idea who this Jarvis character was until I was sent –'

'It doesn't wash, Jimmy. No-one in Rome would take Jarvis's story seriously. How could Jarvis have got any terrorist information, even supposing it were true.'

'It's not true, it's nonsense, Perez told me that. He said Jarvis barely spoke Spanish, never mind Basque. There's no way he could have got that kind of inside information.'

'So why did he spin the story to Perez?'

'God knows. Maybe he liked to make things up, make people think he was some kind of important bloke. He told Perez he used to be a university lecturer and that now he made his living writing crime thrillers.'

'None of which is true.'

'No, but there's an element of truth in it. He was a teacher, remember.' Jimmy saw his chance to get the conversation well away from himself. 'Which brings me back to the call I put into you. Did Jarvis do time?'

'We're trying to find out.' They sat for a moment. Jimmy could see that Suarez was thinking but he didn't want to know what she was thinking about. Or did he? Then she turned to him. 'Look, Jimmy, forget Jarvis, forget Mercer and Henderson. Just concentrate on getting well and getting out. Out of this apartment, out of Santander, and out of Spain. My boss knows you're here now and he's taken it badly but at least I'm not suspended. He's taking legal advice about how to deal with the killing of your intruder. At the moment it's just an intruder, a struggle, and an accidental death. You were in a holiday let so we're letting the papers assume you're a tourist. Maybe our people will decide to throw the book at you or maybe they'll get in touch with your people in Rome and try to sort something out. Just hope the right choice gets made.'

He couldn't stop himself from asking.

'You worried about me?'

She looked at him in that odd way again and then it was gone.

'No, I'm worried about the body count. Two is already too many. I want you on your way, back to Rome doing whatever it is you do for your professor. I want you somewhere that's far away from here.'

It wasn't the answer he wanted to hear but he knew it was the right answer for them both.

The phone rang. Suarez got up and went inside to answer it. After a short while she came back and sat down.

'That was my boss, he wants to see you.'

'At the station?'

'No. I told him the doctor said you couldn't move around a lot until the wound healed but that you could leave hospital if you had someone to look after you. I had to tell him you were here.'

'How did he take it?'

'He didn't fire me.'

'But he'll know it's all wrong, that you're bullshitting him. You're a working copper, how could you look after me?'

And he got the look again.

'Never mind what my boss thinks. He's coming here.' She looked at her watch. 'He'll be here in about half an hour. He told me something else.'

'Yes?'

'You were right, Jarvis did time. For having sex with consenting but under-age girls at his school.'

'Was he an English teacher?'

'What the hell does it matter what he taught?'

'I think it matters. How about whether he and Mercer did time together?'

'We're working on it.' She paused. 'My chief said it was good thinking on my part to check if Jarvis had a record. I sort of didn't get round to telling him it wasn't my idea.'

Jimmy grinned.

'Don't worry, it's not like you did anything bad, like

killing someone. You only lied to get me out of hospital. And any credit wouldn't do me any good, so why not take it?'

Suarez smiled at him and picked up her drink.

'Were you any good as a detective?'

'Best in my year, I was told.'

'Who told you that?'

'McBride.'

'How would she know?'

'Oh, you'd be surprised what she knows.'

'Well you made a good call on Jarvis, thanks.'

'Just exchanging favours.'

'Exchanging favours?'

'I'm staying here aren't I?'

Jimmy hoped for the look or a smile but nothing came, She just took a drink and looked straight ahead when she spoke.

'Where else was there? Your place is currently a crime scene and there's a spare bed here.' She put her glass down and stood up. 'If my boss is coming I better get going again. I'll phone and try to find out where we stand on finding out whether Mercer and Jarvis did time together.'

Suarez went into the living room to make her phone call.

Jimmy sat for a moment then picked up his glass and tried to swirl the ice in his orange juice again, but it had almost melted. He put his glass back. He felt empty and flat, like a disappointed child who expected a treat which hadn't materialised. He reached across the table, grimacing as the stitches pulled, and picked up the glass of brandy and lemonade that Suarez had left. He took a big drink then reached back onto the table and pushed it back to where it had been. The stitches pulled again.

'Shit.'

He ignored the pain, he wasn't a child and there would be no treats, life had to go on. Somebody had set him up to be killed. Why? What did he know that made him so dangerous? He knew Henderson, Mercer, and Jarvis had to be connected, and he knew that it had to have something to do with the porn. It had to. But he couldn't prove it. He looked across at the brandy and lemonade. For God's sake, he wasn't even interested in proving it. So why was he thinking about it? The little voice from deep inside his head, a voice that had niggled him all his life, niggled again – because Suarez was thinking about it. He was doing it for Suarez, because if he did it for Suarez then maybe …

Shit.

But this time it wasn't the stitches. He looked at the brandy and lemonade again, then picked up his orange juice and finished it.

He stared out at the other balconies and let his mind run. He was too tired to fight it. Did he care for Suarez and, more importantly, could she ever care about him in the same way? He'd never even looked at another woman while Bernie was alive. But Bernie was dead … Well, whatever happened, or didn't happen, he wasn't going anywhere and he had to think about something so why not the case? At least it took his mind off other things, almost.

Like Suarez said, Henderson, Harry, and Jarvis had been careful at this end, so why take any chances now? Why set up a killing? There was already one murder investigation going on, why bring in a hired killer and set another investigation going, a related investigation? Another killing had to turn up the heat on Harry and Henderson. So what did he know that made him dangerous? He knew Harry and all about his past. But Harry's past wasn't any kind of secret. He broadcast it, for God's sake: ex-London villain turns writer. It was his fucking trad mark, not a secret. What else? Henderson met up with Mercer and they both lied about it. Of course they fucking lied about it, and the lie would work fine for them

114

as long as they both stuck to it. No, he couldn't see it. Why bring in a killer? That was heavy stuff, importing someone. Why? But nothing clicked into place, nothing stacked up next to anything else. It made no sense, no more sense than any of the rest of this bloody farce. But someone wanted him dead. And that meant he needed to find out who and why or next time whoever they sent wouldn't miss.

He looked at the brandy and lemonade again and nearly reached across. But then an idea flickered onto the edge of his mind, an important idea ...

Before he could catch it Suarez came back and it was gone.

'They're onto it, they should ...'

'Fuck.'

Suarez sat down. The look was back and there was almost a smile.

'Is that a suggestion or a comment?'

Jimmy felt confused and embarrassed. Was it an invitation, a joke, or was she just pissing him about?

'It was something that came to me, an idea. It had to do with Jarvis, maybe something he said or something Perez said about him. But it's gone, it just sort of went when you came out and started talking.'

'It doesn't matter. Jarvis, Henderson and Mercer are none of your business. They're police business, Spanish police business. Your business is persuading my chief that you really did kill that guy by accident, that you know nothing about why he broke in and tried to kill you and that you should be allowed to leave as soon as you're fit enough. That's enough business to be going on with.' She picked up his glass. 'And don't think I didn't see you drinking this. You're off alcohol for a couple of days.' She finished what was left in the glass. 'Don't make me have to lock up the bottles while you're here.'

But he wasn't really listening.

What was it? It had to be something to do with Jarvis. Was it about what Jarvis, Henderson and Mercer were up to? He concentrated, but the idea stayed hidden just beyond the horizon of his mind and Jimmy's thoughts moved back onto the familiar rails. Jarvis was dead and Henderson was only ever an accountant. Jimmy was sure that Henderson had never been convicted of anything, let alone done time. Prison would have broken him. And Henderson couldn't have killed Jarvis, he didn't have the nerve. That left Harry. If Harry was still up to no good and had killed Jarvis then he could probably set up a professional kill. Jimmy's thoughts ran on. And Harry would like to see me dead, just for old-time's sake. But this wasn't down to old-time's sake. It had to be Harry who wanted him dead. Who else was there? He turned his head and looked at Suarez who was sitting back in her chair with her eyes closed. Maybe she was right after all and he should get out of Spain, but he wouldn't go to Rome. He'd go to England. Whatever it was, that was where it must have started so that's where he'd go. Suarez said it first and Suarez was right, maybe the break would come in the UK, maybe they hadn't been so careful there. But first he had to persuade Suarez's chief he'd snapped a total stranger's neck by accident. A nice clean job. Maybe too clean to be an accident. Had he just got carried away and forgotten for a second that he didn't hurt people any more, not even people who broke in and tried to stick knives in him? Maybe it was like riding a bike, something you never really forgot. He looked again at Suarez with her eyes closed. No, it really had been an accident, it really had. The problem was, there were still times when he had trouble believing himself, that he was telling the truth, the whole truth and nothing but the truth.

Chapter Sixteen

'Why are you still here taking an interest? Why haven't you gone back to Rome?'

It was Saturday night and they were eating dinner in a little restaurant in one of the backstreets of the town not too far from the blocks of flats where Suarez lived. It was a place the locals used and it didn't get tourists.

Jimmy ate while he tried to think of an answer to her question. He didn't want to say out loud that he was staying mainly because of her. So long as he didn't say it out loud he could pretend it wasn't really true, just a piece of make believe.

The pause got too long, she was waiting for an answer.

'Are you trying to get rid of me, get me out of your apartment? I'll go to a hotel if you like.'

'No, I don't want you out, I just want to know why you're hanging on. The day before yesterday my chief told you that officially it would go down as a break-in, a struggle, and an unfortunate accident. He also told you he wanted you gone, that if you stayed he might find evidence that changed his mind. And here you are looking like you're thinking of becoming a long-term resident.' She gave him the look. 'It's nothing to do with me, is it?'

Jimmy nearly choked as he suddenly swallowed the food in his mouth. He reached out hurriedly for his wine and took a drink. When he put the glass down she was still giving him the look and waiting for an answer.

'No, it's nothing to do with you. Why would it be anything to do with you?'

117

She sat back.

'Well you certainly know how to pay a girl a compliment, Jimmy.'

Jimmy felt at a loss. Everything he said came out wrong.

'No, I didn't mean it that way. All I meant was …'

She leant forward, put her elbows on the table and rested her chin on her hands. Her blouse hung a bit further open. Jimmy could see the top of her black bra on either side of her cleavage. Was she doing it on purpose? She couldn't be doing it on purpose. He was old enough … well never mind how old he was. She wasn't doing it on purpose.

'It may come as a surprise to you but there have been men who have found me attractive.'

'I didn't say you weren't attractive.' He took another drink of wine. He felt as if he was slipping out of his depth. He was no good at this sort of thing. 'I didn't mean …I think you're very attractive. It's just that …'

'In fact one man thought me so attractive he asked me to marry him.'

She sat back and her bra and cleavage retreated from view. Jimmy was sorry they had gone, he missed them both.

'What was your answer?'

He knew it sounded idiotic but it was all he could think of, except her cleavage and bra and he couldn't very well ask to have them put back on view.

'I said yes.'

That brought him down with a bump.

'Yes?'

'I married him.'

There was a brief pause.

'You're married?'

'I suppose so. I never bothered to get a divorce and he was a Catholic with a big C so no divorce court for Carlos.

And even if he'd wanted one his mamá wouldn't have permitted it.'

'I didn't realise you were married.'

'As far as I'm concerned I'm not. I'm not a Catholic any more, not with a big C or a little c, not with any kind of c.'

'What happened?'

She sat forward again, pushed her empty plate to one side and put her elbows on the table. Jimmy looked, but somehow this time there was nothing to see. Maybe it was a knack she had. He carried on eating his fish.

'I was eighteen, he was English, no, not exactly English. He had been born in England but his family were Spanish, they had a restaurant in London, Croydon. He was here on holiday, we met, fell in love and, bingo, he asked me to marry him and I said, yes. One of those whirlwind things.'

'He swept you off your feet.'

Her face split in a smile.

'You wouldn't say that if you knew Carlos. No, if any sweeping got done it was by me. I was eighteen and a virgin and my hormones were ticking like a bomb. He was good-looking, had a good business, and I would get to live in London. At eighteen it seemed enough.' Jimmy didn't bother to point out that living in Croydon wasn't exactly living in London. 'Also I thought I'd get to learn the restaurant business.'

'So what went wrong?'

'Babies and motherhood.'

Jimmy stopped eating. Apart from a husband did she also have kids somewhere?

'Do you have kids?'

That brought a loud laugh and the laugh caught the attention of a waiter and a few others. Jimmy felt embarrassed, put his fork down and pushed his plate aside as the waiter came. The waiter spoke to Suarez who

119

nodded. The waiter took the plates and left.

'No, Jimmy, don't look so worried. I didn't abandon any babies. Carlos didn't want me to learn the restaurant business or any other business, he just wanted me to have babies and I didn't want babies.'

'So where did motherhood come in?'

'We lived above the restaurant. So did his mother and his father, also his unmarried sister and his uncle Franco, they all worked in the restaurant. The whole lot were under Mamá's thumb. When she said jump they said, how high? The men were all cardboard cut-outs, take the restaurant out of their lives and they disappeared. But I liked his sister. She was older than Carlos but Mamá had already squelched two men who had been interested in her so she had resigned herself to being cheap labour for the rest of her life or at least until Mamá died, which looked like being never.'

'So what did you do?'

'I walked. I went to the till one day after we finished doing lunches. It had been very busy so I took all the cash that was there and walked. It was enough to get me back here. I looked around for work and finally became a cop. There you are, Jimmy, you've wormed my life story out of me on our first date. You must be a real charmer, mustn't you?'

All of a sudden Jimmy felt relaxed. He didn't know why, maybe it was because she had told him about herself. She hadn't needed to do that. Now, whatever he felt about her didn't matter because all he had to do was tell her about himself and let it go wherever it would go.

'So, what about James Costello? What's your life story?'

'I thought this was our second date? Or is it our third? I lose count.'

'What?'

'Our first date was the afternoon we met, remember?'

'So it was.'

There was a silence. She was waiting.

'That fish was good. I like fish.'

Suarez sat back.

Was she disappointed? Did she look disappointed? Jimmy wasn't sure.

'Yeah, Jimmy, the fish is good here.'

'I like fish.'

She was looking at him. But this time it wasn't a nice look.

'So, we go back to the beginning. Why are you still here?'

That's right thought Jimmy, let's get back to the beginning, why am I still here?

'Because I've still got a hole in me that isn't healed. I'll go as soon as it's healed enough to travel. Tell that to your chief if he asks. And I can still go to a hotel if you want me to. I can walk OK now. The stitches don't pull.'

'You know, I think that might be the best idea. You don't need me for anything and I see now that you're more of a private person than I thought you were. You aren't comfortable with anyone too close and it's not a big apartment. Maybe a hotel would be better for us both.'

She summoned the waiter who brought the bill. She looked at it, took a wallet out of her handbag and dropped some notes onto the tray he held. He thanked her and left.

'You OK to go now? We're all finished here aren't we?'

Are we, thought Jimmy, are we finished?

'You don't know me, and if you got to know me I don't think you'd like me. It would be nice to think that you liked me. If you do, I'd like to keep it that way.' He forced out the words he'd promised himself he'd never say. ' Because I like you.'

Suddenly her face changed and she gave him the look again. Then it changed again, her face seemed to soften.

121

'Like you like fish?'

'Fish?'

'You like fish. You just told me.'

Now it was Jimmy's turn to smile.

'It was just something to say. I needed something to say.'

'What did you want to say? And if you mention fish I will kill you, you're not the only one who knows how to break a neck.'

She was back leaning on the table with her chin on her hands and her bra and cleavage were there again but more so. It has to be a knack, thought Jimmy, but how does she do it? He leant forward and put his elbows on the table. The view was even better.

'Listen, I'm not anybody to get involved with. All those things that your lot found out about me, they're true, the bodies in Lübeck, everything, and there's more, plenty more, and none of it's good. And if that's not enough let's just say that I'm bad luck. One way or another I've hurt everyone I've ever cared about so now I don't want to care about anyone any more, there's just too much pain.'

It wasn't coming out right. The words were right but it wasn't sounding how he wanted it to sound.

'Jimmy.' Her voice was soft. 'Are you trying to get into my pants? Because if you are, I can tell you you're doing some terrific job. Jimmy Costello, man of mystery. Jimmy Costello, dangerous to know. Jimmy Costello hurt by life, handle with care, be gentle, damaged goods.'

He knew it hadn't come out right.

'Am I still going to a hotel?'

The cleavage and bra disappeared again as she sat back.

'No, even if I have to tie you to the bed with ropes and stick a towel in your mouth so you can't call for help.'

Jimmy laughed but only a small one.

'Look,' he forced himself again, 'Seraphina.' Thank God he'd remembered it. 'I like you and I want you to like me, but can we leave it at that for now?'

'We can but we don't have to.'

'Yes we do.'

'Are you sure?'

Jimmy nodded.

'Because if I remember how it works I think it would pull my stitches something shocking.'

Suarez rocked back into her chair laughing. Heads at other tables turned and looked but this time Jimmy didn't care. He'd made her laugh.

Suarez came back to the table still smiling.

'Well, I don't want you to suffer on my account, although I'm pretty sure we could manage without you having to go through any pain barrier.' They sat for a moment then Suarez spoke again, this time there was no smile nor even any look. 'Why don't we go back and open another bottle of wine and then, do you know what I'd really like?' Jimmy shook his head. 'I'd like you to tell me about your family, your wife and children. Nothing else. Would you do that, just tell me about them? Leave anything else for another time.'

'Yeah, I'd like to tell you about Bernie and the kids. I haven't talked about them, not properly talked about them, for a long time. Bernie would have liked you.'

'Would I have liked her?'

'Yes, I think so.'

'Good, that's good, Jimmy. Now let's go and open that bottle.'

They got up and left the restaurant. As they walked through the streets a thought came to him. He felt better because now he knew what it was he wanted. He wanted a journalist.

Chapter Seventeen

Jimmy sat at the back of the church. His shirt and slacks were damp and his hair wet. There had been a sudden, heavy shower about five minutes after he had left Suarez's apartment and he'd come out without a jacket because the morning was already warm. He hadn't seen the threatening black cloud because it had cunningly hidden itself behind the other apartment blocks. Anyway, his mind had been elsewhere. The shower stopped before he reached the church, the sun had come out and he'd dried off a bit but inside the church it was cool and he felt cold and uncomfortable. Other people coming into church for the Mass glanced at him and he felt a bit foolish to have let himself get caught in the rain in just a short-sleeved shirt, but he'd left the apartment quietly and in a hurry because he wanted to get to Sunday Mass, it was important.

They had passed the church on the way back to the apartment the previous evening and he'd remembered that tomorrow was Sunday. Suarez had read the times of Masses off the notice board for him. Eight was the first and he'd woken early enough to slip out of the apartment and get to the church with plenty of time to spare. He'd lit some candles, one for Bernie, one for Michael, one for Eileen and the kids, then sat down in one of the back benches and thought about him and Suarez.

The church was filling now with a congregation, which was like all Catholic congregations he had ever known. The majority were women and children and most of the men present were middle-aged or older. It was the young adults who, with a few exceptions, were conspicuous by their absence. He waited for the Mass to begin and thought some more about Suarez. Why did he feel about her the way he did and, stranger still, why did she seem to feel anything for him? She was young and attractive, she didn't need a broken down has-been. Her lover should have been someone young and good-looking, someone successful, like her. How could she –

The bell rang and the priest came out on to the altar, preceded by the altar servers. Everybody stood up and the Mass began. Jimmy stopped thinking about Suarez and began thinking about what he always thought about in Mass, the whole stupid, meaningless mess that was his life. The words from the altar, though in Spanish, were the same, his memories the same, the regrets the same, the same meaningless mess that each day he tried to bully, cajole or pray into some sort of order or meaning. But he knew that however long he tried, and however hard, he would never even come close to achieving by his own efforts what Suarez had achieved in one act of gentleness and compassion. That was why it had been important to get to Mass, for Suarez, to say "thank you" for something that was completely human but had given him hope that somewhere there might indeed be something divine.

The Mass went on and when the time came he didn't go to communion, he slipped out of the back of the church into the sunshine. He wanted to try and be there when Suarez woke.

Jimmy felt the fear jump into his chest when he turned the corner and saw two police cars, their lights still flashing but sirens silent, parked outside her apartment block. There was a uniformed policeman at the entrance and across the road, in front of an identical block, a small crowd had gathered. The kind of crowd he recognised from his days as a detective, the inevitable collection of inquisitive watchers who gathered at the scene of some disaster. Something had happened, something bad.

All he could think was, please God, don't let it be Suarez. But he knew it was, and he knew it was nothing to do with God. He crossed the road and joined the edge of the watchers. One or two turned to look at him but he was of no interest, just a stranger who, like them, was curious to see what was going on. Another police car arrived, a black SEAT, along with an ambulance. This time there were no flashing lights and no sirens. Jimmy recognised the man who got out of the SEAT, greasy black hair, squat and in an ill-fitting suit. Suarez's boss. The man went to the uniformed policeman at the doorway and they began to talk. The ambulance crew got out and began to unload their kit. They didn't seem to be in any hurry. Jimmy left the little crowd and crossed the road heading towards the doorway. The uniformed officer looked over the squat man's shoulder and saw him coming. He shouted something to him in Spanish and waved a hand at him to go back. Jimmy kept on coming. The uniform shouted again and Suarez boss turned. He said something to the uniform who went silent and they waited until Jimmy was standing in front of them.

'Suarez?'

Her boss nodded

'Sí, Suarez.'

'Dead?'

'Sí.'

'How? How did she die?'

The squat man looked at him obviously struggling to understand. The uniformed policeman said something, Suarez boss listened then turned back to Jimmy.

'Dos, two …'

He held up two fingers and then his almost non-existent English gave out and the uniformed copper took over.

'Two shots.'

The chief turned to the uniformed man and rattled off

something in Spanish. The uniform looked at Jimmy.

'He says get into the car. That car.' He pointed to the SEAT in which the squat man had just arrived. 'At once. Go.'

Jimmy went to the car and got into the back. The driver ignored him.

The two men from the ambulance disappeared into the building followed by Suarez's boss. The uniformed man stood looking at him. Jimmy noticed the flap of his pistol holster was undone. Then another uniformed man joined him and also began watching him. He didn't care, if anything he was glad. He would be taken to the station where he might get told something. And he was glad he hadn't been the one to find her. He didn't want to see her dead body because he knew it was his fault she was dead. He had acted like a stupid kid, he had gone back to being sixteen, the last time he had fallen in love. He had behaved like a moon-struck, bloody adolescent. And it had killed Suarez. He let his mind run, it was either think about Suarez or think about something else and there was only one other thing to think about. Whoever sent the killer with the phoney Romanian passport wanted him dead, and wanted him dead in a hurry. The Romanian had missed so he should have been ready for the second time. Or he should have got out, like Suarez told him to. If he had got out she would still be alive. But he had hung on, pretending to himself … Except it hadn't been a pretence. Suarez had cared about him, cared enough to … He stopped thinking. Suarez wouldn't be pushed out of his thoughts so he stopped thinking about anything.

The front door of the car opened and Suarez's boss got in. He turned and looked at Jimmy then turned round, picked up the handset and made a call. He motioned to the driver and the car pulled away. Jimmy looked at the crowd on the opposite side of the street as they watched him go. Now they were interested in him, now he wasn't just a stranger to be ignored. Now he was somebody of importance.

Jimmy sat patiently in the interview room. It was clean and air-conditioned. The chair he was sitting on was comfortable and the table in front of him had a plastic cup of water on it. Since his arrival everybody had been polite and very non-threatening. There had been a murder and he was helping the police with their enquiries. He was co-operating and they appreciated his co-operation. So why did he feel uncomfortable?

He was being interviewed by an English-speaking officer. A youngish man in a white, short-sleeved shirt who smiled a lot for no apparent reason. He had smiled throughout the initial formalities and he was smiling now as he got down to business. So far, Jimmy hadn't felt like smiling back.

'Where were you at half-past eight this morning?'

'At Mass, the church was about a fifteen minute walk away from Inspector Suarez's apartment. I don't know what it's called. She was shot at half-past eight?'

'Yes. Two shots, the first killed her. She was in bed.'

Jimmy knew she was in bed. That was where he had left her when he had quietly got up just before seven to get himself ready and go to Mass. In bed, naked, and fast asleep.

'Someone heard the shots?'

'Several people. We have the description of a man leaving the building. He wore a raincoat, dark glasses and a hat. It was not a good description, but good enough to know you were not the man. You need not worry, Señor Costello, you are not a suspect in this investigation.'

'I'm just helping with your enquiries.'

'Yes. You are helping us with our enquiries.' Another pointless smile. 'What was the nature of your relationship with Inspector Suarez?'

Jimmy picked up the plastic cup from the table and

sipped the water. It was a good question. Were they friends, colleagues, lovers or strangers, or the whole lot rolled into one? How could it get like this in just a few days? It had taken him over two years to go to bed with Bernie for the first time and then only because George was in hospital and lent them his flat. This time it had taken a few days.

'We met when she brought a message from her superiors –'

'We know when and why you first met.'

'Then you also know that she got me a place to stay when it was agreed I should act as an observer on the Jarvis murder. It was a holiday let which belonged to her cousin and was vacant for a week or so. While I was there a man broke in and tried to kill me. And you also know that he was the one who ended up dead but before he died he stuck a knife in me. I told Suarez I didn't want to stay in hospital so she let me stay at her apartment until I could get back into her cousin's place.'

Jimmy stopped. He could leave it there but that wouldn't help. The autopsy would show that she had recently had sex, and a DNA test would show Jimmy was the one she'd had it with.

'Yes, Mr Costello?'

'Yes what?'

'The rest, Mr Costello.'

'There is no rest. I stayed in her spare room. This morning I got up and went to Mass –'

'Why did you go to Mass?'

'Because it was Sunday. I go to Mass on Sundays.'

'You are a Catholic?'

'Yes, I'm a Catholic, and Catholics go to Mass on Sunday.'

'Not all Catholics.'

'No, you're right, not all of them, but I do. Is my going to Mass relevant to your investigation?'

'Seeing as it coincided with the murder of Inspector Suarez, yes, it is.'

'You mean it gives me an alibi or you think I wanted to be somewhere else when it happened?'

'It could do both if it can be confirmed.'

Jimmy knew it would be confirmed. A stranger sitting at the back of church in a wet shirt at Sunday Mass got noticed by somebody. He'd be remembered.

'Were you intimate with Inspector Suarez?'

'Intimate?'

'Did you have sexual relations with her?'

Another smile, but not so pointless this time.

Jimmy paused. If he lied he tied himself into her murder more than he already was. If he answered truthfully there would have to be explanations, and he had no explanation. He had no idea himself how it had happened.

'Was she known to be of a promiscuous nature?'

The smile got switched off.

'I beg your pardon?'

'Was she well-known for sleeping around with casual acquaintances?'

A glint of anger appeared in the young man's eyes.

'She was a colleague, Mr Costello, a well-regarded police inspector.'

'Then why do you think she would have jumped in bed with me? We hardly knew each other for God's sake. Or do I strike you as the type attractive young women can't resist and fall for on sight?'

The officer looked at him. There were no smiles now but no anger either. Jimmy was glad he was still a bit dishevelled. He had never looked any oil painting but now, the way he looked, he guessed the force of his argument was at its high point. He ran his fingers through his grey, cropped hair. It was enough.

'The spare bed had been slept in, but not necessarily

last night, and it looked as though her bed could have been shared.'

'Well if it was, I wasn't the one sharing it.'

'You slept in the spare room?'

'As it happens, no.'

'No?'

'We had dinner together. She wanted to cheer me up, getting knifed can lower your spirits a bit. We had some wine with the meal and we talked.'

'About what?'

'She told me that she had been married, to a guy in England, Croydon, who ran a restaurant. But it didn't take and she came back here and joined the police. Then we went back to the apartment and opened some more wine and talked some more.'

'About what?'

'About my wife and kids. I was glad to talk, I hadn't talked to anyone about them for a long time and she was a good listener.'

'You have a wife and children?'

'Had. My wife died of cancer and my son died in Africa. He was a missionary priest.'

'I'm sorry.'

'Why? Everyone says they're sorry. Why is that? You didn't know him or my wife and you don't know me. Bernie died of cancer and Michael died of something else, something tropical, I don't know what. My daughter lives in Australia with her family. We talked about them and we drank, no, we didn't drink. I drank, she listened. I don't know how long we talked or how much I drank. I don't even remember going to sleep. All I remember is waking up in the chair with a blanket over me and everything tidied away. I assumed she had gone to bed after I passed out. I made some coffee and just sat around until it was time to go to Mass. If she had someone in with her last night he came late and I have no idea who he was. That's it.'

And that was it, most of it. Except that they hadn't drunk much and he hadn't fallen asleep in the chair. He had fallen asleep beside her, and she had been right, he didn't pull his stitches and there had definitely been no pain. Now he had to wait. If they let him go he had to be out of Spain before the results of the autopsy came through.

'Wait here, Mr Costello.'

The young man got up and left. Jimmy waited. When the interviewing officer returned it was with Suarez's boss. The boss spoke in Spanish and the young copper translated.

'He says you were asked to leave. Why didn't you go?'

'I've got a knife wound that isn't healed. I didn't want to travel until I was sure I'd be all right on the journey. I wanted to go, believe me, after what had happened I wanted to go.'

The chief spoke again, spoke quite a lot.

'He says you should leave, Mr Costello. It seems possible that your presence in her apartment was the cause.'

'The cause?'

'One explanation of Inspector Suarez's murder is that you were the target, not her. Whoever sent the first assassin may have found out where you were and tried again and Inspector Suarez was unfortunately in the way. We have covered up your killing of the intruder, we will not cover up for this one and we do not want there to be any possibility of what might be a third attempt on your life. Everything is messy enough as it is. You seem to have powerful friends in Rome who might complicate things for us if you remain here. Go back to your friends, Mr Costello. Inspector Suarez was one of our own, we intend to find out who was responsible for her murder. If you have told us all you know and can help us no further we would like you to leave Santander and leave Spain, at once.'

'If you think I was the target can't I stay and try to help? Maybe I know something I don't know I know.'

The officer unpicked the sentence then spoke to the Suarez boss who listened, looked at Jimmy, then shook his head and said something.

'Leave, Mr Costello, leave while you still can.'

Was it advice or a threat? Either way Jimmy breathed more freely, he hadn't overdone it, but it was a close call. Suarez's boss said something to the interviewing officer then left. Jimmy wanted to get going, but first he had a question.

'Whoever it was, how did they get in?'

With the senior man gone the interviewer didn't seem to mind talking.

'It appears the door was kicked in. There was a good security chain but it wasn't on.'

'No, I took it off when I went out to church.'

Christ. Not only had he caused her death, he had let the bloody killer in. Suarez should have listened to him. He was still bad news for anyone close to him.

'OK, I'll get my stuff from the apartment and the house and I'll get the first plane I can.'

'Everything at Inspector Suarez's apartment must remain. Any clothes you have there cannot be removed. A car will take you to the house you were using, you may take anything you like from there and then you will be taken to the airport. Come with me please.'

Jimmy followed him out of the interview room, along the corridors and out to a waiting car.

'Goodbye, Mr Costello.'

Jimmy got in and it pulled away.

It was Harry, it had to be. His paid killer had missed so Harry had decided to do the job himself. It was risky but the weather had clinched it. The rain meant he could wear

133

a coat and hat. Go in, do the business and get out. Sleepy neighbours slow to get out of bed, all they would get would be a big man in a coat and hat leaving the building. Once he was in and saw it was only Suarez on her own, he'd have to gun her because she'd have recognised him. Then he'd ridden his luck and would probably get away with it. The police would have a hard time putting anything together as long as Henderson stayed quiet. And Henderson would do that, he had too much to lose if Harry went down. The police weren't going to get anywhere, Harry was too wise, he'd been through it all before.

But I'm not the police, Harry, so I don't have to do it by the book. I'm going to nail you for this, Mercer, I'm going to fucking nail you if it's the last thing I do.

Chapter Eighteen

Professor McBride's voice was sharp.

'Mr Costello, where are you? I've been trying to reach you for some considerable time.'

'Yesterday I was helping the police with their enquiries. After that I was escorted to the airport where I spent until early evening sitting in Departures with a minder and then I was put on a plane. I landed over an hour and a half ago and I'm knackered.'

The edge disappeared. Jimmy could almost feel her relax.

'You are back in Rome? Good, then now you can –'

'No I can't, because I'm not in Rome. I'm in London.'

There was a moment's silence while Professor McBride let it sink in. Jimmy guessed the news would get up her nose so he was ready for it.

'What on earth are you doing in London? I went to considerable time and trouble to ensure you were able to leave Santander and return to Rome.'

'No you didn't, you went to considerable trouble to ensure I could leave Santander and go to London. I know that has to be right because I'm here in London and not in Rome.'

Jimmy could almost hear her silent frustration and annoyance rising to danger levels. But she controlled herself. She was good at control.

'What are you doing in London? You were told to talk to Fr Perez and then come straight back. Despite that you stayed on and once again managed to involve yourself with the police. Mr Costello, it was only with great difficulty that I was able to –'

'What do you know about Jarvis's death?'

She paused for a moment but then answered his question.

'Nothing. Until I was told he was dead, murdered, I only knew what was in Fr Perez's letter.'

There was a moment of silence from Jimmy's end.

'OK, if you say so.'

'I do say so. I also say return at once to Rome. You have done what I wanted.'

Jimmy rang off and put the mobile away. He began to take her words apart. It wouldn't be a lie, but it would point him away from the truth, not at it. She said, "You have done what I wanted". She hadn't said that he'd done what she'd sent him to do. Was there a difference and if so did it matter? What had she asked him to do? To go and find out what he could about what Jarvis had told Fr Perez. But Jarvis was dead when he arrived. What had she told him to do next? Join in with the police investigation. Then what? Talk to Fr Perez about Jarvis and then get back to Rome. So what did she want him to think he was doing? Running the ETA thing to the ground by finding out if it was connected to Jarvis's killing? But then she tried to get him pulled back before he had any kind of chance to make some real progress. Was she pulling the plug on what had been a waste of time from the beginning or was she using him again, just like before? But if she was using him then what the hell was she was using him for? It couldn't be anything to do with Harry's business, could it? Why would she be interested in an ex-con and a porn racket? Unless … Porn had long fingers and all sorts of people got caught up in it, even priests, even senior clerics.

The Bakerloo Line train he was sitting in rattled noisily into Maida Vale station. Next stop would be Kilburn Park. Jimmy was heading for his old North London neighbourhood. In fact he was heading for Kilburn High Road, where he hoped things hadn't changed too much. He needed at least one face to be the same. The train began to move. He gathered up his holdall, stood up, and got ready to get out at the next stop. The holdall sagged on its straps, it was almost empty. He never took many clothes with him when he travelled, what he stood up in and a couple of changes of underwear and shirts and things. Whatever else he needed, he bought, but he never needed much. There hadn't been much of his gear left at Suarez cousin's house, and his jacket was impounded in her apartment, so he was still in short-sleeved shirt and slacks with some underwear, two more shirts and two handkerchiefs in the holdall. There was also a toothbrush which he'd bought at the airport. It was summer but this was London not Spain. He would need to pick up a coat somewhere when he left the Underground.

Jimmy came out of Kilburn Park station, walked up Cambridge Avenue and turned into Kilburn High Road. It didn't look so very different and he didn't look so very out of place. A man in a light, short-sleeved shirt didn't turn any heads but today the English sun was busy playing hide and seek behind the clouds and a wind that had an edge on it came and went. Some hardy souls were dressed like him, but not many. He stopped outside a charity shop. The stuff in the window looked classier than he remembered, there were some quite nice things. He went in, it was all very tidy and well laid out. He walked to the men's rail and put down his holdall. There were plenty of shirts and they looked like good ones. He took one down and looked at the label. Marks and Spencer, he was impressed. He put it back and looked at the jackets. There was a snappy, light brown cord jacket that might fit. He took it down and tried it on. It fitted. He went to the mirror, it looked good on him, sort of arty. He looked inside at the label. Wolsey. Things had certainly changed from the last time he needed a coat to keep warm and got one from a charity shop on this road. He went back to his holdall and went to the counter. A bright young blonde smiled at him. He smiled back.

'I'll take it. I don't need a bag, I'll wear it.'

'It looks good on you, you look like a writer or something. Here, turn round and I'll cut off the price tag for you.'

Jimmy turned and she came out from behind the counter with a pair of scissors and snipped off the price tag which hung over the back of his collar.

'Six pounds. That's good for that jacket, you're getting a bargain.'

Jimmy pulled out his wallet from his hip pocket and took out a twenty pound note. The bright blonde took it and handed him back his change, a five pound note and nine heavy pound coins.

'Sorry, that's my last five.'

Jimmy felt the weight of the coins in his hand, then he slipped them into his trouser pocket.

'Not to worry, I'll have a couple of pints, that'll thin them out.'

The bright blonde grinned at him.

'Good idea.'

Jimmy left the shop and walked on down the High Road until he stood opposite a big Edwardian pub, a London classic. The name on the front was The Hind. He was pleased, it had gone back to its original name, no more Liffey Lad. Thank God that joke was over. He looked at his watch, two o'clock. He hoped they'd changed the beers they sold as well as the name and had something worth drinking, proper London beer. It had been too long since he'd tasted a decent pint. He crossed the road and went in after looking up at the name on the small sign over the door. It wasn't Eamon Doyle any more, the Irish period was well and truly over. George was still the landlord, but now he was using his real name.

Inside it was still very well done out, one big room and still one big bar at the far end of the room. But now there were raised areas with dark-stained pine balustrades around them to give the illusion of separateness, in one or two smaller areas they might even give a sense of privacy. The place wasn't crowded, just gently busy. There were what looked like locals drinking, reading papers or talking, and a sprinkling of male and female suits. He walked towards the bar. He passed a group of four pretty young girls sitting at a table talking and laughing together in a language Jimmy didn't recognise, but sounded like Russian. He passed an elderly couple who were sitting with the remains of a finished meal in front of them, looking at the dessert menu. He liked it. It was as it should be at the tail-end of a Monday lunchtime. He stopped and looked at the bar. Two young girls in black T-shirts were working behind it. The shirts had 'The Hind' printed in big gold letters across the chest and a picture of what Jimmy guessed was some sort of deer over the name. He looked around and then he saw him, sitting by himself reading a paper at a table well back from the main entrance near a door marked 'Staff Only'. Jimmy walked across the room, pulled out a chair, put his holdall beside it on the floor and sat down. The paper lowered and George looked at him.

'Hello, Jimmy, nice to see you again.'

He folded the paper and put it on the table.

'Hello, George, you're looking well.'

They were about the same age, but where Jimmy looked crumpled and lived-in, George was smart and well-groomed, his stocky body nicely filling out his expensive suit.

'I'm doing well.'

'I see it's still your name over the door.'

'Not just over the door now.'

He waved a hand and one of the girls came out from

behind the bar. He called to her when she was halfway across the room.

'A pint of Directors, Kristina.'

She nodded and went back towards the bar. Jimmy watched her go to the bar and saw the black handles of the beer engines.

'You've got Directors back on?'

'Yeah, and London Pride, and always a couple of guest ales. There's a market for it now so we can keep it properly.'

'And it's all yours now is it? What happened, you buy someone out or did you have to shoot somebody?'

George laughed.

'No. You were always the violent one, not me. I was the one with brains, remember?' Jimmy remembered. 'No-one got hurt, well, not exactly no one. I suppose you could say Nat got hurt, disappearing like he did in a cloud of smoke. And there was the inevitable squabbles after that, a few heads got cracked but there was nothing serious. It was in my name when Nat ran things. Once he'd departed this world I just kept it in my name.'

'Your own name?'

'Oh, yes. That Irish shit didn't last too long. The trade moved on and I moved with the times. Good food, good beer, and the odd live act in the evenings.'

'Any jazz?'

'Yeah, I still like jazz and it goes down well. Plenty of pubs do live music but we're getting to be the place where you hear good new jazz played. It gives the place tone and lets the yobs know they wouldn't fit in.'

The beer arrived. Jimmy picked up the glass almost reverently, he wanted it to be as good as he remembered. He took a drink. He wasn't disappointed.

'That is a nice pint, George, a very nice pint.'

'I told you. Appearances can bring in the customers but it's the quality brings them back. The food's just as good as the beer. Nothing fancy, not too pricey, but good stuff. You fancy a meal?'

'No thanks, George, I've come to ask a favour.'

'I guessed you'd come for something. There was always a favour when you turned up.'

'It's not a big favour, nothing you'll have to break sweat over.'

'I'm glad to hear it. But before you tell me what it is, maybe you can tell me why should I do you any favours?'

'Because I'm asking nicely. Should I ask differently?'

George smiled.

'Be your age, Jimmy. We're too old for that. You could always take me and I guess you still could, but you'd probably give yourself a fucking hernia in the attempt. Besides, I have decent young blokes who deal with any rough stuff, you might still be a bit of a handful for them, but nothing more than a handful. They could take you. You haven't come back just to go to hospital, have you?'

'No-one needs to go to hospital. All I'm looking for is a contact.'

'Go on then, ask your favour. If it's not too much trouble I don't mind helping out a mate. If I'm sure it's not going to be too much trouble.'

Jimmy took another drink.

'How much is it a pint now?'

'Never mind, you're not paying. Ask your question.'

'Can you get me a journalist?'

George laughed.

'What you going to do, sell your life-story to the papers?'

'I just need a journalist.'

'A bent one?'

'A good one.'

'Ah, now that won't be so easy. I could get you a dozen right now who'd write any story you like if you paid them enough, but a good one? Does he have to be straight?'

'Not so long as he's good.'

'Do I get to know why you need a journalist?'

'Remember Harry Mercer?'

George trawled his memory.

'Harry Mercer? Oh yeah, muscle for Denny Morris. Last I heard he was doing a stretch for trying to knock over a bookies up north somewhere.'

'Birmingham.'

'Like I said, up north. Anywhere beyond St Albans is up north as far as I'm concerned. He was a mug to go off his own patch. What's Harry got to do with anything?'

'He killed somebody.'

'A lot of people got killed one way or another over the years, why rake up old times?'

'Because it happened yesterday morning.'

George looked surprised.

'I would have thought Harry would be too old to still be at the muscle end of anything. He must be nearly seventy by now. Who'd he kill?'

'It doesn't matter, he was trying for me.'

George moved uneasily in his seat.

'Shit. Are you going to be trouble, Jimmy? I won't have any trouble.'

'Don't wet yourself, it wasn't anywhere near here. It was in Spain. I came across Harry by accident and, well, it looks like we had a little falling out and he forgot to mention it. He thinks I'm pushing my nose into his affairs so he wants me dead.'

'Fuck me, Jimmy –'

George's voice carried and the elderly couple looked angrily across at them then put down the dessert menu, got up, looked at them again in a disapproving and shocked way then left.

'I think you've just lost a couple of customers. Last time I was here you got rid of your barman because he used language like that in front of the customers.'

'If they've never heard it before they're the only ones in London who haven't, so sod them. And last time you were here I got rid of that barman because you kicked his teeth out. I don't want any more blood on my carpets. They really are mine now and I'm legit. Almost.'

'All I want is a journalist to help do some digging at this end, someone who can ask questions and get answers.'

'What's between you and Harry is between you and Harry. I don't want any part of it.'

'I told you, Harry's in Spain, none of this will come to London.'

'It had better not.'

'Is that a threat, George?'

'No, Jimmy, it's a fucking promise.'

It was Jimmy's turn to smile. Still the same old George.

'Just get me my journalist and I'll be on my way.'

'I'll see what I can do. You got a number where I can reach you?' Jimmy gave George his mobile number. 'Where you staying?'

'A hotel I suppose. I only just got in. I came straight here, I haven't sorted anything out yet.'

Jimmy finished off his pint and stood up.

'It's a good pint, George.'

'Have another, still on the house.'

'No thanks, I'm knackered. I'll get a room and have a kip.'

Jimmy put his hand to his side, the wound was troubling him. George watched him.

'Damage or old age?'

'Knife.'

'How's the other bloke?'

'Dead.'

George laughed.

'Still the same old Jimmy. What did he die of?'

'Broken neck.'

'I see, natural causes. Like I said, Jimmy, I reckon

you're still good enough to be a handful, even to the likes of my lads. Go and get your kip and I'll get back to you.'

'How long?'

'Is there a hurry?'

'I don't want to hang about and you don't want me hanging about so why not get it done?'

'OK, I'll try and hurry it up. See you, Jimmy.'

'See you, George.'

Chapter Nineteen

The pub was getting busy with the evening trade when she came in and stood just inside the door looking around. George watched her. She went over to the bar and asked something. The girl behind the bar pointed to George's table. She turned and came across.

'You George?'

'That's right.'

She sat down.

'A mutual friend sent me. He said you wanted a journalist.'

George sat back and looked at her. For a start she was too young, early or mid-twenties, but it was hard to tell because she wasn't anything like his idea of feminine. She looked arty: a linen jacket, roll-neck sweater, and glasses. Her hair was black and short. George was vaguely surprised she wore a skirt, not trousers. She looked more like a bloody writer than anything else.

'I know a man who's putting a story together. I think it will be a good story, maybe even a big one. I would like it if you would talk to him.'

'Oh yes, and why would I want to talk to him?'

'I told you, he's putting together a good story, one that people, important people, would be interested in.'

'What makes you so sure?'

'Because I know him, he doesn't piss about. He's been away, abroad, for his health. The climate in London disagreed with him. If he's come back there'll be trouble and it'll be plenty of trouble if past form is anything to go by. He asked me to get him a journalist so I put the word out.'

'OK fine, if you say so then I'll talk to him.' George didn't say anything, he just sat looking at her. She wasn't what he had been expecting. She got tired of waiting. 'So let's hear what you've got so far?'

George decided he didn't like her. Still, she had been recommended, so George got on with it.

'Like I said, I know this bloke, a mate from the old days who turns up and says he needs a journalist. I said I'd get him one. So here you are.'

'Wonderful. But I haven't come for a job interview or to talk about the old days or to have a drink with your mate. I've come here because you put the word out. So what's the fucking story?'

No, he didn't like her. She was ... well she wasn't what he expected, and for a woman, not feminine. Still, she'd been recommended.

'You don't look like my idea of a reporter.'

'And what do you think a reporter should look like? A bottle-nosed souse in a slept-in suit with matching gravy stains?'

George was certain now, he really didn't like her.

'How long have you been around?'

'Since Adolf Hitler wore short trousers. Look, I told you, I didn't come here to be interviewed or pass the time. The man who phoned me –'

George decided it was time to see who she was, who she really was.

'I know who phoned you. The question is, do you know the man who phoned you?' She took off her glasses, pulled out a handkerchief and polished the lenses slowly. George had weighed her up now she was trying to do the same for him. He gave her a second before he carried on 'Because if you know who recommended you, you'll know not to fuck me about. If you're any good that is.'

She restored her glasses and put away her handkerchief. George watched her. She wasn't so bad looking when you got used to her but she didn't make the most of what she'd got. Pity.

'Fair enough, I won't fuck you about if you don't fuck me about. OK? What am I here for?'

George decided that was fair.

'This bloke, my mate, wants to look into something. It's definitely criminal and probably nasty. It's not happening here, it's something over in Spain and there's already dead bodies in the works. Whatever information he's going on he's looking for a connection at this end and he wants help to sort it out, someone who can ask the questions in a way that'll get answers. With me so far?' She nodded. 'So, if you were any good as a journalist would you say that what I've given you might be a story?'

'I'd say it's part of a story and with holes in it. Why would anyone over here be interested in people dying in Spain?'

'Because it involves a bloke called Harry Mercer. Harry used to be a big mate of a bloke called Denny Morris. Spain is where Harry lives now'

The young woman began to look interested.

'I've heard of Morris, he was a heavyweight back in the old days. Disappeared didn't he? Got put in hospital by some sort of psycho and then disappeared when Nat Desmond took over.'

'That's right. How come you know about Denny and Nat, you're too young to ...'

'I do my homework, George. I like to know how we got where we are today. How's your friend connected to Harry Mercer?'

'He was the psycho who put Denny in hospital.'

That stopped her in her tracks for a couple of seconds.

'And now?'

'Now there's shit between him and Mercer. One of

them's going to kill the other. It's a sort of hate-hate relationship. Mercer's already had two goes, he got someone to stick a knife in my mate but that only got the hit man's neck broken. Then he tried himself, but he missed. There'll be blood all over the carpets before long. But I don't want it on my carpets. As far as anybody is concerned I'm just doing a favour for old time's sake, understand?' She nodded, she understood. 'Well, do you want to talk to my mate?'

'Does he have a name?'

'Costello, Jimmy Costello.'

'I'll need to ask around, see what some people think.'

'That's all right, a certain caution does no harm. Do your asking and be here tomorrow, same time, and tell me if you're in or out. If you're in you'll be all the way in and there'll be no way out if it turns sour, and with Costello involved it could turn very sour. Understand what I'm saying?'

'I understand, George.'

'Good. Now piss off.'

The young woman stood up smiling.

'You don't like me, do you? I don't fit into your neat little box of types do I?'

'No I don't like you, but don't worry, it's nothing personal, I don't like most people. Just be here tomorrow like I said.'

The young woman walked away and George watched her go. He knew who had made the recommendation and George respected his judgement. If he said she was OK then she was OK, linen jacket and all. But she didn't look like a journalist, she looked like a writer, or maybe an artist. Oh well, it would all be up to Jimmy now.

Thinking about it, George decided he didn't much care who came out on top just so long as there was no blood on the carpets at this end. Not on his carpets anyway.

148

Chapter Twenty

Two nights later the same young woman was sitting at the same table, but it wasn't George she was talking to. It was Jimmy.

'I spoke to George a couple of days ago and did some checking.'

'And?'

'People that matter remember you.'

'I'm nothing special, I never was. Why would anybody remember me?'

'The word is that you turned up a few years ago and by the time you left some very influential people were getting their hands dirty trying to scrape shit off the fan.' Jimmy shrugged. He didn't care what she'd heard. 'Also, I was told that the car bomb that got Nat Desmond was down to you.'

He cared about that. It was one thing getting called a bent copper, especially if you were one, but it was another thing altogether getting your name linked to terrorist games.

'Not me.'

'Maybe not you personally, but I was told you were the one that saw that it got done.'

'Whoever told you that doesn't know his arse from his elbow and if that's the kind of contacts you have you'll be no good to me. I need someone who can tell fact from fiction.'

The young woman looked round the big bar. It was another busy night and there was a nice mix but they had a table to themselves and George had made sure their talk would be private so long as they didn't shout. Across the room George was sitting by himself reading a paperback with a cup of tea on his table. He looked up from his book to where they were sitting. The young woman nodded to him. George ignored her and went back to his reading.

'Your mate George doesn't like me. Why would you say he doesn't like me?'

'George doesn't like most people, it's nothing personal.'

'Do you think you'll get to like me?'

Jimmy couldn't see the point of the question, but whatever it was, it wasn't a come-on.

'I don't know you. I don't want to know you. But if I knew you I probably wouldn't like you.'

She changed the subject. She wanted to get alongside him if she was going to work with him. She needed to get a feeling for the kind of person he was and she could see it wasn't going to be easy at short notice.

'They say this place was a gangster's pub in the old days. That it got used by the likes of Lenny Monk and Denny Morris. They were supposed to be real hooligans and nasty with it.' Jimmy didn't respond. Lenny Monk and Denny Morris were a long time ago, and both were now dead. 'They say it was from this pub that you took Denny out and beat the living crap out of him and put him in hospital.' Jimmy still left it. 'I'd give a lot to get the full story on that, so would my editor, so would a lot of editors. The inside story of the fall of Denny Morris and the rise of Nat Desmond. I know people who would pay a lot for that story.'

'You'd have been a kid when all that happened. Why would ancient history like that interest you or anybody else?'

'Listen, Jimmy, George told me some things about you, interesting things.'

Jimmy looked across at George.

'George has a slack mouth. It'll get him into trouble one of these days.'

'No, you've got it wrong. I'm good, believe me, and I'm on the way up because I'm young and I'm hungry. I needed to know that this is something that could help me get where I want.'

'And where's that?'

'The top. Where else is there?'

How many times had Jimmy heard that? 'I want to get on up there where everyone will see I'm the best.' How many people had he seen step on family, friends, and anybody else, until it was their turn to be stepped on and be a rung on the ladder for some bigger bastard to stand on.

He started listening to her again. She was still telling him about how good she was going to be. 'I don't want to piss about following the same stories as everybody else. I want to stand out from the crowd. Old-style London gangsters make good copy, there's a market for that sort of nostalgia. When I came to see George I wasn't much interested in what he wanted, I was interested in George and the guy who recommended me to him.'

'Why, what's interesting about George?'

'I've heard of George, he's somebody in this town and when he put the word out he was looking for a journalist I was recommended to him by –' she said a name. It meant nothing to Jimmy.

'Means nothing to me and George told me he's legit these days. Almost.'

That got a smile.

'Of course he is, if he says so, and I'm sure he says so. Anyway, I wanted to meet him, every little helps. Then he told me a few things about you. He knew I'd only take an interest if there was a sweetener in it for me so he gave me a few bits and pieces.'

'Enough to get you interested?'

'I'm here, aren't I? It was you who asked for me, not the other way round. You want a journalist and I want to move on up. Why can't we both get what we want?' Put like that, it seemed reasonable enough. But if you put shooting yourself in the head the right way it could seem reasonable enough. 'Like I said, I've talked to people and I know you were a bent copper and you were well into those gangs. It's funny though, because people who remember those days will talk about the likes of Monk, Morris, and Desmond, but nobody seems to want to talk about you.'

'I told you, I was nobody.'

'Too damn right you were nobody. I got someone to look at your official file at the Met. He said it had been filleted. According to your file you spent all your time as a Detective Sergeant doing bugger-all.' She sat back, pulled out a large handkerchief, took off her glasses and gave them a polish. 'You're an interesting person, Jimmy, someone with a past, a past I could use. If I can help with whatever you're up to I want to be paid, properly paid, and not just with money.'

'Don't tell me you want my body?'

That almost got a laugh, but only almost.

'No, you can keep your trousers on. I want you to co-operate with me on the truth about the old days. There are names out there, big, respectable names, who got where they are now by mixing with people who were definitely not respectable. I want names, dates and places. I think there's a lid to be lifted and I want to do the lifting. That's my price, take it or leave it.'

She leaned forward and took a sip of her drink. It was lemonade with a dash of lime, no ice. She didn't seem to drink proper stuff.Then she sat back and waited.

So, thought Jimmy, this is what journalists look like today. Twenty-something, jeans, leather jacket, non-drinker, non-smoker, and probably with a fucking degree in Sociology or some other bloody ology.

'You got a degree?'

'Yes. Cambridge. Politics and Economics, why?'

Jimmy didn't answer, what did it matter? Was she any good? That was what mattered. Jimmy didn't need to think about it for very long. This was probably the best offer he'd get and he wanted to get on with things.

'OK, I'll tell you what I want and you can tell me if you can do it. If you can, I'll co-operate all you want when it's over.'

That was what he said. What he thought was – and I can kick your arse up through your neck when it's all over if you try to get anything about me or my past into print.

'Oh no, Jimmy, I want something on account. What's to stop you getting what you want and then telling me to shove my questions about you and the old days up my editor's arse?'

So, maybe not so green as she was cabbage-looking after all. Well, that was a good sign. An idiot would be no good to him.

'What do you want?'

She thought about it.

'How about Nat Desmond? What was that car bomb really all about?'

So Jimmy told her to get him another pint of Directors and they sat in the Hind drinking while Jimmy told her why the IRA had car-bombed a top London gangster. When it was over she looked impressed.

'So you used the IRA to get Desmond off your back? How were you linked to the IRA?'

'I wasn't, I used a contact who was. I wanted a favour from them, they wanted a favour from me in return. I gave them Nat.'

'And why was he a favour to the IRA?'

'Nat was clever. In the end he was too clever. His trouble was that he wanted it all, the money, the power, to be the one at the top. And at the end of it all he wanted a pension plan that would protect him when he decided to retire and enjoy the profits. Nat was really just a violent accountant who got into bad company. He'd been passing any information he picked up on terrorists coming in and out of London to Special Branch. He had the contacts so he got the information. The IRA owed him a visit. The car bomb was their visit.'

'I see.'

No you don't, thought Jimmy, but it was close enough.

'So, now can we get on to what I want? I've had a hard fucking week and I'm tired.'

'Sure.'

'Harry Mercer worked for Denny Morris, we knew each other. I hadn't seen him for ...' he tried to work it out but gave up ' ...a long time. I came across him recently in Spain. Never mind what I was doing there, I just came across him. He was linked to a bloke called Arthur Jarvis who got a bullet in the back of his head.'

'George told me there were already bodies in the works. Jarvis is one of them?'

Jimmy nodded.

'Mercer was also linked to another bloke called Henderson, a semi-retired ex-pat who owns an accountancy firm in the Midlands. Harry says that these days he's a writer but I think he's a wholesaler of hard, nasty porn. I need to be able to prove that Jarvis, Henderson, and Mercer are linked. I can't do it in Spain because they've been too careful, so I've got to do it at this end. I need to find out how they met and how they set up what they're doing. Jarvis was a teacher who did time for having sex with some of his under-aged pupils. Mercer did a stretch for trying to knock over a bookies in Birmingham. They probably met inside, that's the likeliest bet. Henderson has an accountancy firm in Coventry. I would guess he handles the money end but I don't have

154

any leads on how he got involved.'

'Why?'

'Why what?'

'Why are you interested? There's plenty of porn out there, putting a couple of providers away won't change anything. What's in it for you?'

'When I turned up, Mercer must have added two and two together and come up with five. He was never strong on brains so put me down as trying to fit him in the frame with the local police for his porn racket.'

'How was he wrong? You are trying to fit him in.'

'But I wasn't, it was just a coincidence that we met, but Harry isn't taking any chances. Just before I left Spain Harry tried to top me but he was unlucky and shot the wrong person. One way or another he'll try again, this is my way of stopping him.'

'Another of the bodies?' Jimmy nodded. 'I see, so you're pleading self-defence, not the pursuit of justice?'

'If you like.'

'Why didn't you just take what you've got to the Spanish police?'

'They've already got it, but like I said, Harry and Co. have been very careful. Jarvis is dead and Henderson is too scared of Harry to do anything.'

'Did Mercer kill Jarvis?'

'Maybe, I don't know. I just want to make the connections at this end so the Spanish police can roll them up and put Harry where he won't be a problem to me any more.'

'And as you're not a copper any more you can't just swan around the UK, kick in a few doors and ask questions like you did in the old days so you need someone who can get answers for you. A journalist. Me.'

'You.'

'OK, my editor will stand up for that. What we've got is an ex-pat porn king living the high life on the Costas on

155

the proceeds of dumping filth onto the internet. Add his gangster past, a teacher who poked his under-aged pupils and a bent accountant and you've got the beginnings of a story, but there's still holes in it. It'll need some writing to make it any good, but that's my job.' She held up her drink. 'Cheers, we've got a deal.' She took a drink and put her glass down. 'I'll ask your questions and get your answers for you.'

She leant forward and put out her hand.

Jimmy shook the hand, but not with any enthusiasm. He felt the same as George, he didn't like her. She was cocky, brash and too full of herself. She reminded Jimmy of a young George all those years ago when they had first met. But he had liked George. Maybe she would grow on him.

'What do I call you.'

'Rosa. Rosa Sikora.'

'Sikora, that's Polish isn't it?'

'As Polish as Hammersmith makes them.'

'OK, Rosa, when can we start?'

'I'll need twenty-four hours to sort things out with my editor and tie up a few loose ends but then I can get going on it. Is that OK?'

'Fine. The first thing I need to know is where Jarvis did his time.'

'Sure, I can do that. What's his first name?

'Arthur'

'I'll have it for you in twenty-four hours.'

Jimmy stood up. His side was still hurting. He should rest it. Rosa looked at him.

'You OK? Pain in your side?'

'It's nothing. It's just old age, I'm slowing up.'

'George says different. He says Mercer sent a bloke to stick a knife in you.'

'And I still say George has a slack mouth and it'll get him into trouble one of these days. Don't you start suffering from the same complaint if we're going to work together.'

Rosa smiled.

'Is that a threat, Jimmy.'

Jimmy smiled back.

'No, sunshine, not a threat, a fucking promise.'

And Jimmy left The Hind and went back to his hotel to get some rest. He had his journalist. Now he could get on with nailing Harry Mercer.

Chapter Twenty-one

Leicester prison was an architectural monstrosity which stood beside a busy main road. The frontage it presented to the world, although the world did its best to ignore it, was grim and massive. Its dark stone walls were topped off with battlements and crenellations designed to give the impression of a medieval fortress. In this it failed miserably. It looked exactly what it was, a Victorian penal institution. The big, black doors under the arched main entrance were flanked by two turreted towers, and it was through this portcullis-style gatehouse that new inmates were delivered by white vehicles with small, neat windows, which resembled horseboxes arriving at a better-class cross-country event.

To one side of the main gate towers stood an eight-foot, corrugated, aluminium fence or screen which, compared to the solid mass of the main building, had an air of permanent temporariness. Through a door in this fence visitors to the prison could reach the new Visits and Administration centre. Quite why such a fence was needed at all was something of a mystery, the most likely reason being, however, that it screened the modern new addition to the prison from the public gaze as the authorities did not want to advertise that public money had been spent improving the lot of people who were friends or relations of convicted felons.

Jimmy's bag was searched when he and Rosa had arrived in the new centre, confirmed they had a meeting a Mrs Morrissey in Administration and were given their passes. The bag contained a camera and a spare lens. Rosa had given it to Jimmy before they set off from St Pancras station that morning.

'You have to have a good reason for being there so you're going to be the photographer, but for God's sake don't touch anything. It's expensive kit and I want to give it back to the bloke I borrowed it off all in one piece. Just try and look like a newspaper photographer.'

'How's a newspaper photographer supposed to look?'

'Comatose.'

'Come again?'

'Press photographers go comatose unless they've got something to shoot. They can switch off what passes for their brains over long periods of time. Just keep hold of your bag and look as if you've switched off your brain and you'll look exactly like a press photographer.'

After the brief search they were taken to an office and introduced to a neat, middle-aged woman. She gave them a formal, polite smile but her voice was distinctly on the chilly side.

'I have the information you asked for. I could have quite easily sent it to you so I don't quite understand why you took the trouble to come all the way from London.'

Rosa took over and Jimmy tried to look comatose.

'Because we need more than just the information we asked for, although thank you for that.'

'More?'

'Yes. May we sit down?'

Mrs Morrissey unbent a little.

'Of course.'

They all sat, Mrs Morrissey behind her desk, Rosa and Jimmy opposite.

'My editor wants me to do a piece on modern prison methods. He feels, and I agree with him, that the public are pretty fed up with horror stories about our public services. Not that they aren't true, but he feels the balance has swung too far, that it's time to look at where public money is being well spent, where the public is getting good value.'

'I see.'

But obviously she didn't.

'The trouble is we need to find a good focus for the thing, not just cold facts and figures. The reading public wouldn't be interested in statistics, what we need is something human. That's why we came, to look for some human angle to deliver the story of your success here.'

'Our success?'

'Yes. But bear with me, Mrs Morrissey, it'll all become clear, I promise.' Jimmy was impressed. Rosa was winning her over with her charm offensive and what she was saying sounded good even to him, and he knew it was bullshit. 'Could we perhaps start with the information we asked for?'

Mrs Morrissey turned to her computer screen and did what she had to on the keyboard.

'Here he is. Harold Reginald Mercer had been here four years when Arthur William Jarvis arrived. Jarvis served two years of a three-year sentence. He got full remission.'

'So they served two years together?'

'Correct.'

'Mercer served how long after Jarvis was released?'

She turned back to the screen and fiddled with the keyboard again.

'He served another eighteen months.'

Jimmy did a quick calculation and the words were out before he could stop them.

'Harry got remission!'

Rosa looked angrily at him. Jimmy shut up and Rosa took over again.

'So Mercer got remission, Mrs Morrissey?'

'Parole.'

Jimmy heard it, so it had to be right, but it didn't make

160

sense. Harry wasn't the sort who got parole. He always had been, and was always going to be, a danger to society. Rosa went on.

'Would any of the current warders remember either man?'

'Yes, several.'

'You see, what we need is a picture of this man Mercer's life in prison.'

'Why?'

'Because Harry Mercer came into prison a hardened criminal, but left a reformed character. How did that happen? How, after a life of crime, did Leicester gaol turn him round? That's our story, Mrs Morrissey. That's the success I mentioned earlier.

'I see. Then perhaps you should talk to the Governor.'

She said it like it would be a treat.

'No, not the Governor, although I'm sure he does an excellent job. What we need is someone who was close to the day-to-day routine, who knew the prisoners and all the little things that never get into reports but make prison life what it is for those serving a sentence. What I think we need is a warder who could not only fill in the facts but what lay behind the facts.'

Mrs Morrissey leaned forward slightly and her manner became confidential. She was definitely on board now.

'You can talk to one of the warders if you like but the person I recommend you speak to is an ex-warder, John Carter. He retired two years ago. He knew what went on in the jail almost as well as the prisoners did, certainly more than the other warders.'

Rosa leaned forward and became confidential as well.

'Do you mean he was being paid off?'

It was a mistake. Mrs Morrissey sat back with a flush of anger on her face.

'Absolutely not. John was never involved in anything like that. I merely meant that his long service gave him an excellent understanding of what went on. He was respected by prisoners and staff alike.' St Screw of Leicester, thought Jimmy, feast-day the thirty-first of February. Mrs Morrissey continued obviously still very huffy. 'I would never have mentioned his name if I thought you would ...'

'Quite, quite, Mrs Morrissey, I apologise. I'm afraid that as a journalist I don't often get to see the best side of people and, like the police, it can sometimes warp your view of the world. I'm sure it would be most helpful to talk to Mr Carter if he has the knowledge and experience you say he has.'

Mrs Morrissey was prepared to be mollified.

'What exactly is your story going to be about?'

'Like I said, Harry Mercer came into Leicester a career villain, violent, dishonest and dangerous. When he left he had changed his life around. He is now a successful writer and lives in Spain. If you go on to Amazon you can see his books there. That's our story, if we can get it – how the gangster turned crime writer. What I have to do is gather background info, make the inside of the prison come alive and show how it can help as well as punish. Your Mr Carter sounds as if he would be an excellent source to fill me in on how Leicester gaol helped turn round a hardened criminal so that he used his past experiences in a way that brought him success and gave pleasure to his readers.'

Mrs Morrissey gave a small but genuine smile. Rosa had won her over. Jimmy was impressed, she was good. She lied well. Maybe it was something she got taught at Cambridge as part of her degree. Being able to lie well would be a big plus for any aspiring politician or economist, even if they finished up as journalists.

'Well, that all sounds very ...'

But Mrs Morrissey couldn't find the right word so Rosa just kept on going.

'Do you have a contact number for him?'

'Oh, I really couldn't pass out that sort of information.'

But Rosa knew better. Why tell her about Carter if she didn't want her to make contact. She just wanted a bit of coaxing.

'I'm sure he could be a big help and I may be able to use his picture in the feature. He must have had some part in setting Harry on his new life if he was as respected by everyone as you say he was. That sort of commitment and achievement deserves recognition.'

Mrs Morrissey smiled again and folded.

'I can give you his phone number but don't say I was the one you got it from. I'm only trying to be of help. If you weren't a reporter trying to show people that prisons aren't always what people think I wouldn't dream of …'

'Thank you.'

Rosa had her notepad out and a pen poised. Mrs Morrissey gave her the number.

'Thank you. You have been a great help.'

Rosa and Jimmy got up.

'I'm glad to have been of assistance. It will be nice to get some positive news in the press about us at last. People don't know how difficult the job of the Prison Service –'

But Rosa was finished and wanted to get on.

'Goodbye.'

'Oh, yes, goodbye.'

Mrs Morrissey got up and took them out of the office and walked them down to the visitors' entrance. Jimmy's bag got searched again. Were they putting on a special show because they were the press? What did they think he might be trying to smuggle out? One of the inmates. He got the bag back, they handed back their passes and left the gaol.

Out on the busy main road they walked a short way until they came to a side street where a Georgian terrace stood opposite the high, blank side wall of the prison. It was a quiet street without the rush of traffic of the main road. They walked up it far enough to leave the worst of the traffic noise behind them and Rosa made a call.

'Hello, my name is Rosa Sikora, I'm a newspaper reporter and I'm researching a feature on a writer who spent time in Leicester prison some years back. I understand your husband was a warder … oh, sorry, your father. I understand he was a warder there until two years ago?' She listened for a second. 'Do you think it would be possible to meet up with your father and ask him a few questions?' She turned to Jimmy. 'She's gone to get him.'

'Will he agree?'

'Oh, yes, they always agree. People like to talk about themselves, so long as they don't feel personally threatened they always … Hello, Mr Carter, my name is Rosa Sikora. I'm researching a feature on a man called Harry Mercer. Do you remember him? Good. Mrs Morrissey gave us your name and number and said we should talk to you, that you knew the prison while Mercer was there better than anyone. You will? Fine, but I'm afraid it has to be today, we have to be back in London by late this afternoon. When would you be able to … half an hour would be great. Where should we meet? The Marquis of Wellington pub. Where is that? On the right of the London Road past the station. Don't worry, we'll find it. Wonderful, see you at the Marquis in half an hour then.'

She put away her mobile.

'Where's this pub?'

'You heard, on the London Road.'

'And this is Leicester, not Kilburn, so where the bloody hell is the London Road?'

'Not far from the station. Apparently you can't miss the pub, it's got a very distinctive frontage. We'll get a taxi at the main road.'

They went back to the main road but all the traffic was heading one way, the wrong way, and there were no taxis.

'Great. A one-way system. Do we walk?'

Rosa looked at the traffic.

'Looks like we do.'

Jimmy unslung the camera bag.

'Right, then you can have a go with this.'

Rosa took it and slung it on her shoulder.

'It's not so heavy. I thought you were supposed to be a tough guy.'

'Tell me it's not heavy when we're sitting in this Marquis pub and you've carried it all the way, then I'll call you the tough guy.'

Chapter Twenty-two

The front of Marquis of Wellington pub wasn't anything special at street level, but above the ground floor windows it was metalled black with raised silver decorations and in the centre a raised roundel containing a profile of a man's head, obviously the Marquis himself. Above all the decoration there were attractive bow windows, all of which promised something exceptional inside. Sadly, any distinctive flourishes finished at the front door. Inside it was like most other big city pubs with the usual open-plan arrangement and one main bar. However, for those rare souls who wanted some degree of privacy there were a few partitioned booths by the windows. Rosa went and sat in one of the unoccupied booths, unslung the camera bag and put it beside her. She massaged her shoulder and made a face at Jimmy, who smiled and then went to the bar and looked at the beers. He chose one and ordered a cup of tea for Rosa. When the beer had been pulled he took it to the booth, sat down and tasted it.

'It's not a bad pint this. Everards, I've never heard of it, must be local.'

Rosa looked around. There were a few people at tables, mostly on their own. 'It looks an OK sort of place. Did you see the front as we came in? Very individual. See the roundel over the door?'

'What's a roundel?'

'Strangely enough, a round thing. There was a picture of the Duke of Wellington in it.'

'So why is it called the Marquis of Wellington, not the

Duke?'

'How should I know.'

Jimmy left the business of pub names and got to the business in hand.

'Now we know Jarvis and Mercer did time together.'

'You guessed right.'

'What we need now is the internet.' He looked at Rosa. 'Have you got something we can use?'

She gave Jimmy a look of commiseration.

'You're a bloody antique, you know that?' She took out a tiny netbook computer and switched it on. 'What was it you wanted?'

'I wanted to find out when Harry's first book got published.'

'We don't need the internet. I saved the pages about Mercer's books from Amazon. I thought it might come in handy.' She found the pages and then looked up. 'That's interesting.'

'Don't tell me, let me guess. It got published before Harry got his parole.'

'No, but you're close. Two months after. How did you know?'

'Because Harry was muscle, never brains, and there's no way he'd ever turn into a writer. He didn't become one in prison or out. A fiver to a fish tail says Jarvis wrote Harry's first book based on stuff Harry told him inside and when Harry came out Jarvis went on writing them.' Jimmy took a thoughtful drink. 'Which makes it all a bit of a bugger.'

The tray with the tea things arrived. Rosa thanked the barman and started to pour.

'Why? It makes sense and it makes the connection you wanted. What's wrong with it?'

'It's hardly likely Harry would top Jarvis if he needed him to write his books. Unless, maybe …'

But there was no easy way round it. You didn't kill the

167

bloke who gave you your cover unless, maybe …

But, no, there was no easy way round it, not as it stood.

'You really want Mercer to go down heavy, don't you? Is this personal?'

'Wouldn't you call sending someone to stick a knife in you personal?'

'You know what I mean. Is there another reason, other than Mercer thinking you're poking into his porn racket?'

'No. I told you, Harry and I hadn't seen each other for years until a week ago.'

A man in his late fifties came in and stood by the doorway looking around. Rosa got up and went over to him.

'Mr Carter?'

'Yes.'

They shook hands.

'We're over here.' They came to the booth. 'What will you have to drink?'

'A pint of Original. Thanks.'

'Get Mr Carter a pint will you, Jimmy?' Jimmy looked at her, she gave him a smile. 'We won't need you to take any pictures just yet.' She turned her attention back to Carter. 'Good of you to come at such short notice, Mr Carter.'

Jimmy got up, went to the bar and ordered a pint of Original. It was the same beer he had ordered for himself.

'Local brewery, is it?'

The barman nodded and carried on pulling the pint. He wasn't the chatty type. Jimmy paid for the beer and took it back to their table. Carter was already talking. He paused when Jimmy came and took the glass.

'Thanks.' He took a drink and resumed. Jimmy sat down and listened. 'No, Jarvis never had much trouble. He wasn't a proper paedophile, he didn't molest little kids. He just bonked a few willing girls who weren't quite sixteen. I mean, it goes on all the time doesn't it? You see it on the news and in the papers. I mean, they give out condoms and the pill and stuff like that to them at school these days. Hardly worth putting knickers on for some of them, the amount of time they must have them off. I'm glad it was different when Kathy was a girl.'

'Kathy?'

'My daughter. I live with her. No, with Jarvis it was a technical crime, nothing nasty. And he was a nice bloke, big, good-looking, you could see how young girls would fall for him. He taught drama he said, and they let their imaginations run away sometimes. He just took what was offered. He shouldn't have been in prison at all really but I suppose it was because he was a teacher. If he hadn't been a teacher he wouldn't have drawn a three-stretch but he said the papers made a fuss, blew it up, set out to crucify him. You know what the bloody papers are like?' He smiled sheepishly. 'Oh, of course you do. I didn't mean that you would do anything like …'

'Don't worry about it, Mr Carter and, yes, I'm afraid I would do something like that. The news by itself often isn't enough to sell papers and it is sometimes the sad duty of reporters like me to goose it up a bit. It's a naughty old world and you can't change it. But I don't need to tell you that, not if you've spent your working life as a prison warder. So, tell me about Harry Mercer.'

'Oh, Harry fitted straight in when he turned up. He hooked up with a couple of long-stretch blokes who ran things and started doing the heavy work for them. Harry the Hammer they called him. When Harry came to collect, you paid. Not that he was violent in the normal run of things, only when it was called for.'

'Did he study?'

Rosa didn't mind Jimmy cutting in this time.

'Study what?'

'Did he do any courses? Open University, stuff like that?'

That got a big grin.

'Harry? Not Harry. He wasn't the studious type. He might have read a few of the betting slips he collected but that was all.'

'What about Jarvis, was he the studious type?'

Carter thought about it.

'Yes, I remember now, Jarvis was the one who did some sort of course. It may have been the Open University. English it was, I know because I helped him by getting some of the books he needed from the library service.'

Rosa picked up the questioning again.

'Did Jarvis and Harry ever share a cell?'

'No.'

'Did they seem friendly?'

Carter paused.

'Not friendly exactly.'

'What?'

'Well I got the feeling that they talked, that they had something going, but they kept it all very much to themselves if they did. They had nothing in common that I could ever see, and I never came across anything that I could actually put my finger on, but you get a feeling for things after a few years. I'd say something was going on, but as it never caused trouble I left it alone.' He remembered something else. It was coming back. 'And I'll tell you something else that seemed odd at the time. There was this young tearaway came in after Jarvis had done about a year. Drawn a stretch for GBH. Violent, fancied himself, a troublemaker. He started on about Jarvis when he found out what he been sent down for. I remember him saying how you should take a file to a paedophile and he made sure Jarvis heard it. That was about as far as his brains or his idea of joke went. He was just using Jarvis as an excuse to show everyone what a hard-case he was, but he was obviously going to do him some damage. Then

Harry stepped on him. We couldn't prove anything, Harry was too clever for that. But the young hard nut spent a month in hospital and had to have his jaw wired. He wasn't such a hard nut after that and Jarvis never got bothered by anybody again. Nothing was said, but after what happened to the tearaway, nothing much needed saying did it?'

Jimmy took a drink.

'Nice beer, this Original.'

'Yeah it is. It used to be called Old Original but they changed the name. I don't see why.'

'Would you be surprised if I told you that Harry took up crime writing?'

That got a laugh.

'Harry? It wouldn't surprise me, it would bloody well amaze me. I told you, Harry's idea of reading material stopped at betting slips or page three girls stuck to his cell wall. He didn't even read a newspaper that I can remember. Harry couldn't write a book if his life depended on it.'

Jimmy looked at Rosa.

'Our information seems to be wrong then.'

Rosa carried on.

'What about visitors? Did either of them get anyone regular?'

'I don't remember. There's so many visitors over the years. You don't remember them, they just get to be a blur of faces.'

'Does the name Henderson mean anything to you?'

Carter gave it some thought, then brightened.

'Yes.' Jimmy and Rosa gave each other a look. 'There was a bloke called Henderson. A runty little feller, bald with glasses, harmless. Did time for bigamy.'

'Bigamy?'

'Yes, which was a laugh because no one could see how he could get one woman to marry him never mind two. He

171

was Scottish, a sailor.'

'Not an accountant?'

Carter laughed.

'No, he worked on cruise ships, a steward I think. Mind you, as I remember, now that you ask, he did have a way with him. Could make people laugh.'

Whoever this new Henderson was, he wasn't the one they were looking for. Jimmy finished his pint. They had what they needed. It was time to move on.

Rosa agreed, she finished her tea and pushed away the cup.

'Thank you very much, Mr Carter. You've been very helpful.'

Rosa and Jimmy got up. Carter looked up at them.

'Is that it? Is that all you wanted to know. It doesn't seem much to me. I could tell you plenty more about what went on. Stuff you could –'

'Thank you, but we've got all we need.'

Rosa was about to turn and leave when Jimmy stopped her.

'Hang on. Don't forget the camera. It's not heavy.' She didn't move, Jimmy gave her a smile. 'I got the drinks, remember.'

She picked up the camera bag and slung it over his shoulder. Then they left. Carter sat at the table with a bemused look on his face for a moment then stood up and took his drink to the bar where the barman was reading a paper. He didn't like drinking on his own.

The barman looked up. He could see that the glass was still almost full.

'Yes, sir?'

'One bloody pint. It was hardly worth the effort of coming. Bloody newspaper reporters.'

And, seeing that nothing was wanted except conversation, the barman returned to his paper. He wasn't the chatty type.

172

Jimmy and Rosa set off down the London Road towards the station where they had arrived earlier and taken a taxi to the gaol. When they got inside Jimmy looked for the Customer Enquiries booth. It was on the far side of the ticket hall.

'Hang on here, I want to find out something.'

Rosa unslung the camera case, put it down beside her and looked up at the big departures board. The next London train left in twenty minutes. She looked across at Jimmy, who was talking to someone in the enquiry booth. When he came back his phone went off. He took it out and looked at the name. It was Professor McBride. He switched off the phone and put it away.

'Someone you don't want to speak to.'

'A woman I know. She thinks I should be somewhere else. Never mind her. Henderson's firm is in Coventry. We can catch a train from here, change at Nuneaton. It would take us about an hour.'

'You're joking?'

'Why not, we're finished here and it's early yet,' he looked at his watch, ' not even two. Why not go on to Coventry?'

'And do what? Find Henderson's business, walk in without an appointment and say to whoever's there, excuse me, tell us all you know about a sex offender called Jarvis, a career villain called Mercer and your boss's involvement in wholesaling hard porn in Spain.'

Jimmy shrugged.

'You're the reporter, you think of something.'

Rosa stood for a moment.

'I've thought of something.

'Good, what?'

'I've thought of what a pillock you must be to think I'd set off for Coventry without any way of getting what we want. Unlike the police, I don't carry a warrant card, so I can't just barge in and beat information out of people. You

173

go to Coventry if you want, I'm going to be on the next train back to London and here,' she picked up the camera case, 'you take this fucking thing. It's heavy.' Jimmy took it. 'Come on, it's platform three.'

She didn't wait for him. Jimmy slung the bag over his shoulder. It didn't seem so heavy, he couldn't see what she was moaning about. Then he set off after her, maybe she had a point, they would need a story, a way in, but that was her job. He couldn't think of a story so he didn't try, he left it alone and switched his brain off. To anybody who took any notice he looked just like a newspaper photographer.

Chapter Twenty-three

'I was surprised when I got your call yesterday, but it was a very pleasant surprise. We've never been in the running for an award before, although I have to say I've never actually heard of it. The Small Businesses Good Service Award.'

Rosa got real conviction into her voice, as if there really was an award.

'I can understand that, Mr Dredge; this is only its second year and last year was really nothing more than a try-out, but I assure you it will rapidly gain prestige in the trade. Too few people realise how important good services are to the sustaining of small business profitability. The simple fact is that twice the number of small business failures are directly down to poor service facilities when compared to marketing or production problems.'

'Indeed? So many.'

'Fact, I assure you, researched fact.'

'I see. But how did we get chosen?'

'Our business editor uses a firm that monitors the performance of businesses that fit the category of the award. He picks three of the top ones and I get sent to interview whoever is in charge and choose which one wins.'

Mr Dredge passed over the inherent nonsense of Rosa's explanation and cut to the heart of what she had said, the bit he was really interested in.

'I see, you are the one who actually chooses?'

'Yes.'

'And have you been to the other two?'

'Yes.'

'May I ask who they are?'

'No, sorry, I can't tell you that.'

'No, of course, I quite understand.'

Mr Dredge was the senior accountant at Henderson-Kenwright & Co. but he didn't look like an accountant, he looked more like a cartoonist's idea of an on-course bookie. He was a balding, chubby man with a checked jacket, yellowy-green waistcoat, florid bow tie, and a face that fitted his ready smile. A friendly man you could trust, a bookie you'd be happy to bet with.

'So, how do you decide?'

Jimmy sat and watched Rosa in action. It was a good idea, the award. It put Dredge on their side from the word go and, considering she'd only thought of it the previous day when Jimmy had phoned her, she made it all sound very real.

'That's quite simple. We talk to one of your clients.'

'I see.'

'Neat and effective, after all it's the opinions of your customers that are the most accurate indicator of the service you provide.'

'Of course, I can understand that.'

'The truth is, Mr Dredge, there isn't a lot of money in awards unless they're big awards, the sort the public care about, and providing services to small businesses is, to put it bluntly, not headline-grabbing stuff. You and I know how vital it is but, well, as I say, not the stuff that makes headlines. We're doing it because we think it's important but we can't put too much into it in the way of resources. So this morning you get the two of us and we go home with whatever you've told us and, hopefully, one interview with a satisfied client and we take it from there.'

'Yes. And the award itself?'

'Five hundred pounds.' You could see the

disappointment on his face. Five hundred pounds wasn't much, not much at all. 'I'm afraid it's not much.'

Dredge gave a weak smile barely trying to hide his disappointment.

'No indeed.'

He still looked like a bookie, but now a bookie who has been asked by a stranger to extend credit. Rosa was ready for his response.

'No, the money isn't much. But then again it's not really about the money.'

He brightened up.

'No?'

'No, it's about the publicity. A feature on the winner in our business section, a big feature.'

The smile returned, the stranger had turned out to be credit-worthy after all.

'A feature?'

Rosa nodded.

Dredge thought about it.

'And do you choose the client you interview, or do I?'

Rosa slightly lowered her voice. She was becoming confidential.

'Mr Dredge, I'm going to let you into a little secret. It isn't only about who gives the best service. The feature on the winner needs to be good copy, something that will be interesting to a wide audience so we choose the winner by choosing the most attractive of the satisfied clients.'

'I'm sorry, I don't understand.'

'Let me explain. If you were accountants to a small engineering firm who made, say, widgets. It would be difficult to see how their high opinion of your services could be written up into a good feature. But say you were accountants to a club that celebrities frequent,' She let it sink in. 'You can see how that would take very little writing indeed to have a very wide appeal.'

Dredge saw. He smiled.

'Yes, I can see what you mean. Unfortunately I'm afraid our customers are almost all of the widget-producing variety. Solid rather than spectacular.'

'That's a pity. It wouldn't have had to be an actual cat-house, you understand, just something to hang a story on. A local celebrity, a firm with some sort of angle we could play up, like a small publisher whose books people might have read.' Rosa waited but Dredge didn't respond. She edged forward. 'A publisher who had an author whose name the public would recognise.' She waited again.

Dredge perked up.

'There is a publisher.'

'Is there?'

Rosa's surprise was good, it looked almost genuine though Jimmy thought it a shade overdone. Dredge took it at face value.

'Yes, it's a firm not far away, Leamington Spa, Tate and Wiston.' The enthusiasm went out of his voice. 'But they publish mostly trade journals and specialist books. I doubt very many of your readers would have –'

Rosa turned to Jimmy.

'You're the book reader, Jimmy. Does the name Tate and Wiston ring any bells?'

Jimmy was no actor, but he did his best. He didn't try surprise, it would come out like shock, or as if he was having an attack or seizure, so he went for a straight delivery.

'I think I know the name. They publish Harry Mercer, the crime writer, don't they?'

Rosa did more surprise.

'A crime writer. That sounds interesting. Harry Mercer? Never heard of him. How about you, Mr Dredge?'

'No, I'm afraid crime-thrillers aren't something I read.'

'OK, Jimmy, for the benefit of us ignorant ones, who is Harry Mercer?'

Jimmy spoke his party piece just as she'd rehearsed him.

'He was a London career gangster, got sent down for armed robbery and while inside he turned his hand to writing. He's written four books so far and these days he lives in Spain.'

That was it, not an Oscar performance but he'd got the words out. Now Rosa could get on with things again. She turned back to Dredge full of enthusiasm.

'Great, a celebrity ex-gangster virtually on your books, Mr Dredge. Could you get us an interview with whoever heads up …what did you say the publisher's called?'

'Tate and Wiston. I could try, I'm sure they'd like to help. Shall I phone them and set up an appointment? What would be a suitable date?'

'I'm afraid it's like I said, there's no real money for this, so today is all we get for you and your client.'

'I see.'

'Why not try this publisher and if it's no-go then we'll move onto the next most likely. I must say though, if you can swing it for us I think we may finally have our winner. The other two firms couldn't come up with anyone who could compete with a gangster turned best-selling author.' She had Dredge where she wanted him now so she gave him the final push. 'Have a go, use your charm. I think you'll find it will be worth it. You know what our circulation is?'

He didn't so she named a figure, it sounded ridiculous to Jimmy but it landed Dredge all right. He pulled a roll-file to him and flicked through the roll until he found the number. He made the call.

'Hello, Mr Jardene, it's Gordon Dredge of Henderson-Kenwright, I have a small favour to ask. We're being put up for a new industry award, the Small Businesses Good Services Award. I have someone from the newspaper who are sponsoring it here with me now. She wondered whether she could speak to one of our clients, preferably a satisfied one.' He gave a brief laugh, the Jardene character must have made a joke. 'Of course, very amusing. As they are only up from London for the day I thought of you. Could you give them –' He looked enquiringly at Rosa. She flicked her fingers up twice. '– twenty minutes some time around lunchtime? It would be a real help and I think we would both benefit from the result. There will be a feature in the business pages and the paper's circulation is –' Dredge told him the circulation. It was a real help. 'You can, at one today. That's so good of you, Mr Jardene. Thank you.' He put the phone down. 'So, one today.'

'Great. How do we get to Leamington Spa?'

'By car?'

'No.'

'Taxi?'

Rosa shook her head.

'We'd never get it past Accounts if it was over ten pounds.'

'Then train is your best bet. There are regular trains from Coventry. Once at Leamington, get a taxi and ask for Copthorne Terrace, number thirty-two. It won't cost anywhere near ten pounds.' They all laughed politely. 'Tate and Wiston are on the first floor. You will see a Mr Jardene, that was him on the phone.'

Rosa stood up, so did Jimmy. She put out a hand.

'Thank you so much, Mr Dredge, and perhaps I should add, congratulations.'

Dredge simpered as they shook hands, a pleased bookie after a good day at the races.

'Oh, thank you, but perhaps a little premature, although I'm sure Mr Jardene counts as a satisfied client.'

'It's in the bag.'

Jimmy felt like clapping. Someone should be applauding her performance. She was a born actor. Mr Dredge held out his hand to Jimmy.

'Goodbye, Mr …'

Rosa hadn't introduced him so Dredge had no name for him and Jimmy didn't give him one, just shook his hand. He looked as if he was about to follow Rosa then stopped.

'One last thing, Mr Dredge, who actually owns this firm, Henderson or Kenwright, or is it still a partnership?'

'Mr Henderson is the owner, he bought out Kenwright some years ago, but he's not active in our day-to-day running any more. He lives in Spain now,' he smiled at a thought he'd just had, 'like our writer, Harry Mercer. Quite a coincidence isn't it?'

Rosa smiled and edged closer to the door. Jimmy didn't smile or follow her.

'So Mr Henderson's retired?'

'Yes, I suppose you could say he's retired. Nothing official but he doesn't have any sort of active role any more.'

'But he pops back occasionally to keep an eye on things?'

'No, we haven't seen him for …' Dredge had to do think about it, ' … slightly over two years. I have his full trust and, if I say so myself, the firm is in very safe hands.'

Rosa could see that Jimmy's questions were beginning to unsettle Dredge.

'I'm sure it is. Jimmy's a great one for background, Mr Dredge, but we really have to be going. Thanks.'

Jimmy joined Rosa who stood waiting by the office door, she took a firm grip of his arm and they left. Dredge sat back into his chair a happy man.

'Thorough devils,' he said to himself. 'Still, I suppose it all helps.'

And he got back to work.

Outside the offices of Henderson-Kenwright Rosa stopped.

'You nearly fucked that up, you know that?'

Jimmy shrugged.

'I got what I wanted.'

They began to walk.

'Next time for Christ's sake stick to the agreed fucking script.'

Jimmy shrugged again and they set off in silence heading for the station. Although Henderson-Kenwright's offices were in the city centre they were located in a row of pleasant three-storey Edwardian buildings over the road from which was pretty park filled with trees and well-maintained lawns and flower beds. The station was only five minutes walk away through the trees and flowers but at the far end of the park the scenery changed abruptly. They left the park and took a pathway which led down steps into an underpass. Overhead was a busy ring-road and on the other side of this road you emerged into a mass of grey, slab-like, concrete and glass. This post-war redevelopment was a place of tall office buildings with small, unlovely retail outlets at street level. They bought their tickets in the station and found they had forty-five minutes to kill until the next train to Leamington came in, so Jimmy suggested a quick drink. He'd spotted a big old pub not far from the station which somehow had been missed by the planners. It was twenty-five to twelve but the Rocket pub was open. Inside it was empty of customers and the man behind the bar looked up from his paper and gave them a welcoming smile. Jimmy bought drinks, a pint and a lemonade and lime, and took them to the table where Rosa had sat down. Once he was seated Rosa raised her glass.

'Cheers. Despite your injury-time efforts that all went very well. I think I made a bloody good job of slipping our marked card onto him. If anyone asks he'll say it was his idea to choose Tate and Wiston.'

Jimmy put down his pint. It wasn't bad. Pedigree, a Midland beer. Not Directors or London Pride, but drinkable, very drinkable.

'It was a good idea and you did it well. Even I could almost believe in the award the way you pitched it. What will your editor say when Dredge finds there's no such award never mind any splash in the business pages for the winner?'

'If I get the story I promised him, the one about Mercer, he'll say, "fuck off and if you've got a problem we'll see you in court". If I don't get the story he'll apologise humbly to Dredge and then tell *me* to fuck off and I'll never work on a London paper again.' But she didn't seem worried about it either way. Was she really that cocky? 'And while we're busy handing out congratulations, well done you for making the connection. What made you think of Henderson Kenwright and the publisher?'

'I did some looking when we got back from Leicester. Henderson's business is in Coventry and it just so happens that Harry's publisher is in Leamington Spa, a few miles away. It was too much like a coincidence so I checked what else they publish. It's like Dredge says, all trade stuff, journals and business books. Why would a publisher like that take on an unknown crime-thriller writer? They have no marketing to plug it into because it doesn't fit in with anything else they do. What sort of publisher does all trade stuff but takes on one solitary crime writer? Does it sound on the up and up to you?'

'So you reckon someone persuaded this Tate and Wiston outfit to publish Harry's stuff and that someone was Henderson.'

'It was worth a close look. If we can confirm it then we've got all three of them hooked into each other.'

Rosa was impressed, this guy thought things through. But then, he'd been a copper, a detective and, by all accounts a good one, if bent. From what amounted to virtually nothing he had sorted out how Jarvis, Mercer and Henderson were linked.

'What was all that stuff you asked before we left?

About Henderson being retired and did he come back at all?'

'I was told in Spain that Henderson leaves Santander about six times a year, he tells people he goes back to the UK to check on his business. Now we know he doesn't, so where does he go?'

'You should have been a reporter, there's more money in it than police-work and it's not so dangerous. Do you want me to introduce you to my editor?'

'Do you think he'd give me a job?'

She laughed.

'Get the whole of this story and he'll give you mine.'

She took a drink. Jimmy looked at his watch. It was nearly time to be getting back to the station.

'You're a bit young to be a reporter on a London paper? How did you get so far so fast?'

'I told you, Jimmy, I'm good and I'm in a hurry. Also I'm prepared to do whatever it takes.'

'Sleeping with the enemy?'

'It's been known to happen. Like I said, you do what it takes, if you don't there's others who will. These days talent on its own isn't enough.' Jimmy gave her a look. She gave him one back. 'Don't worry, I haven't got you marked down for a bit of pelvis-pushing. You're just someone who might get me a good story.' Then the look changed and Jimmy knew that sort of look now. 'But keep going the way you are and I might throw in a freebie at the end of things.' She finished her drink, pushed the glass away and stood up. 'Come on, let's get going to see this Jardenebloke.'

Chapter Twenty-four

Copthorne Terrace had been built in the glory days of Leamington Spa when Regency society flocked to its healing waters to flirt, gossip and display. The terrace was a long row of what had once been classic Regency elegance, but now the facades were shabby, stained and peeling, a Regency dandy fallen on hard times. This was back-street Leamington, not much-photographed Landsdowne Crescent, nor the gleaming white of the well-maintained fronts that looked across the Parade at Jephson Gardens where visitors walked among trees and flowers on the banks of the gently flowing River Leam.

The houses of Copthorne Terrace were now bed-sits, small flats and low-rental office space. Number thirty-two, where Tate and Wiston occupied the first floor, looked bigger and better maintained than most; the white of the frontage had been repainted as recently as ten years ago, almost yesterday compared to the majority of its neighbours. Inside the offices of Tate and Wiston it was much the same as the fronts themselves, a standard of office organisation was obviously maintained, but not too high a standard. Shelves were stacked with piles of magazines, journals and pamphlets which had obviously been there for some time, forlornly waiting the attention which would never come.

Mr Jardene fitted well into his surroundings. He was a small man of indeterminate middle-age, anything from forty-five to sixty-five. His suit had been good when new but it was now far from new. His desk was the one really tidy thing Jimmy or Rosa had seen since they had entered the offices. He was a raft of order afloat on a sea of incipient chaos.

'We are a very small publisher you understand.' He waited a second for his visitors to recover from the shock of this bombshell. They recovered. 'Ours is a rather specialist business, trade journals and magazines for the smaller business associations.' He picked up a magazine and offered it to Rosa who took it. *The Commercial Meat Haulier's Gazette*. It had a picture of a juggernaut on the front. Rosa gave it back. 'But it is steady work and the few books we publish are very focussed so they do quite well, in a specialist market sort of way.'

Rosa got down to business. Commercial Meat Hauling, though fascinating in itself, would have to wait for another time.

'I understand you publish the crime-fiction of Harry Mercer?'

A shadow passed over Mr Jardene's face. He looked as if she had tactlessly mentioned some past infidelity committed by his wife, forgiven but not forgotten. He pursed his lips as if he was sucking a wasp.

'It appears under the Tate and Wiston imprint. In that sense you could say we publish Mr Mercer.'

It hadn't been the response they had been expecting but Rosa pushed on.

'It's a bit unusual for a publisher like yourselves to do something quite so different from your main work isn't it?'

'No.'

'No?'

'No, not unusual. Un*heard* of in any respectable house.'

'Could you explain?'

But Mr Jardene disliked the subject. He wasn't in a cooperative frame of mind. That much was obvious.

'I thought you had come to discuss our opinion of the

186

service we get from our accountants, Henderson-Kenwright. Something about an award?'

Rosa moved ahead carefully. It would be easy to lose him and she didn't want to lose him.

'Yes, in a manner we have, but Mr Dredge was the one who told us you published Harry Mercer and it might make a good piece in the feature.'

'The feature?'

'We will do a feature on Henderson-Kenwright if they win the award.'

'Well I don't see that the books of Mr Mercer will be of any interest to anyone. They are certainly not best-sellers.'

'Oh, we were told they were.'

'Then I suggest you check your source.'

'I see, how well do they sell?'

'Hardly at all.'

Rosa was struggling, Jimmy could see that, but he had no way of helping. He was struggling himself.

'I'm sorry, I don't understand.'

'They are badly-written rubbish. No, sorry, I'm afraid I'm letting my feelings get in the way of my judgement. They *were* badly written rubbish, the first two. The third was just about readable and the last one had some small merit. For anyone who likes lurid crime-fiction, that is.'

'Could you explain, Mr Jardene? What you seem to be telling me is that you have published a series of books in a genre in which you have no interest or expertise, that the writing doesn't merit their being published. They don't sell yet you have published four.'

Mr Jardene decided to relent. Here were people who looked as if they would listen sympathetically to him.

'The decision, I assure you, was not mine but, as I said, they appear under our imprint., but that is all. Design and production are carried out elsewhere as are sales, publicity, and marketing, if there is any publicity or marketing which I doubt. I have as little to do with the wretched things as possible.'

'So if you don't want them published by Tate and Wiston, who does? Is it vanity publishing, does Mercer pay to have them published?'

The idea of Harry paying for the vanity publishing of his books almost made Jimmy laugh out loud, but Rosa was doing well now so, with an effort, he remained outwardly comatose.

'Indeed not. I would have resigned rather than stoop to vanity publishing. The very idea!'

'OK, Mr Jardene. You told us your mystery tale, now can we get to the bit where you rip off your false nose and whiskers and reveal who committed this dastardly crime?'

It was a clever move and she got the reaction she wanted. Jardene gave a small smile.

'It was Mr Henderson's idea. He seemed very taken with it and when he explained it to me I could see that, as an idea you understand, it might work. A series of crime thrillers written by a reformed criminal using his first-hand experiences. With the right publisher and with a good editor it might have worked.'

'Mr Henderson was the one who wanted them published?'

'Yes.'

'But why with Tate and Wiston? Like you said, it needed the right publisher and an editor who had experience in crime-fiction. That doesn't sound like Tate and Wiston.'

'It isn't and wasn't, but unfortunately we are the only publisher owned by Mr Henderson. So we got stuck with it.'

There was a pause. Mr Jardene nursed his sorrow while Jimmy and Rosa were thinking. Jimmy decided it was his turn to speak.

'How long have you been with Tate and Wiston?'

'Twenty-one years.'

'And how long has Mr Henderson been the owner?'

'A little more than seven years.'

'Did Henderson-Kenwright get to do the firm's accounts after Henderson bought the firm, or before?'

'Before. Henderson-Kenwright were our accountants when I started with the firm. That was when old Mr Henderson ran the business.'

Jimmy did the calculations. Henderson had bought the business one year before Jarvis had been released from prison. While Jimmy was thinking, Rosa kept the questions going.

'If the first book was badly written and didn't sell why did Mr Henderson go on?'

'He said he had given Mercer a three-book contract.'

'OK, but why book four?'

'I don't know but, as I said, the quality of writing improved from book to book. From an abysmal start, admittedly, but book three was almost readable and book four, though trashy and desperately in need of a good editor, might have been commercial in the right hands.'

'You obviously found the whole thing distasteful, so why read them? You seem to know them very well.'

'They appear under our imprint. I wouldn't dream of having our imprint on anything I hadn't read myself.'

'A matter of professional pride?'

'Not at all. I am a publisher, my most valuable skill is the judgement of the quality of the material we accept for publication. I wouldn't dream of taking someone else's assessment of the quality of something I publish.'

'Or appear to publish.'

'Quite. I know the books are rubbish because I have read them myself.'

Jimmy cut in.

'Are we finished here?' They looked at him. 'I think we're finished here.'

Rosa decided she agreed. She stood up.

189

'Thank you, Mr Jardene, you have been more than helpful.'

Jardene stood up.

'And if Mr Dredge asks how things went?'

'I'd have to say Henderson-Kenwright have fallen back in the betting, right back.'

Jardene smiled.

'Yes, I rather think I would say that as well.'

'Fine, then we'll be on our way.'

'Can I phone for a taxi?'

Jimmy answered.

'No thanks, we'll walk.'

'As you wish.'

They all shook hands and Jimmy and Rosa left the offices, went down the stairs and out into the street where they headed in the direction of the centre of town, a couple of streets away. Jimmy suddenly stopped.

'Hang on here.'

He turned and hurriedly walked back to number thirty-two. Rosa saw him go in. She waited and after a few minutes Jimmy reappeared and came back up to her.

'What was that about?'

'There was one more thing I wanted to ask Jardene.'

'Obviously. What?'

'I wanted to know who did the cleaning?'

They resumed walking.

'You think that place gets cleaned?'

'Not the inside, but the windows do, once a month. A local firm do it.'

They walked on in silence for a minute.

'Are you going to share it with me?'

'Acme Property Services.'

'Not the bloody window cleaners. Why did you ask the question? Is whoever cleans the windows important?'

'I don't know, it might be. Come on let's find somewhere to get a drink and I'll explain.'

They went to the bar of a big, white-fronted Regency hotel on the main street opposite the public gardens. It was comparatively quiet and was big enough for them to get a table where they wouldn't be overheard. The beer this time was Bass, as classic as the Regency interior of the hotel. Rosa had tea.

'Henderson bought Tate and Wiston before Jarvis came out of prison. That means he's been part of Harry's game from the word go. Harry must have set it up in prison. He took my advice after all.'

'Advice?'

'Years ago I pulled Harry and some others for a security van job. I told Harry that he was getting too old for violence and he should learn a trade when he got sent down. As it happened the case never came to court, some sort of cock-up by the prosecution. But when Harry next went down he must have decided he wanted something quieter but still profitable. I think he decided to become a porn wholesaler but he needed a legitimate front and a way to explain the money. When Jarvis turned up inside Harry found his front. Jarvis was educated, a teacher. Harry probably sounded him out to see if he would write the books so Harry could re-invent himself as a gangster turned writer. Jarvis knew his teaching career was over and he needed a source of income so he agreed. Harry provided him with genuine information and general background and Jarvis cobbled together the first book. Somehow they got Henderson on board.'

'Any idea how?'

'No, not yet, but he had to be on board because he bought Tate and Wiston. They needed a tame publisher for the books to get into print.'

'Like Jardene said, they wouldn't have seen the light of day with a genuine publisher.'

'No, and Harry didn't want them to. He just wanted them out there.' Jimmy smiled to himself. 'He was lucky

Jarvis was such a bad writer. If he'd been a good one Harry might have got to be somebody important in the literary world and that kind of attention –'

'Would put the lid on his real business plan.'

'You can be a best-selling crime-writer, or a hard porn retailer, but not both, not at the same time anyway.'

'I see what you mean. The books were bad and didn't sell but that didn't matter, it was even a plus because no one took any notice of them and Henderson hid away the income from the porn racket in the accounts at Tate and Wiston.' Her mobile rang. 'Yeah? Things are going fine, we're making real progress. If he keeps going like he is then my guess is he'll get all the way on the story.' She smiled at Jimmy. 'You should give him a job. We've made the connection between Jarvis, Mercer and Henderson and we know the books were just a front, done by a publisher Henderson owns. No, that's as far as we've got but like I say, we're getting there. What do you want me to do?' She listened. 'OK, I'll pass it on.' She put away the phone. 'That was my editor, he was impressed. And he had a bit of news for you. The Spanish police want to talk to you.'

'Official?'

'No, there's no official request as yet, no warrant or anything like that, but he's got a tip that the UK police have been asked to locate you and, when found, hold you until the Spanish decide what they want to do. Apparently it's all very low-key at the moment. Seems the Spanish can't make up their mind how they want to play it. They want to talk to you but they don't want to make it public.'

'I see.'

'Well I don't, and neither does my editor. Why should the Spanish police be after you?'

'I told you, Harry sent someone after me and I killed him. I didn't mean to but I did.'

'And that's why they're after you? No other reason?'

'I don't know of anything else.'

'Then why are they taking it so gently, gently? If you topped a guy in Spain why not put out an arrest warrant?'

'The bloke broke into the house I was staying at. I heard him and was ready for him. He got a knife in me but I still broke his neck.'

'I see. You're a very violent man, Jimmy, I'll have to remember that. So what happened?'

'I was interviewed by the police and they decided it was self-defence. It looks like they may have had second thoughts.'

'Sure it's just that? Nothing else?'

'No, nothing else.'

But he could see she didn't believe him. Why didn't she believe him? Whatever it was she decided to change the subject.

'All right, now explain to me about the window cleaners.'

You're bloody good, thought Jimmy, but you're not perfect, and I think you've just made a bad mistake. But he decided that, like Rosa, it was best left alone, for the moment.

Chapter Twenty-five

There was a decent service from Leamington to London Marylebone but Jimmy insisted on going back through Coventry. He said he wanted another pint of Pedigree at the Rocket. Rosa didn't like it but agreed. It wasn't worth arguing over. When they got there the Rocket was busier so they sat outside on a small patio where three wooden tables were set behind railings out overlooking the railway lines. The station was quite close, down to their left. Jimmy had a pint. Rosa passed on another drink and sat while he drank slowly. Finally she decided she might as well get something out of the delay.

'I still don't see it about the window cleaners.'

'I told you.'

'Tell me again.'

'Window cleaners get paid.'

'Cash in hand, that gives us nothing.'

'No, it's a contract.'

'So they're on a contract, where does that get us?'

'The Acme lot in Leamington are sub-contracted. While we were waiting for a train at Leamington station I phoned them.'

'I didn't see you do that.'

'You were in the toilet.'

'Hiding things from me now?'

'They were very co-operative and told me that the window cleaning contract for number thirty-two Copthorne Terrace had been given them by Universal Building Maintenance, a Coventry firm. They gave me the number and I phoned them and, surprise, surprise, Henderson-Kenwright were also clients.'

'Great. So now you know who cleans Henderson's windows. Is that progress?'

'It might be.' Jimmy looked at his watch and stood up. 'I'm going to see Dredge.'

'Why? You'll miss the next train.'

'I'll tell him he's not going to get any award.'

'He never was.'

'I know, but it will give me an excuse to ask him about his windows.'

Rosa gave a shrug. If he was determined to go they might as well be on their way.

'OK, let's go and break the bad news.'

'No, you stay here.'

He didn't mean it to come out like an order but it did and she noticed.

'Why?'

'Because it doesn't need two. Just me making a courtesy call.'

Rosa didn't like it and this time she wanted to argue.

'Very clever. In and out and, oh, by the way who looks after your windows? You sure you don't need me to ask the question properly?'

Jimmy could see she wanted to be there when he talked to Dredge but he wanted her to stay put.

'I'll think of something.'

She still didn't like it but she decided not to push it. She could see Jimmy didn't want her along.

'OK, Jimmy, have it your own way, you've got us where we are now so I suppose you know what you're doing. I'll stay here and have a drink and when you're through I'll meet you down on the station.'

Jimmy walked through the pub and out onto the main road, but instead of turning right towards the Ring-road underpass he walked left until he could see down the side of the pub. Rosa was at the table on her mobile and talking hard and somehow he didn't think it was to any editor.Jimmy turned and set off to Henderson-Kenwright's offices.

'I'm sorry, Mr Dredge, it didn't work out. Apparently Harry Mercer isn't anything special as a writer. In fact he's a dead loss so far as I can see. If he was any good, pulled in serious money, I suppose you would have noticed it in the accounts so maybe it's not such a big surprise.'

'I see, oh well, easy come easy go and, as you say, if there had been any serious money going through Tate and Wiston's books I'm sure it would have been noticed here. We don't get many celebrities.'

'And apart from Mercer, Tate and Wiston aren't exactly an exciting outfit. Not if appearances are anything to go by.'

'What you see is what you get. They keep going and turn in a small but steady profit.'

'Maybe Mr Henderson bought them as an investment?'

'An investment?'

'Property. The firm may not be much, but maybe the property is?'

'Mr Henderson doesn't own their property. The offices are rented. Commercial property of that sort, flats, small offices, is not a good investment. Capital can be better employed elsewhere.'

'But this place, he owns this? Mr Jardene told me it's a family firm.'

'The family did own it but these days the sensible thing to do is sell the property then lease it back.'

'Sorry, why is that the clever thing?' Dredge liked to talk, to show how smart he was, so Jimmy let him talk.

'That way, the capital value of the property is released and can be invested and the occupier is relieved of all maintenance charges. If the roof blew off it wouldn't be our responsibility to put it back on.'

'I see.' Jimmy thought about taking it further, trying to get the name of the company that Henderson had sold the property to, but decided that was a step too far. He stood up. 'Well, sorry again that things didn't work out but you've been most helpful.'

'Not at all, it's a pity of course but there you are. If nothing else it provided a nice variation to an otherwise rather dull routine.'

Jimmy left Dredge's office and walked out into the street. He looked at the park, the way back to the station. But he stood, thinking. He had the feeling he was getting close now.

The publisher was a good front for Harry but it wasn't really any use to launder cash from the porn racket because the accounts went through Dredge's office and big money would have been noticed and looked into. But a property company sounded like the sort of outfit who could move big sums about without too much bother and somewhere there was a company that owned Henderson-Kenwright's property. Could he winkle out the name of the property company from the maintenance outfit? Harry had his cover as a writer, if he and Henderson owned a property company they had the other half of what they wanted, a way to clean their money. Then a thought struck him, a name popped into his head. Maybe he didn't need to ask Universal after all, maybe he had already been told the name of the company. What he needed now was a newsagents and a phone book. He turned away from the park and headed in the opposite direction from the station towards what looked like the city centre.

Jimmy sat in a pub. On the table beside his pint there was a copy of the paper Rosa said she worked for and a copy of the local Thompson's Directory. Jimmy looked at the open Thompson's and made a call.

'Universal Building Maintenance? Yes, my name is

Parker, I'm from Iberian Property Holdings, I would like to query your last invoice concerning one of our properties which you service in Coventry.' He waited while he got transferred. If his guess was right he was almost home and dry. 'Hello, yes, Parker from Iberian Property Holdings, I have a query about your last invoice for the Henderson-Kenwright window cleaning contract. Thank you.' He took a drink from his pint, closed the directory and pulled the paper to him. 'You've got it on the screen?' Bingo! 'Good. Can you confirm the amount? Thank you, that's fine, there's no problem after all, a mistake at this end. Goodbye.'

Iberian Property Holdings, they owned the house Jarvis rented in Santander, and now he knew they also owned Henderson-Kenwright's offices. It had to be Henderson and Harry. And they were based in Gibraltar so not subject to any UK oversight. Very neat. Jimmy opened the paper, found a number and made another call.

'I want to speak to one of your journalists, a Rosa Sikora.' There was a pause. 'You sure, no one of that name. I know she's journalist somewhere on a London paper and I need to contact her. The National Union of Journalists? Thank you, I'll try them, do you have a number? Great, thanks.' He dialled again. 'Hello, I'm trying to contact one of your members, a Rosa Sikora, it's in relation to a story she was researching but I've mislaid her contact details. Yes I'll wait.' He waited. 'No member of that name? No, it's not Joseph Sikora, she's definitely not a man. OK, thanks.'

Jimmy put away his phone. Well, whatever Rosa did for a living she wasn't a working journalist; that, or her name wasn't Rosa Sikora. Either way it was bad news but not altogether such a big surprise. She'd played the part well, but from the beginning there'd been nothing solid to back up her being a reporter, no editor to talk to him about the story, no background work through colleagues. And why didn't she know Harry's books were no good and sales almost non-existent? A few calls would have given her that. Unless of course she already knew. And wasn't it nice that she could suddenly drop everything and go swanning off with him simply because he asked her to?

He thought about the phone call she'd got after their meeting with Jardene.

From the way she behaved when she'd told him the Spanish police wanted to talk to him he was sure she'd known about the bloke with the broken neck, but she didn't know how the police had reacted or what they might want. Whoever called her was pushing her to get information. What had she actually contributed? Where Harry and Jarvis did time together and the idea for interviewing Dredge. Other than that, she'd been a fellow traveller in a position to keep a close eye on everything he did and see where he was going.

So, who would think it worthwhile to get George to put a minder alongside him? He went back to Harry. Harry was part of the set-up, but he wasn't bright; vicious, but never bright. Henderson was bright enough, but not brave enough. He'd never have the bottle to begin a criminal career no matter how much it might make him. Jarvis didn't count, he was just the writer. So there had to be someone else, and it could be that someone who put Rosa beside him. The porn thing had to have a London end. Harry didn't have the brains but he had plenty of friends who had all the brains, the bottle and the money to get the racket going. And Harry would have told London about my turning up in Spain out of nowhere which meant that when I arrived and put the word out through George that I wanted a journalist, somebody saw to it I got Rosa. Whoever gave Rosa to George was the London end. That was who she'd been talking to when she'd told me it was her editor, and that was who she was talking to after I left her at the Rocket.

Jimmy decided it was time to see George again.

He ignored what was left of his pint. He hadn't drunk much of it but it wasn't a very good pint, it wasn't very well kept. He'd only bought it so he could ask for the Thompsons and sit at a table while he made his calls. He looked up one more number then stood up and took the Directory back to the bar and left the pub. He stood outside and called the taxi firm whose number he had got from the Directory.

'How much for a cab from Coventry to Leicester. OK, pick me up as soon as you can, I'm outside the Black Bull pub in the city centre. It's just round … You know where it is? How long? Good.'

He put away the phone. Rosa would be getting worried now, but she wouldn't risk another visit to Dredge. She'd wait until she was sure he'd gone and then head on back to London. Jimmy stood and waited. Ten minutes later a minicab pulled up. Jimmy opened the door.

'Leicester?'

The driver nodded. Jimmy got in and the cab pulled away.

At the station Rosa, as Jimmy thought, was indeed worried and was back on the phone.

'He's been gone too long, he must have tumbled me somehow. How should I know? I just did as I was told. I tagged along, let him lead and followed where he went. Now he knows the publisher is a front for Harry and he's got the name of the service outfit that looks after Henderson-Kenwright's office so he'll probably get to the property company in Gibraltar. I told you, he's good, he'll get all the way. He's put Mercer, Jarvis and Henderson together, and he's probably got enough as it stands for the Spanish police to give the whole thing a good going over and you don't want that, do you?' Rosa listened. 'Hang on. If you want him stopped he's got to be stopped quickly and that means here in the UK, and that sort of work isn't

my side of things. I'm supposed to be brains not muscle.'
She listened. 'All right, I'll wait and see if he comes back
but I doubt he will. Your best bet is to get him in London,
if he goes back to London.'

Rosa put her phone away just as another London-bound
train pulled in. She stood and watched as passengers got
off and passengers got on. The train pulled out, the
platform cleared of arrivals but began to fill up almost at
once with others making their way wherever they were
going at the end of the working day. But Jimmy wasn't
one of them.

No, thought Rosa, there was no way he's coming back.
Somehow he's tumbled what was going on. If he went
straight back to London there was still a chance to nail
him. But only if he went back to the Hind, and Rosa didn't
believe he'd be such a mug as to go back to the Hind, not
if he'd worked it out that it was George who'd palmed her
off onto him. And she was pretty sure he'd worked that bit
out all right.

She gave herself a small smile, a bit of her hoped he'd
make it. He had something about him, not much, but
something. Maybe she really would have given him a
freebie if they'd worked together for much longer. Yes, he
was different somehow, had something about him.

Jimmy sat in the back of the cab watching the
motorway pass by. George had set him up. What did that
mean? Was it a favour or had there been pressure? Or was
it just money? He gave up. George had the answer so he'd
have to wait until he could ask him, ask him nicely. Harry?
The whole thing was too clever for Harry. Harry recruited
Jarvis in Leicester gaol, but he must have been told to be
on the look-out for a suitable candidate to have moved so
quickly when Jarvis turned up, if what Carter the Leicester
screw said was right, which it probably was. And
Henderson? Well if Henderson was already into porn he
was a cherry ready to pick, he wouldn't have had any

choice. He was probably blackmailed into it. But none of that got him anywhere further. What about the other end, where the product got made? The bloke who had knifed him in Spain had had a Romanian passport, a false one, but he had probably come from that part of the world. No, he had been prepared to go as exotic as Leamington Spa but sod anywhere else, and definitely sod bloody Romania.

He looked at his watch; he had been on the road almost three-quarters of an hour. Soon he would be in Leicester, but by now Rosa would have contacted London. He thought about his plan, the one he'd worked out on the way back from Tate and Wiston. It wasn't a good plan but if it worked he'd get what he wanted and maybe get out alive. No, it definitely wasn't a good plan but there was no other and there was no point in running. Running wasn't a plan, it was just running. He knew, he'd tried it. Everything depended on who it was in London that was behind the racket. He hoped it really was somebody with a few brains and not some bloody hooligan. Someone with brains might see what he was up to, someone like George. But if George was linked into it he'd be on the edges somewhere, that was always where George felt comfortable, picking up tasty bits of the action but never getting caught in the frame.

The cab passed some signs for the M1 going north and south, and then came to a big roundabout. The driver passed the slip-road for the M1, went under the motorway and came out the other side on the outskirts of Leicester. Not long now, soon he'd be at the station and he could make his call. Then he'd be on his way to London. He thought about Rosa. She'd be on her way to London as well by now. He'd liked Rosa, he didn't think he would, but he did. She was sharp and clever and good at her job. She had something about her. If she'd been serious about that freebie maybe he'd have taken it.

Jimmy's mind ran on. Funny really, sex had never

mattered that much between him and Bernie, just something they did when he felt like it. It had been different with Suarez, not just something they did because he felt like it. Different. What was happening to him in his old age? Never looked at another woman for all his married life and now what? Hop into bed with any young thing that fancies him? Why was it different now, and why didn't he think of it as a sin? But sex and sin took a back seat when Jimmy saw a direction sign for the station. He leaned forward.

'Make it the station.'

The driver nodded and they went on. He needed to get ready to make his call. A lot depended on that call, not least his life.

Chapter Twenty-six

'Hello, George.'

George tried to keep the surprise out of his voice but failed.

'Hello, Jimmy, where are you?'

'Oh, round and about.'

'In London?'

'Maybe. I'm somewhere, it doesn't matter where. Tell me, George, how much did you get?'

George didn't bother to pretend, he knew well enough what Jimmy was talking about.

'Nothing. On my life, Jimmy, nothing. The word was out that if you showed they wanted to be told. You showed so I told them. What else could I do?' There was a pause. 'Listen, you're dead if you come back here. Run, Jimmy, run somewhere far away from London and far away from Spain. Go and see your daughter and her kids in Australia. You've disappeared before, do it again. It's not like the old days, it isn't like it was with Denny. This lot aren't just violent, they've got themselves tied into everything. Come back to London and you'll be fucked inside two days maximum. And the law will be part of it so don't think of running to them.'

'Don't tell me there's bent coppers on their books.' Jimmy laid on the artificial shock with a trowel. 'I won't believe there's coppers on the take in the Met.'

'Very funny. I mean it, I can't help you, no one can. You can't fight these blokes. They don't sit in some pub of an evening or in some club getting pissed. They have offices in places like Canary Wharf. They go to the fucking opera and ballet for God's sake. They're respectable now, they're in the finance business. They make their money work. They'll get you and –'

'I've got a deal.'

There was a pause at the other end.

'A deal?'

'Yeah, a deal.'

'What sort of deal?'

'Never mind what sort of deal. I want to talk to someone.'

'And say what?'

'Harry's got to go down. I don't mind if it's just Harry who falls, but he's got to go down and he's got to go down hard, all the fucking way.'

'Harry?'

'Harry. I want to talk to someone,' a thought came, 'make it Rosa.'

'Rosa? The reporter I got for you?'

'That's right, George, Rosa the reporter.'

'Why her?'

'I know her by sight and I think she's got brains. If she'll listen maybe I'll get my message across. I don't want to talk to someone who thinks with his fists and can't pass on a message that isn't a punch in your face or a boot in the bollocks.'

There was another pause. Jimmy knew what the pause meant, it was George thinking if there was anything in this for him. Jimmy could hear the wheels turning.

'I'll talk to somebody and see what I can do, but I can't promise.'

'That's all right, I don't want a promise. I want a meet, at Birmingham New Street Station, half-past ten. If Rosa doesn't show I'll do the other thing.'

'And the other thing is?'

'I walk into the nearest cop-shop and turn myself in.

Rosa said the Spanish police want to talk to me. If my only other choice is running I'd rather hand myself over to the Birmingham law and take my chances. Whoever you talk to, George, make them understand, I've nearly got enough to get Harry and I know where to look for the rest.' Jimmy let it sink in. 'Do you think your friends would want me to talk to the Spanish police?'

George knew the answer to that one.

'Whereabouts in Birmingham Station?'

'Let's keep it simple. She stands in front of the departure board where I can see her. And it has to be just her, nobody else. I've got a mobile number for her and when I'm satisfied she's on her own I'll phone her and tell her where to go.'

'You in Birmingham now?'

'What do you think? I had to wait until she got fed up of waiting then I caught the first train out. I'm all set at this end, ready and waiting. Pass on the message to your friends and tell them to get Rosa on the move.'

Jimmy put his phone away. He had his ticket so he set off for the platform where in ten minutes he would catch a direct train from Leicester to London St Pancras International.

It was just after eleven when George came out of the back of the Hind pub. The open door threw a light across the small, dark yard where he parked his car, a silver Jag. When the door closed the yard returned to darkness. George didn't need any light to get to his car, he knew exactly where it was. He walked towards it and put his hand in the pocket of his overcoat to get the key.

It was easy, Jimmy had no problem taking him from behind. With his left hand he pushed George hard forward and George, surprised, staggered and fell against the car. With his right hand Jimmy slammed George's face onto the roof of the car. George almost bounced off the car and

Jimmy stood back, his fist raised, as George turned. He'd been waiting in the dark long enough for his eyes to adjust to what little light there was, George would still be blind. He could see that George was trying to get his right hand inside his jacket. Jimmy took what he could get. He hit George hard in his throat. George made a choking sound, put his hands to his throat and something clattered to the floor. Jimmy took aim, he had time now, and kicked George hard just below his left knee. George was struggling for breath through his damaged wind-pipe but the kick got all his attention. The cry of pain got all tangled up in his damaged throat and came out as a rasping croak as his leg folded and he went down into a crumpled crouch against the side of the car. Jimmy bent down and picked up what had fallen, a small revolver. He stood back and looked at George who was on the floor trying hard to get his breath and hold his damaged knee at the same time. He wasn't doing very well at either.

Jimmy squatted down beside him and peered at his face. There was blood over it, coming mostly from his nose. He moved slightly back and waited. After a few minutes George managed to look at him.

'Don't worry, George, you'll live.' He held the gun where George could see it. 'A cannon at your age? I thought you were brains, not violence.' He dropped the gun into his jacket pocket, leaned forward, hauled George up, got his foot behind each leg, pulled them out and sat him gently as he could on the ground with his back against the Jag. George grunted in pain but settled. Jimmy looked closely at him, he needed him to function and he was worried he'd overdone it. George's nose was still bleeding both from the nostrils and from a cut across the bridge of the nose. Jimmy could also see there was a cut over his right eye. There was a little blood coming from his mouth, probably have a split lip inside. He would look a real mess in the morning. If they both made it to the morning.

'Breathe slowly, George, small breaths at first.' George's eyes focussed on Jimmy's face and he tried. It wasn't easy but as he tried it began working. Jimmy waited until George's breathing became steady enough for him to talk. After a couple of minutes George finally seemed to pull himself together and looked as if he could pay attention. 'Hello, George. I see you don't stay on till closing time and count the takings. Become trusting in your old age haven't you?'

George tried a smile but gave up. It hurt his lip.

'Hello, Jimmy, I thought you said you were in Birmingham.'

His voice was a husky whisper.

I should pack this sort of thing in, thought Jimmy, any harder and I could have done him some permanent damage.

'I am, George, I'm in Birmingham meeting Rosa Sikora who's going to agree to everything I say while she puts me on the spot for the team that'll be with her.'

George managed the smile this time, it hurt, but he managed a small one.

'Nice one. But where does it get you?'

'How you feeling now?'

'How do you think? Fucking awful.'

'Come on, George, we've got to be on our way.'

Jimmy helped George to get up and gave him a minute to get himself together. Then he went to the back of the car and picked up a small holdall. George watched him. Then George's phone went off.

'Switch it off, you're not taking calls tonight. You're otherwise engaged.'

George got out his phone, switched it off and put it away.

'We going somewhere?'

'Yes, you're driving me down to Ebbsfleet.'

'Ebbsfleet? Why the fuck are we going to Ebbsfleet?'

'It's where the Eurostar stops.'

'And what would you want with the Eurostar?'

'I'm a trainspotter, always have been, remember? Get in and don't forget that I'm the one with the gun now so behave yourself.' George began to limp slowly round the car. Jimmy watched him. George fumbled out his keys and opened the door. 'I hope this motor of yours is an automatic. I made sure you had a good right leg but it's going to hurt like shit if you have to change gears.' George didn't respond but he also was glad that it was an automatic, because pressing the clutch would have hurt like shit too. They got into the Jag and George started the engine.

'OK, Jimmy, you're the pilot on this one. How do I get us to this fucking Ebbsfleet place?'

'Don't you know where it is?'

'Heard of it, that's all.'

'Use one of those gadgets then, one of those place finder things.'

'A sat-nav?'

'That's right.'

'I haven't got one, I don't need one in London, do I?'

Jimmy smiled at him.

'George, we're going to Ebbsfleet and you can piss about all you like but we're still going. You know the way all right and if you don't then find some signs or I'll get out that little cannon of yours and blow your fucking brains all over your fancy fucking car. I haven't got much to lose have I? You told me that yourself.'

George gave him a glance and decided he did, after all, have an idea of the way. The car pulled out of the yard into an alley and then out on to Kilburn High Road.

'I get out of London occasionally these days, maybe I can find it for you.'

'See, George, you can still work things out, you're still the one with the brains. Just get me there.'

'I'll get you there, Jimmy, though God knows what it'll cost me if anyone finds out.'

'Well don't let anyone find out.'

George gave a grunt; he wasn't up to a sarcastic laugh yet.

'OK, we point south-east and keep going, and if we fall into the Channel we'll have missed our turning.'

Jimmy grinned. Still the same old George.

'Take it easy, we're not in any hurry and you don't want us picked up for speeding.'

'No, God forbid I get a speeding ticket. That would be real trouble.'

They drove in silence through the bright lights and busy streets and on, through central London heading for the M25. Once on the motorway it was easy going, the traffic very light. From the M25 they turned onto the M2 and headed for Dartford.

George felt recovered enough to talk.

'Why did you come back? I told you, London's not a healthy spot for you at the moment.'

'Whoever's after me will have a team up in Birmingham covering Rosa. Your mates might be big-time, have fancy offices and front as respectable these days, but they're still just villains. If they want me they still have to send out a heavy mob to get me, that hasn't changed. And if the best blokes they could rustle up at short notice are all in Birmingham I figured I could get in and out and on my way without any trouble.'

'But why? Why not just go to an airport and take a plane to somewhere?'

'Because Rosa told me the Spanish police want to talk to me and have a request out for me to be detained, so I figure airports aren't such a good bet. To be on the safe side I figured I'd give St Pancras International a miss. She said it's all being done very softly-softly at the moment so I reckoned if I got going in a hurry and got a good start I'd

210

be OK, which meant I needed a lift. Naturally I thought of you. Somehow I felt you owed me something.'

George could understand how Jimmy might see it that way.

'Does that mean we're square now and no hard feelings?'

'No hard feelings, there never was. You did what you had to do so I did what I had to do. You were due a smacking so you got one.'

'You risked your life coming back to London just to give me a smacking?'

'No, there was something else.'

'What?'

'I told you, I needed a lift.'

'Why not just hire a car and drive yourself?'

'I couldn't do that.'

'Why?'

'I don't have a driving licence any more.'

'Good God almighty.' And George started a laugh which quickly deteriorated into a cough which hurt almost as much. When he had got his throat under control he smiled. 'Still the same old Jimmy, still just the same.'

Chapter Twenty-seven

It was ten-past three in the morning and George's Jag stood in the car park of Ebbsfleet International station which, bathed in the eerie glow of fluorescent light, looked to Jimmy as God-forsaken a place as anyone could wish to find. It was a vast expanse of black neatly edged with pale kerb-stones and covered with white lines demarking each of the hundreds, maybe thousands, of parking spaces. There weren't many cars parked and the whole place had an almost abandoned look. The first Eurostar wouldn't arrive until five forty-two, another two and a half hours. Jimmy stared ahead looking at nothing in particular. George put his hand into his coat and took out a packet of cigarettes, Jimmy didn't take any notice, he had the gun and George had already lit up two or three times since they'd arrived. George lit his cigarette and opened the window.

'Filthy habit, George. You should give it up.'

'Not as filthy as some I could mention.'

'True, and not as hazardous to your health.' George smoked on for a while and Jimmy looked at nothing in particular. Then George threw the half-smoked cigarette away. 'What's up? Decided to take my advice and pack it in?'

'No, funny thing but they seem to hurt my throat. Can't think why.'

George closed the window and they sat in silence and let the time pass. Both had plenty of experience of sitting waiting. After half an hour George pulled out another cigarette and tried again. Once again he threw it away half smoked but this time left the window open. The car was getting stuffy.

'I've done you a favour. Probably saved you from cancer.'

'Thanks, I'll try and return the same favour one day.'

And again they lapsed into silence. After a while a man came from somewhere, got into one of the few cars and drove off. They both watched him.

'It's all go here, isn't it?'

'Just one damn thing after another.'

The sky was lighter, morning wasn't far away. Through the open window they heard the birds of Ebbsfleet begin their dawn chorus. George tried to stretch. Jimmy moved so his arms didn't come near him. George turned to him.

'Don't worry, I'm not going to try anything, just trying to iron out a few kinks. I haven't spent a night sitting in a car for a long time.' He bent down and massaged below his left knee. Then he sat up. 'I can't say I ever got used to the waiting, sitting like this, at night in a car with nothing to say, just waiting for the job to begin. I thought I'd done with all that kind of thing. I *had* bloody well done with it until you came back.'

Jimmy didn't respond. He hadn't liked the waiting either. Waiting for just the right time to move in and make the pull. It was like George said, sitting with nothing to say and nothing to do but wait. Some seemed better at handling it, seemed to be able to just switch off. Like newspaper photographers. Jimmy pulled the gun out of his pocket, opened the chamber and held it so the bullets slid out into the palm of his hand. He dropped the bullets into the back behind his seat and held the gun out to George.

'Here you are, let's do a swap.'

'What sort of swap?'

'Your gun for your phone.'

George got out his phone, handed it to Jimmy and took the gun. He snapped the chamber shut and looked at it.

'Stupid bloody thing. If it ever does go off I'll probably shoot myself. I hope I don't hit anything important.'

He put it back into the shoulder holster.

'Why carry it? You were never the violent type and I can't see you shooting anybody, not in cold blood.'

'No, me neither. But they said I had to stop you if you turned up. How was I supposed to do that? But if I didn't, well, you know how it is, so I got the gun. Didn't do me any more good than the knife did that time in the Hind.'

'It didn't put you in hospital this time.'

'No, that's true, but this time you needed me so you couldn't very well put me in hospital could you?'

'No.'

They sat for a moment.

'They'll come for you, Jimmy, you know that? They won't let you close down their racket, it makes too much money. It's not just the porn, it's what goes with it.'

'I know. But I really do have a deal. That wasn't just a story to get Rosa and the heavy mob out of the way. I have a deal and I want you to tell them what it is.'

'What deal?'

'The same one.'

'Just Harry going down hard?'

'That's right. What do you know about all this?'

'Not much. I know who put the word out on you and that hard porn is only one of the things they're into. I got the word like everybody else; give them the nod if you turned up.'

'OK I'll tell you my story and if you believe it you can pass it on.'

'What's my believing it got to do with anything?'

'Because it'll be true, or true enough. If I don't convince you, you won't convince anyone else.'

'Fair enough, tell me your story.'

'Harry gets involved with a team who try for a bookie's up in Birmingham and as a result goes down for a ten stretch. He knows that when he comes out his days as any kind of muscle are well and truly over so he looks around for a new line of work. He meets someone inside who's in for running porn. They talk about it and Harry thinks, that's the work I want. But he's got a lot of form so the law will be keeping an eye on him. What he needs is a new life, a legitimate life that provides a good income. Then Jarvis turns up. They talk and Harry tells Jarvis about himself. Jarvis makes some remark, something like, "if you could put it in a book it would make money". Something like that, about writing up his experiences and Harry thinks, why not? He's not interested in becoming a writer but even though he's not too bright he can see it would be a good front. The books wouldn't have to sell because that's not where the money will be coming from. All he needs to do is have books out there with his name on so he gets Jarvis to agree to do the writing in return for looking after him. Jarvis thinks, why not? After all, he's in for sex offences and all he knows is teaching, nothing else. How is he going to make a living when he gets out? Harry tells his porn mate that he's got a business plan but he needs somebody to handle the money side of things. He gets given the name of a good client of the porn merchant, Henderson.Henderson is vulnerable and, with a bit of pressure, he'll drop. Harry's got time to serve but he coaches Jarvis so when he comes out the first thing he does is put the bite on Henderson – join us or we'll give you to the police. Henderson folds. He likes his porn and doesn't want to give it up, but also he's greedy. He smells the money so he sets up the publishing end by buying Tate and Wiston who are already on his books. That's the cover for Harry as a writer set up, but it's no good for laundering any serious money. So Henderson sets up a property company in Gibraltar called Iberian Property Holdings, easy enough to get to and well away from official prying eyes. When Harry gets out he moves to Spain and starts setting up the production end, probably in some ex-Eastern Bloc country. My guess is Albania or Romania or somewhere like that. Harry's in charge of the buying and selling, Jarvis gets a house rent-free and a regular income while he does the writing. Henderson handles the money through the property company and everything is hotsy-totsy until I turn up at the same time that Jarvis cops a bullet in the back of his head and Harry thinks it looks like things are beginning to unravel.'

Jimmy stopped and waited. He let George chew on what he had given him so far. George wasn't in any hurry to comment so they sat in silence for a few minutes. Then George came to life.

'Did you do it? Did you top Jarvis?'

'No. I'd never heard of him till I got asked to go to Santander and talk to him. First thing I knew about him was that he was dead.'

'What were you doing there? What was this Jarvis geezer to you?'

'Never mind about that. It wasn't anything to do with Harry's racket. I was asked to talk to Jarvis about something to do with the Church.'

'The Church? Your Church?' Jimmy nodded. 'What's the fucking Church got to with this? I thought we were talking about wholesaling porn?'

'I told you, it doesn't matter what I was there for. It turned out to be a load of bollocks anyway. The problem is, while I'm there I bump into Harry and when I do I'm keeping a local detective inspector company and we're asking about Jarvis. Harry jumps to the natural conclusion that his racket is in the frame. I'm somehow tied up with the local coppers and maybe I'm positioning myself to come on to him for a bung to keep me sweet about the whole thing. Whatever I'm doing I'm bad news.'

'How else would he would figure you? You always took your bung to stay sweet.'

'So he decides the best thing to do is have me topped. He's got plenty of the right connections in that part of the world now so he can get someone to do the job at short notice. But the guy he sends misses and I'm still alive. Harry tries and again it's a miss. Two pops at me and the bodies pilling up means now I really am pissed-off at Harry so I head off for London to do some digging about him and Henderson and their nice little earner. And that's it, that's the story I will tell to the law. Just Harry, Henderson, Jarvis and no one else. I came to the UK and made the connections between the three of them. I found out about the writer thing being a front and now I'm buggering off to Gibraltar to confirm they own a company called Iberian Property Holdings. When I've done that I'll take everything I've got to the Spanish police so they can roll up Harry and Henderson. What do you think?'

George didn't answer for a moment.

'So did Harry kill Jarvis?'

'George, for God's sake just stick with what I'm giving you. Forget Jarvis. Harry didn't want him dead, he wanted him alive and writing his bloody books.'

'So who did kill Jarvis?'

'How do I know? The man in the fucking moon. I told you, forget Jarvis.'

Reluctantly, George did as Jimmy asked.

'OK, Harry and Henderson get rolled up. How does that go down well with the London end? It still sounds like you're closing down their racket.'

'Only temporarily. There'll be nothing in what I tell the police to tie into any London end. If the police follow up my story all they'll get is Leicester gaol, Henderson-Kenwright, Tate and Wiston, and Iberian Property Holdings in Gibraltar, and all of that gives them nobody except Harry and Henderson. Harry'll be no loss, as things stand he's not going to be much good to anybody with no one to write his books for him so maybe now is a good time for London to think of a new face to handle that end of the business anyway.'

George began to see where Jimmy was going.

'So this end, London, and the production end wherever it is, get moth-balled while the coppers do the investigating and once Harry and Henderson are safely banged up the operation can get set up again somewhere else.'

'Exactly. No real harm done, just temporarily closed for refurbishment and staff training. All very business-like, all very Canary Wharf.'

George almost managed a grin but his lip still wasn't up to it.

'I like it, Jimmy, it's neat, believable even. OK, I'll try to sell it for you. I don't say I will, but I'll try.'

'Thanks. I'll go to Gibraltar by train, that will give London long enough to get stuck in to covering their tracks and telling the production end to do the same. By the time I get what I want, hand it over and the Spanish police start talking to Harry and Henderson, London should be free and clear.'

'I understand.'

'Just one more thing. None of this works if Harry gets a sniff of him being set up to take the fall. Him and Henderson have to be there to go down so the police think it's all wrapped up.'

'The people at this end are many things, Jimmy, but stupid isn't one of them. Harry will drop if you do everything just like you say you will. What if he decides to talk?'

'You know your mates here in London better than me. If Harry tried to talk could he put the finger on any of them? Could he have any of them put away?'

'I doubt it.'

'And if they knew he'd tried to grass them what would happen to him?'

'I see what you mean. Well, I guess you've got it sorted. All I have to do now is get them to see it your way.'

The sky was light blue now and bright, the sun was up and the day had begun. Jimmy looked at his watch, it was a quarter to five.

'Time to be on my way.'

'One last thing, Jimmy.'

'Yeah?'

'Why?'

'Why what?'

'Why are you doing this? What's in it for you? As far as I can see there's no way any money comes to you, all you get is Harry and Henderson banged up. Why is that important?'

'You could say I get my pay-off from someone else.'

'Who?'

'A friend, I'm doing it for a friend, George. Let's leave it at that, shall we?'

George shrugged. It wasn't his business one way or the other.

'If you say so, sunshine.' Jimmy reached over to the back seat, picked up his holdall and got out of the car. George lowered the window and leaned across. 'Good luck, mate. You're still going to need it.'

'Thanks. By the way, George, clean yourself up before you go out in public. The state your face is in you'll frighten the horses. See you.'

Jimmy walked away carrying his small holdall. George moved the rear view mirror. Jimmy was right, his face was a mess. He readjusted the mirror started the car and pulled away. His last view of Jimmy was him walking across the car park towards the glass and steel of Ebbsfleet International. George thought about his parting words, "See you".

'No you won't, Jimmy lad. Not any more you won't.'

219

Chapter Twenty-eight

Jimmy sat in the Eurostar looking at his reflection in the window as they passed under the Channel. Even if George went straight to the station, or into the town and found a public pay-phone to call his mates in London ,they couldn't stop him now. Eurostar was the fastest way into central Paris, he'd be there just before nine local time. And they couldn't get anybody local to be at the Gare du Nord to pick him up because all they could give any Paris talent would be a verbal description, useless to any watcher as the Eurostar disgorged. He was safe for the time being.

Above him on the rack was the new holdall he'd bought when he arrived in St Pancras from Leicester. He'd bought everything else there that he'd need to get him on his way and see him through the next few days. He'd stocked up on Euros and, as he always did these days, he'd had his passport with him. He'd been able to keep his little appointment with George, do the business, catch his train and get on his way. If he'd made the right move at the right time things should start going his way now. He was the one ahead of the game and they were the ones having to play catch-up.

The train suddenly emerged from the blackness of the tunnel into the light of a clear French morning. Jimmy adjusted his watch to French time. He knew nothing about the railway system in France or Spain but the way he looked at it was, how difficult could it be to get a train from Paris to Spain and then on to somewhere near Gibraltar? Thank God the EU had paper-free borders.

Even if the Spanish police were looking for him they weren't looking too hard. He still wasn't in the frame for Suarez's murder. Their problem was that they'd had him, questioned him, and chosen to kick him out. Then they'd found that he'd been shagging one of their own who'd suddenly got two bullets in her. He could see how they'd want to know what that was all about, but he could also see how they weren't in a big hurry to go public on it. They'd look for him and up the pressure if they had to until they found him and when they did he had no doubt that the question would finally get asked: what exactly was your relationship with Inspector Seraphina Suarez? He only hoped he could come up with some sort of answer.

Jimmy looked out of the window and pushed Suarez and the Spanish police to one side and made his mind go back to the London end. Even if it was the way George said, and the people he was up against were the supermen of English crime, no outfit was powerful enough to find one bloke who was somewhere on a train or a plane or a coach in France or Spain. No he was clear, now it was up to George to sell them his deal.

Jimmy thought about what George had told him, all run out of flash offices in somewhere like Canary Wharf, tickets to the opera and the ballet. Things must really have changed, it wasn't crime like he was taught it. But that had been long ago and things did change. It was people that stayed the same.

Jimmy tried to doze, it had been a long and tiring night and there was a lot of travelling to come. He closed his eyes, stretched out his legs and let his mind wander. It didn't wander very far.

The problems would begin when he got to Gibraltar. From what he knew it was a bloody tiny place, not somewhere he could melt away into the crowds or blend in, not somewhere to try to hide and then pop out and do what he had to do. And even if he could, it wouldn't help because all they had to do to nail him was have one man watching the door of whatever office he needed to visit. He settled further down and kept his eyes closed. Yesterday was already ancient history and it would be a long day, and there were more where that came from.

But his mind wouldn't switch off.

How long would it take to get to the bottom of Spain? Probably two or three days, maybe more. It depended on how often he stopped. But that was to the good. It gave them time to do what he'd suggested. It also gave them time to think that he might change his mind; that he might give himself up to the Spanish police and pass on what he'd already got. Yes, things were, at last, running his way, but only just.

His mind wanted to begin again so he opened his eyes, turned and in the window, against the darkness of some trees, caught a brief glimpse of someone, a man old enough to know better. He looked away. He kept telling himself he was too old for all this, yet he kept on doing it. Why? He thought about it and the same answer came up as it always did. What else was there? There was no one he cared about now except his daughter and the grandchildren he had never seen, and they were on the other side of the world. She didn't want to know him, she'd gone as far away from him as she could get. No, there was no one really. And he didn't want anyone to care about him. Suarez had cared, but she'd been a glitch in the machinery, a hiccup, a one-off moment when he almost wanted to rejoin the human race. But most of all she'd been a mistake, for both of them. Look at what it did to her. The truth was he didn't want to change. The truth was he didn't want anything. Then he remembered Harry's words when they had met at his villa.

You were right, Harry, I was a toxic bastard. I still am and it's all I ever fucking will be.

222

Chapter Twenty-nine

Jimmy took a taxi from the Gare du Nord to the Gare Montparnasse, where he could catch a train and head to the Spanish border. He looked around and chose a café close by where he could sit for a while, have a big cup of coffee and a warm croissant for breakfast, and watch Paris go about its business in the morning sunshine. The coffee and croissant came and were as good as they looked and smelled. He felt revived after his journey. The sun was warm, not scorching like the Spanish sun, and he felt relaxed as Paris bustled about him. He hadn't seen much of the city but somehow he liked the place. He put a hand into his pocket to get a handkerchief to wipe his mouth and felt something in his pocket. It was George's phone. He had forgotten it was there. He took it out and switched it on. George had missed three calls. Jimmy checked. They were all from the same person, Rosa.

'Shit.'

He called up the last voice message.

'And where the fuck are you, George? I've called you twice already. Costello never turned up and I'm hanging around waiting to be told what to do. Do we stay here or come back or what? Fucking get back to me will you?'

Jimmy switched off the phone and put it away. Suddenly Paris wasn't a pleasant place to sit and have breakfast, relax and feel warm. It was the wrong place. The right place was Santander, and bloody quick. He called the waiter and asked for the bill.

You clever bugger, George. What made you think you needed Jarvis to do the story-telling? You can tell the tale all right yourself, as a writer of pure bloody fiction you're up there with the best of them. Respectable villains who go the ballet, with offices in Canary bloody Wharf, who could go anywhere and do anything. Bollocks, all pure bloody bollocks, but you knew I'd swallow it all. This whole thing wasn't set up by any modern bloody master criminals, it was set up by a very old-fashioned villain working out of a Kilburn pub called the Hind. Jimmy almost laughed to himself at the fool he'd been.

And the best part was that I told you everything I'd found out, showed you how to mothball everything and let Harry take the fall so you could begin again when the dust settled. Well, done, George. Very clever. But you're not home yet.

The waiter brought him the bill. Jimmy paid and left, heading for the station.

He needed to be in Santander, he needed the Spanish police to have what he'd got before George could cover his tracks. He didn't give phoning more than a passing thought, who could he phone? This had to be done personally where he was known if he wanted to get any action in a hurry. What was the quickest way to get there? He went into the Gare de Montparnasse. It was a big, busy station and it took Jimmy a couple of minutes to locate the ticket windows. He saw them and went across. There was a queue at each one. He chose the shortest. After a few minutes he got to the window.

'I want to go to Spain.' The woman behind the window shrugged and said something in French which went right past Jimmy. 'Do you speak English?'

She shook her head.

'Non.'

He understood that. She looked along the line of ticket sellers. Then she said something else. It sounded like, sank. It meant nothing to Jimmy. She said something again, slowly. Gee-shay sank. It sounded a bit Oriental.

Jimmy shook his head. She said the same word again a couple of times and held up five fingers then pointed to her left.

'Five? What, window five?'

'Oui.' Then she said slowly, as if to a backward child. 'Guichet cinque. English there.'

Jimmy understood.

'Thanks.' He left the window and joined the queue at window five. Eventually it was his turn. The man behind the glass was young. Jimmy hoped his English was good.

'Do you speak English?'

'Yes.'

'I want to go to Spain.'

'Don't we all? Whereabouts in Spain?'

'Santander, and I'm in a hurry. How long would it take by train?'

'You would be best taking the TGV. The next one leaves at –' He checked a screen. '– eleven twenty-five. You arrive in Irun at sixteen fifty-five.' He looked back at Jimmy. 'From Irun you would catch a Spanish train.'

'So altogether how long?'

'It would depend on the time from Irun to Santander. I don't know whether there is a direct connection or not. For that information you would need to go to the International Enquiries desk.'

'Make a guess.' The young man gave a shrug and spread his hands, the universal Gallic gesture that said he wasn't even going to try. Jimmy needed some idea of how long it would take. 'It's important, a police matter.'

That brought the young man back into things.

'A police matter?'

'I have been told a friend has been badly injured and the police need to talk to me. Like I said, I need to get to Santander the fastest way I can. Would it be quicker if I took a plane?'

'It could be. It would depend on when a suitable flight

225

was available.'

Jimmy decided to pack it in. This wasn't getting him anywhere.

'How long would it take to get to the airport?'

'Which one?'

'Oh, Christ. How many are there?'

'Two. Charles de Gaulle and Orly.'

'Which would be better for Santander?'

The shrug came again, he was SNCF, not Air France.

'Which is closer if I go by taxi?'

The young man had to think.

'I'm not sure, but by taxi, maybe Orly.'

'Thanks. Where are the taxis?'

The young man pointed and Jimmy saw the sign. He left the window and headed for the taxi rank. Getting to Santander by train sounded too slow. George had a start on him now. But he thought Jimmy was headed for Gibraltar and taking his time so maybe he wouldn't be in too much of a hurry. Jimmy had to beat him to the punch which meant taking a chance on the airport. He came to the taxis and got in the first one.

'Orly airport. I'm in a hurry'

The driver nodded and seemed to understand. The taxi pulled away. The Paris traffic was busy but the driver was either mad, or clever, or both and they made good time clearing the city.

Just under thirty minutes later the taxi pulled up at the drop-off area, Jimmy paid it off and went in. He went to the nearest departure board. There was nothing anywhere near Santander. It was mostly French destinations. The Terminal building, what he had noticed of it, was not so very big by international airport standards and it began to look to him as if he had chosen the wrong airport. He looked at his watch, just after eleven. He looked at the board again. There was an Iberia flight to Madrid due off in six minutes. Sod it. From Madrid he could have got to

Santander or Bilbao. As he looked down the list of destinations the Madrid flight disappeared from the screen. The remaining departures times went as far as 13.16 but there was nothing that might help him so he found a seat and sat down and watched the departure board.

Flights disappeared from the board and flights got added but nothing came that was any good to him. He waited. Then another Iberia flight to Madrid appeared at the bottom of the list. 14.45. Jimmy got up and walked along the Concourse until he found the Iberia ticket desk.

'Do you speak English?'

'Yes.'

'I want to go to Santander. If I catch the 14.45 to Madrid and get a connection what time would I get in?'

'The young woman consulted her screen.

'There is a connection at Madrid for Santander which will get you there by 18.45.'

'I'll take it.'

Jimmy pulled out his wallet and the young woman began processing his ticket. When it was sorted he went through the security check and into the Departures lounge. He looked at his watch again. If his flight left on time it would go in just over two hours. Maybe he would have done better at Charles de Gaulle but even going through Madrid he would probably still get to Santander faster than if he had gone by train. Had he made the right decision? Then he let it drop. Right or wrong, he'd made his decision and he was going by plane. He went to one of the bars and bought himself a beer, found a table, sat down, and began his wait. He should eat, he knew he should get some food inside him but he wasn't hungry so he settled for beer. How quickly would George get going? Jimmy took a drink. Was he still ahead or was he back to being the one playing catch-up? It was an interesting question but one there'd be no answer to until he got to Santander. So he drank his beer and waited.

Chapter Thirty

It was half-past ten and the pub was empty except for a girl behind the bar getting everything ready for opening time. George was sitting at his table by the *Staff Only* door, opposite him was Rosa. She put down her tea and looked at him.

'You're a mess, you know that?'

George knew it. His nose, what wasn't covered by a plaster, was red; his right eye had taken on a shade of deep purple and there was a plaster stretched over it. The right side of his bottom lip was swollen, giving his mouth a sulky look.

'Never mind what I look like.' George took a careful sip of his tea. 'It's you we're talking about. I had you alongside Costello to see where he'd to go with this thing. Somehow you fucked up and that set him running.' Rosa didn't bother to disagree. George wasn't in the mood for a debate. 'But I'm still ahead of the bastard. He's after the last bit, the property firm in Gibraltar, and when he gets that he'll have pretty much all of the Spanish end. But that's all he's got and most important, he hasn't got me. He thinks I'm here dealing for him so he's taking his time which means I can clean up here before anybody comes looking.'

'What happens when he gets the Gibraltar information?'

'What do you think?'

'I think you get closed down and your wallet takes a beating.'

228

'Maybe. But I haven't set all this up for some ex-copper to walk in and blow it away.'

'You said it was this Harry bloke in Spain Jimmy wanted taken down. Why not let him do that? It's not a bad idea, the one he came up with. Lose Mercer and Henderson and let the police think it's all over, then put in someone new and start again somewhere else. Jimmy was right, with Jarvis dead Mercer's lost his cover as a writer. With no books you don't need any publisher so you don't really need Henderson. Any half-decent accountant could run the money end once you'd set up another company.'

George ignored her, he'd been wrestling with the problem of finding the best way to deal with the situation ever since he'd left Ebbsfleet. Rosa's suggestion that he fall in with Jimmy's plan made sense to her because she knew a lot about the Spanish operation, she had to, but that was all she knew about. George knew the whole picture. He wasn't so worried about one poxy little porn operation. What concerned him was the Gibraltar company. It was linked to other companies and a lot more than porn money went through it, not only for George but for a lot of his business associates. Let Costello give Iberian Holdings to the police and too many things might start to unravel. Jimmy's idea was good enough in its own way, but only if he had time to separate out what he wanted to keep from Iberian Holdings and what he'd have to let go to satisfy the Spanish police. That would take some time and it wouldn't be straightforward. Could he isolate everything connected with Mercer and Henderson in the Gibraltar company quickly enough and leave no loose ends? He had no problem with letting the police have Harry. Harry had made a mess of things. He was getting too old and sloppy. For God's sake, he'd even managed to kill a woman police inspector when he'd been told to try for Costello himself, which meant the Spanish police wouldn't cut a deal, not with someone who'd put two bullets into one of their own.

That was a nuisance. If Harry was sure he was going down he might give them George as the man who ordered the shooting and try for a reduction in sentence. It wasn't a big problem, Harry couldn't give them anything that would nail him, but he needed to be free of police interest while he sorted out Iberian Holdings. The company was in Harry's and Henderson's names but Harry didn't know that. When business required it, George had all the necessary documents to prove that he was Harold Reginald Mercer.

Rosa pushed her teacup away. It was finished.

'What about the property firm? Does it give Costello what he wants to clinch everything?' George nodded. 'Is it in Mercer and Henderson's names?'

An idea was forming in George's head.

'Just Henderson's.'

'You know, I think it was a mistake.'

'What was?'

'You shouldn't have sent Mercer after Costello.'

'Never mind that.' George had made up his mind. There wasn't enough time to sort out the company. Costello had to be stopped. 'The point is we're ahead of him.'

'So, what happens now? You send a couple of goons to Gibraltar to wait for him and then do the job?'

George looked at her. She hadn't looked like a reporter when he'd first met her and she didn't look like a killer now, but she'd done an OK job until she'd screwed up. But that was probably more down to Jimmy being clever rather than her being stupid. Maybe she could make up for it by doing another little errand. He thought about it. He didn't have a whole lot of choices.

'No. There's too many people involved already. Jimmy has to be taken care of, but there's another person I need seeing to before I get round to him and I want it done in-house, so to speak.'

230

Rosa knew what he was saying and she didn't like it.

'Fuck that. I told you I don't –'

But George still wasn't in a mood to have a debate about anything.

'Shut it. You came to me, girl, I didn't come to you. I asked for talent, and someone whose judgement I respect recommended you.' George sat back and gave her the best he could manage of a smile. 'You want to be up there don't you, in among the fast money, in among the real action, among the real movers and shakers? A fancy degree and all the ambition in the fucking world but you don't have any patience. You want it all and you want it now. Fine, I can respect that. You've got brains,' the smile went and George lent forward, 'but have you got bottle? Without bottle you're just another wishful thinker waiting to be a fucking casualty, someone who wanted it all but couldn't get it up when the blood started to flow.' He could see he'd made his point. 'If I say I need someone fucking dead all I want to hear from you is who, where, and when? You know quite a bit about me now and you know what's going on. That means you're in and the only way out is somebody finding your body one day and trying to identify what's left by your DNA or your fucking dental work. You know I can make it happen.' George sat back and tried the smile again. 'It's your choice, girly; you dead, or the one I want dead, dead. Take your time.'

Rosa looked at her empty tea cup. She wished she drank. She felt she needed something stronger than tea.

'Get me a drink, not tea.'

George made a gesture to the bar and the girl came over to their table and waited.

'What do you want?'

'You decide. You're the big thinker this morning.'

George turned to the girl.

'A double Scotch, nothing in it.'

The girl left.

231

Rosa sat and waited for her drink but there was nothing really to think about. George was right, she wanted it and she had to take it all or not at all, there was no middle way. She'd paid her way in her first year at Cambridge by doing small-time dealing in cannabis, and she'd worked her way up to Class A drugs by the time she graduated. She found she had a talent for it and had become that rare thing, a student who came out of university considerably better off than when she went in. After graduation she made up her mind to join the bad guys and use her talents where they gave her the biggest returns in the shortest time. That meant either working in the City or working with the friends who'd supplied the drugs. Her friends won.

'I suppose there has to be a first time for everything, doesn't there?'

George's face began to split into a grin but stopped quickly. His fingers went to his swollen lip. He might get away with a smile but it was too soon for anything more.

'Sensible girl. I want you to go to Santander.'

The whisky arrived. Rosa picked it up and took a sip. It burned her throat but she liked it. It was something powerful. She took another sip. If she was in she might as well be in all the way. What other way was there?

'And who do I kill there, Henderson?'

George nodded.

'Good girl. There's only one real trail to follow in this and it's the money. The money leads to Henderson and he really can finger me. Eliminate Henderson and the trail goes cold and gives me time to sort things out. First we lose Henderson and then we'll see to Jimmy fucking Costello.' He put his hand inside his jacket and pulled out a wallet. 'Here's some expenses money.' Rosa took it. 'Go to Harry, tell him I sent you, but don't tell him what's going on at this end. Tell him we're on top of everything here but say Henderson's been in touch with me and I think he's getting ready to blow the whistle and try to save his own neck so I'm getting rid of him. He'll get you a gun. Tell him when and where you'll do it so he can have a solid alibi. Knock over Henderson, ditch the gun and get back here. Finish him off and there'll be five grand waiting for you when you get back.'

Rosa finished what was left in her glass. She felt great.

'There'd better be.'

And she got up and left.

George watched her go. Graduate fucking villains, what was the world coming to? He hoped she was as good as she thought she was. One thing was certain: she was a slippery customer, too ambitious and too interested in other people's business. He thought about where things stood. If she got Henderson he was pretty much clear, if she missed, well, he wasn't getting any younger. Maybe it was time to retire and find a bit of sunshine and female company. He gently felt the plaster on the cut over his eye. He had never liked violence, and he liked it least when he was on the receiving end. Yes, he'd start mothballing things at this end so that when they came looking, if they came looking, there would be nothing that would put him in a court and get a conviction. Careful, that's me, careful and clever. George put his hand in his pocket for his mobile. Then he remembered where it was, and what was probably on it.

'Shit.'

Suddenly he decided that it wasn't mothballing the company needed, it was closing down. Oh, well, nothing goes on for ever. Then he thought about Rosa. No sense in stopping her now. Get him if you can, girl, it'll be good practice, but that's all it will be because it looks like you're going to be too late. I think the damage has already been done.

Chapter Thirty-one

It was almost twenty past seven in the evening and still hot when Jimmy finally walked into the police station at Santander. He had slept through most of the flight from Madrid, his mind finally giving in to the tiredness that had built up over the past days. A uniformed officer was sitting at the duty desk. He looked up from some paperwork as Jimmy came to stand in front of him.

'I understand the police here want to talk to me.' The officer said something in Spanish. 'You don't speak English do you?' The officer shook his head. Or you do, thought Jimmy, but you're not going to speak it to me. 'I'm here to assist the police in their enquiries.' Nothing. 'It's in connection with the death of Inspector Seraphina Suarez of the Santander police.' That got home. 'My name is Costello, James Costello.'

The officer picked up a phone and made a call, it was in Spanish but Jimmy heard his name in there. Then the duty officer put the phone down and stood up, all the time looking at Jimmy. Jimmy got the distinct impression he wanted to say something, something not nice, and that looking wasn't all he wanted to do. From the way he was standing Jimmy was glad there was a desk between them. He was too tired for any rough handling.

The English-speaking officer who had conducted the interview when Suarez's boss had brought him in came through a door.

'Good evening, Mr Costello. We have been wanting to talk to you.'

'You shouldn't have told me to leave in such a hurry,

then, should you?'

'Come with me, please.'

He led Jimmy through some corridors to an interview room. They both sat down and he said something in Spanish. Then he switched back to English.

'I am Inspector Santos. Everything we say will be recorded. You understand, Mr Costello, everything is on record?'

'Am I being arrested? You should caution me if you're arresting me shouldn't you?'

'You are not under arrest. You are assisting us in our enquiries, you are doing so at your own request.'

'That's right, at my own request.'

'The autopsy on Inspector Suarez's body revealed that she had sexual intercourse the night before she was killed. The DNA of the man matched samples which we took from the house you had rented from Inspector Suarez's cousin. It was your DNA, Mr Costello. Can you explain that?'

It wasn't a time for being funny so Jimmy didn't try.

'No.'

Santos looked surprised.

'Do you deny that you and Inspector Suarez had sex?'

'No. I mean I can't explain why we had sex. I hardly knew her.'

'You lied to us, you said you spent the night asleep in a chair. You have deliberately hampered a murder investigation by withholding information and you have also given false information …'

'Which leaves me open to criminal prosecution. I know, I've had to tell people often enough myself. But it's not me you want, is it?'

'Last time we spoke you told me that there was no relationship between you.'

'I know. In a way it was true.'

'You don't call having sex a relationship?'

235

'We had sex, but I don't know why it happened. We were working together, we found we liked each other. Nothing should have happened. I was old enough to be her father. I never meant it to happen. I still don't know how it did.'

'She was willing?'

Jimmy looked at the Inspector, now it was his turn to be surprised.

'You don't think I raped her, do you?'

'There were no signs of force on the body but ...'

He left it hanging.

'Look, you knew her better than I did. Look at me, how old I am and the shape I'm in. Also I have a knife wound in my side. If I had tried to take Suarez by force what would have happened?'

Santos paused. He knew Suarez so he knew what would have happened.

'No, we never seriously considered that possibility. Do you know who killed her and why she was killed?'

'Yes. She was killed by a local British ex-pat called Harry Mercer. He fronts as a writer of crime novels but he's a career villain. His real business is porn, wholesale provision of hard, nasty porn. He works for or with another villain based in London.'

'And the name?'

Jimmy gave him George's name.

'He owns the Hind pub on Kilburn High Road, London. The Met will have a complete file on him. I went to Mercer's house with Inspector Suarez as part of the investigation into the death of Arthur Jarvis. You have all the background to why I was on the case with Suarez, I was put in as an observer?' Santos nodded. 'Mercer got the wrong end of the stick, he thought I had come to poke my nose into his business. My guess is he contacted London for instructions and was told to get rid of me. He hired someone to have a go but it got bungled and the guy wound up dead. Your lot know all about that as well. The London end still wanted me dead so Harry tried, kicked in the door and found there was only Inspector Suarez there. He had to shoot her because she knew him.'

'Mercer knew you were staying with Inspector Suarez?'

'It wouldn't have been too hard to find out if you were looking and Harry's had experience at finding people.'

'If you knew all of this why didn't you tell us?'

'I didn't know it all then. I wanted to get to the UK quick to find out what the connection was between Mercer and Jarvis. I suppose that's why I lied to you. I needed to go to England not hang about here answering endless questions that would go nowhere.'

'All right, what else do you know?'

'Here, you'll need this.' Jimmy took out George's mobile and passed it across. 'It's the mobile of the man who controls the London end. If you run down the calls in and out it will give you most of what you need to tie Mercer to London.' Santos looked at it but left it on the table. 'If I was you I'd put somebody onto watching Harry right now. If he gets a call he'll run.' Santos didn't move or speak. Jimmy reckoned somewhere the boss was listening and the orders would be going out. Harry would get his watcher. 'Harry had a partner here, another ex-pat, Henderson, he owns an accounting firm in the UK. He also owns the publisher who publishes Harry's books. If you check you'll find that Harry's book sales wouldn't feed a cat, never mind fund the life-style he has here. The money all comes from the porn racket and gets laundered through a company called Iberian Property Holdings, which operates out of Gibraltar. The house Jarvis lived in rent-free was owned by that company. If Suarez ever got round to it you might find that the Hendersons had a rent-free deal with Iberian Property Holdings before they bought their fancy new villa.'

'And Jarvis was connected to their operation how?'

'He wrote the books for Harry. They met in prison. Jarvis was a teacher with an extra-curricular interest in bonking his under-age girl pupils and got handed a three-year stretch. Harry recruited him inside. I don't know where they picked up Henderson.'

Santos thought about it.

'Why did they kill Jarvis?'

'I didn't say they did. I don't think they did. I don't know who killed Jarvis but I doubt it was Mercer. Jarvis wrote the books, they needed him. If Jarvis's death is mixed up in this, I can't see how.'

'I see. You will have to make a full statement, everything, including your relationship with Inspector Suarez. You should have come to us sooner, Mr Costello.'

'And told you what? Suarez knew everything I knew before you bounced me out of the country so you had all I had. Everything else I got in England and now I'm giving it to you. If you don't fuck it up you should be able to take them all.'

Santos ignored Jimmy's little outburst.

'Shall we begin?'

'Where do you want me to begin?'

'At the usual place, Mr Costello, the beginning.'

And where exactly is that, thought Jimmy? When I arrived? When I got told to come here? When I first met Professor McBride? When I first met George or Harry? When I was born? Where does anything like this begin?

'I live in Rome and occasionally work for a college there, I collect information, do research. I was asked to come and talk to Jarvis …'

And Jimmy told them everything. He was hungry, weary and past caring about anything including himself. By the time he had finished his statement, signed a copy in English and a copy in Spanish he didn't care what happened to Harry, George or any of them. He didn't even care that Suarez was dead or that she died because she cared for him. She was a copper, she had to take what came with the job. He had come with the job and he got her killed, but he didn't care any more. For a short time he had felt almost part of the human race again, he had been touched by love and it had made him want justice for Suarez. And where had that grand moral pursuit of justice got him? Nowhere. Suarez was still dead. Harry, George and Henderson might get banged up but the porn would still get made and flow from another set of Harrys, Georges and Hendersons. He would go back to Rome slightly more damaged but not really any different. No wiser, no happier, no different from when he had arrived. He sat by himself in the interview room waiting to be told he could leave.

Then something his mum had once said to him came back. He had wanted something and they couldn't afford it. A school trip, a school trip to Dawlish, that was it. He'd sulked and she'd looked at him and said, "Self-pity is the most unattractive of emotions and the least useful". It had taken him until now to see how right she was. Don't feel sorry for yourself, make the bastards who did it feel sorry. Make yourself fucking useful. Then he realised he was hungry, very hungry. If he didn't eat soon he would keel over and if he wasn't allowed to take a piss his bladder would explode.

The door opened and Santos came in. Jimmy looked up at him.

'What always gets worse the more you nurse it?'

Santos stood still and looked at him.

'What did you say?'

'It's a joke. What always gets worse the more carefully you nurse it?'

Santos came to him and held out something. Jimmy looked at it. It was a photo.

'Do you recognise this woman?'

239

Jimmy took another look. It was a surveillance photo of Rosa walking into Harry's drive.

'Yes, she's Rosa Sikora. She works for the London end. When did you get it?'

'She is with Mercer now, as we speak. She arrived there about ten minutes ago. Do you know why she's here and why she's visiting Mercer?'

Jimmy slowly shook his head. Why would George send Rosa to Santander. If she had come to get rid of him then why wasn't she in Gibraltar? Was George cleaning up anything that could lead to him?

'If I were you I'd put somebody on to Henderson's place.'

'We are already watching Mr Henderson.'

'I can't think of anything she'd be doing here except bringing a message from George that's too important to phone or e-mail or –'

'Or what?'

'Or getting rid of the evidence.'

'You mean Mercer and Henderson?'

'No, not Mercer. She couldn't take Harry. Harry's an old hand and anyway, he wouldn't talk unless he was sure he was going down for Suarez's killing. He might talk then to try and work down his sentence but by then George would be clean or well on his way. I think she's come for Henderson. Once Henderson faces any serious questioning and sees anything like evidence he'll spill his guts. He's the money-man and the money's always the best trail to follow. He's my bet for the one who can give you London. If the first thing she's done when she arrives is see Harry my guess is she asking him to get her a gun. Harry can get guns, we know that.'

'I'm afraid we'll need to keep you here a little longer, Mr Costello.'

'Then can I take a piss and get something to eat?'

'I'll see what I can do.'

240

Santos left. Jimmy resumed his battle with his bladder and tried to ignore the clamour of his stomach. How many times had he let someone sweat in an interview room, no food or drink, no toilet break. It wasn't your actual torture but it was bloody effective. The door opened and the officer from reception who didn't speak English came in. He said something in Spanish but Jimmy recognised the gesture. He got up and followed him They stopped outside a door with a symbol of a man on it. Jimmy went in and took his piss. It wasn't the greatest feeling in the world but at that moment he couldn't think of anything that would feel better. He came out of the toilet and they went back to the interview room. On the table was a plate of cold meats, a salad and some bread. There was a paper cup and plastic bottle of red wine. Jimmy went and sat down. There was a fork but no knife and the fork was plastic.

'I don't like wine, got any beer?'

The officer left, closing the door behind him. Jimmy took a piece of salami and popped it in his mouth. He looked at the wine, then poured some into the cup and took a drink. He had been wrong, it tasted great. He took some bread. As he ate he felt better. He spoke out loudly to the empty room and to the silent, invisible listeners.

'A grudge.'

The words bounced off the walls. He continued.

'A grudge gets worse the more you nurse it. So don't nurse it – settle it, or forget it.'

Jimmy took another drink and filled his mouth. Leave it to the police, let them settle it, if they could. He was tired of it so he'd forget it, the whole fucking lot of it.

He carried on with his meal. Things weren't so bad when you actually came down to it. It was a pity about Suarez and he was sorry George was going to get banged up. He liked George, apart from getting Harry to try and kill him. Harry and Henderson didn't matter. Harry knew the risks and Henderson was a greedy little shit who would get what was coming to him. It wasn't Jimmy's job to clean up the world. He had come to find out what Jarvis knew about ETA and now he'd done that. Jarvis knew nothing, he never had. Jarvis was an unfortunate accident. As he finished his meal it suddenly dawned on him. Of course. Now he knew who killed Jarvis. He didn't know why but he knew who. The point was, should he do anything about it? He thought about it and drank some more wine. It wasn't beer, certainly not a London pint, but it was OK. On balance he thought not, do nothing about Jarvis's killer and go back to Rome. It was none of his business who'd done it, nor why they did it. This time he'd keep his nose out of it and head back to Rome. It didn't pay to get involved. Getting involved was for other people and it always led to tears in the end.

Then the small thought that had slipped from his mind when he had sat on Suarez balcony came back to him. He remembered what the old priest had said. "We make a convenience of each other." He smiled as another little bit clicked into place. And that's exactly what the clever old bastard had done, made a convenience of Jarvis. Jarvis was there so he had used him. Clever, devious old bugger, a piece of work McBride would have been proud of herself.

Jimmy finished the wine and another thought floated into his mind which also brought a smile. She was going to throw a fit when she saw his expenses. There was always that to look forward to.

Chapter Thirty-two

When Jimmy woke up he felt both good and bad. He felt good because the sleep had refreshed him, but he felt bad because sitting with his head on his arms on the table had not been such a good position to spend a couple of hours asleep, and now he was paying the price in aches and pains. Also he needed to take another piss. He stood up and looked at his watch. He had been in this bloody interview room nearly five hours. He walked about the room stretching and rubbing himself. It helped but he still didn't feel great. Also his mouth felt like somebody had emptied a vacuum cleaner bag into it. That must have been the wine. He decided he didn't like wine after all. He walked to the door of the interview room opened it and went into the corridor. There was no one there. He went to the gents toilet and went in. An officer was using it. Jimmy ignored him and, after one look, the officer ignored him, finished, washed his hands and left. When Jimmy was finished he did the same and went along the corridor and out into reception. There was a new officer on duty, a sergeant. He looked at Jimmy.

'Do you speak English.'

'A little.'

'How long is Inspector Santos going to keep me here?'

'No idea.'

'Can I get a cup of coffee?'

'Sure.'

'Is there anywhere more comfortable to wait than that interview room?'

'No.'

'OK, and thanks for seeing about the coffee.'

Jimmy turned and made his way back to the interview room. The remains of the meal were still on the table. He didn't sit down, he'd had enough sitting down for the time being. His bum ached from the hard chair. After a few minutes the sergeant from reception came in and put a cup of coffee on the table then left. It was black coffee and when Jimmy tasted it there was no sugar. Jimmy liked milk and two sugars in his coffee. He put it down and carried on slowly walking around the room.

He tried not to think about anything. There was nothing he needed to think about. None of this was his business any more. It didn't matter why Rosa was in Santander. All he had to do was get back to Rome.

The door opened and Santos came in.

'I'd like you to come with me, Mr Costello.'

'Where?'

'To talk to Mr Henderson.'

'What do you need me for? I've told you everything I know and where you can go to back it all up. You don't need me.'

'I think I do. Rosa Sikora was arrested a few minutes ago at Henderson's villa. She was stopped in his drive, searched and was found to be in possession of an illegal firearm. We know where she got it from.'

'Mercer.'

'Of course. He was followed. He went to a bar where certain things are for sale, illegal things. Money changed hands and he was given something. He took it back to his villa where Sikora was waiting. He then drove her to the end of the road where the Hendersons live and dropped her off. He is now sitting in El Sombrero Restaurant arguing with the waiter about something.'

'Getting himself remembered?'

'As you say, making his presence memorable. Once

244

you have identified the Sikora woman we'll pick him up.'

'Why do you want me to identify her? Didn't she have a passport with her?'

'She did but we would prefer also to have a witness identify her.'

'A witness?'

'Of course. When all this comes to court you will be an important witness.'

Jimmy didn't like that but he couldn't see there was anything he could do about it at the moment. He was still supposed to be co-operating.

'OK.'

They left the interview room, were joined by a uniformed officer and went along the corridor and then down some steps to a lower floor. Jimmy recognised the cells. He was taken to a door, the officer unlocked it and opened it. Rosa was sitting on the bed. She looked up.

'Hello, Rosa.' She didn't answer. 'What does your Politics and Economics degree make of this?'

'Fuck off.'

She looked down at the floor. She didn't look clever, sharp or tough sitting in a cell. She was trying to, but mostly what she looked was frightened and defeated.

'It happens, Rosa, you better get used to it. It's one of the risks of the trade. When they charge you and you get convicted and they bang you up in some Spanish jail, think of it as a post-graduate course or maybe more of an advanced work experience placement. And spare a thought for Harry, he's going down for killing a police inspector. They'll throw the book at him and then throw away the key. Harry will pop his clogs in a Spanish prison unless he can bargain some reduction. I hope you didn't tell him what you were up to, because if you did he'll use it.'

She looked up again. This time there was real fear in her eyes.

'You're lying.'

But he could see she knew he wasn't. He had seen people in interview rooms and cells look at him like that too often to be mistaken. She was finished; she'd sing like a canary now. Jimmy stood aside and the door was slammed shut.

'Let her see Harry being brought in or in a cell then interview her quick, she'll fold like paper.'

'We don't need you to tell us how to do our job, Mr Costello.'

Jimmy shrugged and walked away. There was no pleasing some people. Santos and the officer followed him up the stairs. Jimmy stopped.

'Can I go now, I'm getting a bit tired of this place.'

'No, Mr Costello. I told you, we need you for one more job. I am going to interview Mr Henderson, probably arrest him. I would like you to be there.'

'Why, back there in the cells you told me you didn't want my help?'

'No, Mr Costello, I said I don't need you telling us how to do our job. But it would be a great help if you were there when I speak to Mr Henderson. I now know what happened but you actually worked it all out and know all parties concerned. If you tell him where he stands I'm sure he will believe you, believe you much more so than he might believe me. Tell him what you told me and I think your assessment of Mr Henderson will be perfectly accurate.'

He was right, of course. But Jimmy didn't want to meet the Hendersons again. He particularly wanted to avoid meeting Mrs Henderson. He didn't like her, she was not a nice woman..

'Are you asking or telling?'

'It depends on whether you want to stay in the interview room for the rest of the night and probably all tomorrow, or go to a hotel.'

'I see. OK, let's go.'

They left the police station and got into a big black SEAT. They sat in the back. A plain-clothes men was in the front and another driving. It was about one-thirty when they got to the Hendersons' villa. They pulled up at the end of the drive, Santos and Jimmy got out. A man got out from a car parked across the other side of the road, came across and spoke to Santos then stood to one side. The two men in the front of the SEAT just sat there.

'Come on, they're both at home and the lights are still on.'

They walked up to the door and Santos rang the bell. It was Henderson who answered it. Jimmy bet it was always his job to answer the door.

'Good evening, Mr Henderson, I am Inspector Santos, and this is Mr Costello, whom I think you have met before.'

Henderson was already starting to sweat.

'Really, Inspector' he looked at his watch 'it's past one. This is most …'

'Mr Henderson, this is a very serious matter.'

'If it's about Jarvis again I've told the police twice that my wife and I hardly knew Jarvis.'

'It is not about Mr Jarvis.'

'No?'

'No.'

'Is it about the woman inspector who came last time?' Henderson paused, he didn't want to ask, but he asked. 'The one who was murdered?'

'In part, yes.'

Jimmy watched as Henderson visibly began to disintegrate.

'But what could I possibly know about that? I only met her once, briefly.' He looked at Jimmy as if seeing him for the first time. It was a sign of how close he was to panic that he seemed to think Jimmy might actually help him. 'This man was with her. He'll tell you –'

'Shall we discuss it inside?'

Santos pushed passed him and went into the villa. Henderson followed and Jimmy followed Henderson. Jimmy left the front door open. In the large living room Dorothy Henderson was sitting with some embroidery on her lap. She looked at Jimmy when he came in with the same look as last time.

'Sit down, Mr Henderson.'

Dorothy Henderson wasn't weak like her husband and she certainly wasn't going to sweat. She put her sewing down and looked at Santos.

'I presume you are the police. Do you normally give orders to people in their own homes when you barge in at one in the morning?'

'In cases of murder, intent to murder, possession and distribution of pornographic material and money laundering, I invariably do give the orders, Mrs Henderson.'

Henderson almost collapsed onto the settee. She took it better.

'No doubt you have some reason for being here. It had better be a good one because first thing tomorrow, or I should say today, I shall make a formal complaint about the timing of this intrusion, your manner and behaviour and the remarks you have just made.'

Jimmy decided that if he was here he might as well make the most of it.

'You may need to save a little time from all of that to slip in and visit your husband in his cell at the police station.'

She looked at Jimmy with total loathing and was about to speak when Santos cut in.

'Tonight my men have been stationed outside your house –'

'Spying on respectable residents? Do you and your men have so little to do with your time?'

'– and some short time ago they intercepted a woman who was on your drive coming to the house to kill Mr Henderson. The woman is now in custody.'

That stopped her and Henderson gave a low whimper and put his knuckles to his mouth. Dorothy Henderson waited a moment.

'Please explain, Inspector. Why would anyone come here and kill my husband?'

Santos looked at Jimmy. It was show-time.

'Because he is involved with others in a criminal operation to create and sell pornography. He launders the profits through a company called Iberian Property Holdings which is based in Gibraltar. Inspector Suarez and I stumbled onto the operation while looking into the death of Arthur Jarvis. A man called Mercer, a colleague of your husband who poses as a writer, killed Inspector Suarez in a failed attempt to kill me. It was his second attempt.' She looked at Jimmy and he could see she was on Harry's side, she also wanted him dead. 'I went to England and did some digging. Jarvis and Mercer were in prison together. I found that Mercer's writing was merely a front, Jarvis wrote his books, badly as it happens. Mercer's real business was hard porn. I also found that Iberian Property Holdings was a vehicle used to launder the proceeds from the racket. Your husband handles the money and the money leads to a man in London who set up the whole thing.' He turned to Henderson. 'I've told the police about Tate and Wiston and the book sales, Mr Henderson. Mr Jardene doesn't send his regards, he doesn't like you making him publish Harry's rubbish, although he says it's getting better. He says the next one, although with Jarvis dead, there won't be a next one, might even have been commercial.'

Henderson was wheezing and gently rocking back and forward. Santos took over. Jimmy had done his job.

'It was the man in London who ordered the killing of

Mr Costello which, unfortunately, led to Inspector Suarez's death. Now the operation here is fully blown he hired a woman called Rosa Sikora to come and kill your husband. As I said, we intercepted her and she is now in custody.'

Henderson slumped forward and started moaning. He was also shaking. If he heard any more he'd probably pass out. Jimmy decided he hadn't been needed after all. But Dorothy Henderson wasn't giving in so easily.

'Have you any proof of these ridiculous accusations?'

'The gun the woman was carrying which we know was supplied by Mercer. The material on Jarvis's computer. The fact that Jarvis lived rent-free in a house owned by the property company. The publisher. The company in Gibraltar. Do you want any more?'

Henderson came to life,

'I was forced into it. I was blackmailed. I had no choice. I'll tell you anything, anything.' Then he shouted the clincher. 'It wasn't my fault.'

Dorothy Henderson looked at him, it wasn't a nice look for a wife to give her husband.

'Shut up.'

But he wasn't listening.

'They threatened me. I was a respectable –'

'Shut up.' Her voice was raised and was a voice that expected to be heard and obeyed. Henderson looked at her with frightened eyes and shut up. Good God, thought Jimmy, he's about to be arrested on a hat-full of serious crimes and he's still more scared of his wife than what's going to happen to him.

'What did they use to blackmail you with, Mr Henderson?'

Santos' voice was calm and quiet with no hint of a threat. Henderson was about to answer when his wife spoke. He didn't see the problem with the question, but she did.

'Nothing. If there is an ounce of truth in any of this, which I doubt, there was nothing with which anyone could blackmail my husband. We are and always have been respectable people. If, and I emphasize if, there is anything to this,' she looked at Henderson to drive home her point, 'my husband must have been threatened. His life must have been threatened. There could never have been any question of blackmail.' She looked again at her husband who swallowed but seemed to finally take the point. He tried to speak, spluttered a couple of times, then got his words out.

'No, not blackmailed, threatened, with violence. I couldn't refuse. They threatened my life.'

'Who did?' The question came from Jimmy. Henderson and his wife both looked at him. 'Who threatened you with violence? Who made you fear for your life?'

A crafty look came into Henderson's eyes.

'Mercer, Mercer threatened me. He is a very violent man. I believe he has a history of violent crime. If someone like Mercer threatens you then of course you take it seriously.'

'I see, only I have a problem with him threatening you.'

Henderson wasn't up to following but Dorothy Henderson was. Her hat was still in the ring.

'A problem?'

'Yes, you see Mr Henderson started setting up this whole operation, buying Tate and Wiston in Leamington Spa, while Mercer was still in prison.' He turned to Henderson. 'What did you do, go and visit him in Leicester prison so he could threaten you there?' The fear flooded back and Henderson's mouth made speaking movements but nothing came out. 'Perhaps you meant Jarvis? But Jarvis was a teacher who liked young girls. He wasn't such a frightening sort of bloke. Quite a nice bloke by all accounts, except for his little hobby, of course.'

Henderson fell back on the settee, he was sweating and

shaking and now he was dribbling. Jimmy also saw a large dark stain begin to spread across the front of his trousers.

Inspector Santos took over.

'Is there anything you wish to tell us, Mr Henderson?'

'My husband has nothing more to say. You will now please leave. If and when you wish to speak to either of us again, it will only be with our lawyer present. Now leave, I find your presence here odious.'

She looked at Santos then at Jimmy. The look made it clear that in the odiousness stakes Santos was only a place bet. Jimmy was the clear winner. Jimmy saw the look on her face; it was a look he remembered, a look he had never forgotten. It was the same arrogant superiority that had been on the face of the nun headmistress of his primary school when she told him Terry Prosser had named him as the one who smeared shit on the boys' toilets' walls.

Jimmy turned to Henderson.

'Do you own a gun, Mr Henderson? Is there a gun in the house?' Henderson looked at him, confused and still frightened. Jimmy turned to the policeman and spoke slowly. 'It would be easy to check wouldn't it, Inspector Santos, if a license had been issued?' Then he looked back at Mrs Henderson. He wanted to enjoy this so he made sure it sounded Sunday School polite. 'Tell me, Mrs Henderson, is there a gun in the house? Or if you're not sure we could always get a search-warrant.'

The look had gone. Her face now was pale and set. Santos joined in.

'Is there a gun, Mrs Henderson? Please answer Mr Costello's question.'

'Yes. We bought it two years ago when those break-ins occurred in some of the British-owned villas and Mr Naismith was put in hospital. It is perfectly legal, we have a permit.'

'May I see it, Mrs Henderson?'

'Certainly Inspector, although what it has to do –'

252

'Please, just get the gun.'

She got up and went to an ornate chest of drawers by a wall, pulled out the top drawer, reached in and pulled out a gun. She turned. She was holding it by the grip and it was pointing at Jimmy. Now he wasn't enjoying it any more, now he saw that it was his turn to sweat. Santos also saw where the gun was pointing.

'Please, Mrs Henderson, don't do anything foolish.'

She gave him a look of pity.

'I have never done anything foolish in my life, Inspector, except marry a man whom I thought could give me the quality of life I deserved, but who turns out to have been a common criminal, and so stupid that he got caught.'

And, with a quick movement, she put the gun to her temple and blew her brains out.

The sound of the shot crashed around the room as she pitched sideways, bounced off the drawers and crashed to the floor. Jimmy and Santos stood rooted to the spot. Henderson began to scream hysterically. Jimmy looked at the body. There was blood coming from the wound and he noticed that the bullet had made a hole in one of the walls and below the hole were spattered something that looked like flecks of porridge. He felt as if he was going to throw up. Two men ran into the room and stopped. They were the men from the front of the car. Both had guns. They looked at the body and then at Santos.

He spoke to them in Spanish. They put away their guns and left. Santos went to Henderson who was still screaming and slapped him across the face. He didn't stop so Santos hit him again, harder. This time it did the trick. Henderson took one look at the body, buried his head in his hands and began to rock back and forward. The smell of cordite tinged with urine came to Jimmy's nostrils.

'I need fresh air.'

Santos nodded.

Jimmy left the villa and stood in the garden. It was a

warm night, full of the buzzing of cicadas and sweet aromas from the flowers and plants. There was a full moon, the whole place was bathed in a pale silver light. It was beautiful. Jimmy walked to the nearest flower bed, bent over and vomited.

Chapter Thirty-three

Jimmy was asleep in his hotel room when the phone rang. He had no idea how long it had been ringing. He had heard it in his dream as a school bell but he was locked in the boys' toilets with no clothes on and his mother was shouting to him from outside that it was time for him to go and say Mass. He was parish priest and the congregation were waiting to sing for him. Finally it had penetrated his mind that the ringing was the phone. He rolled over and picked it up.

'Yes?'

It was reception.

'One moment.'

Then Santos' voice came on.

'Mercer wants to talk to you.'

'Fuck Mercer, I'm knackered and I'm not the bloody Spanish police.'

'And Mercer still wants to talk to you.'

'Don't I get any rest?'

'I think you should come and talk to him.'

Jimmy struggled into a sitting position.

'I didn't do so well last time you got me to talk to somebody, remember? Or do you want me to take a gun into him so he can blow his brains against a wall as well?'

'Forget that. Mercer says he wants to talk to you.'

'What time is it?'

'Just after six.'

'For Christ's sake, I've been going non-stop for God knows how long. I don't know what day it is never mind what time it is. What good would I be? I couldn't even be sure of staying awake. I've told you all I know, you have enough now. Henderson must have coughed up his lungs as soon as you got him to the station.'

'Henderson's in hospital.'

'What's the matter with him?'

'He's in a psychiatric unit. We brought him in and he fell apart, drooling, making odd noises. He's no good to anyone at the moment. The initial diagnosis is that he's traumatised, deep traumatic shock. With care and medication he might be able to talk to us in two or three weeks, but that's just a maybe.'

'He's faking it.'

'No, he's in a bad way. You saw him at the villa, did it look like faking to you?'

He had a point.

'No.'

'The truth is, no one has any idea how long he'll be like that.'

'And if he starts to come out of it the first thing he'll think of is making it last, maybe making it look permanent.'

'Which is why we need Mercer to talk. He doesn't know about Henderson yet.'

'That his wife topped herself or that Henderson's gone doolally?'

'Both.'

Jimmy sagged. He would have to go, he knew that, but he didn't have to like going. Then he pulled himself together. Self-pity, an unlovely and useless emotion.

'What reason did he give? Why does he say he wants to talk to me?'

'He didn't. He just says he wants to talk to you before he'll talk to anyone else. We need you, Mr Costello.'

'Has Rosa talked?'

'Yes. She's giving her full co-operation. We let her walk past the cell Mercer was in, the door was open. They saw each other. It was like you said, as soon as she got to the interview room she gave us everything she knew.'

'Which was?'

'She was recommended by a man named Joseph McNally, somebody whom she knew to be a criminal, to play the part of a journalist for your friend George, the man you claimed was the London end. Some friend by the way.'

'I take them as they come.'

'She said she was going to get five thousand for killing Henderson.'

That got a small laugh out of Jimmy.

'She didn't know George very well, then, did she? So what you've got is Henderson in the booby hatch for we don't know how long, Rosa with a gun which you can prove was provided by Harry and saying she was sent by a George to kill Henderson, plus what I dug up in the UK?'

'Yes.'

'And you can't make a case with all that without me talking to Harry?'

'We can make parts of some cases, perhaps. But we want it all, including your friend George.'

'Take Harry down to a cell and stamp on his hands. He's got arthritis in both of them. He'll cough to anything if someone with boots dances on his fingers.'

'That's not a serious suggestion is it?'

It wasn't. But the way he felt it was close.

'All right. Send a car in an hour.'

'Why an hour?'

'Because I'm going to get a shower and something to eat and drink and have a piss and a crap. I've been to your interview room before. This time I want to be prepared. Harry's not going anywhere.'

Jimmy put the phone down then picked it up and dialled room service.

'Can I get some coffee and sandwiches? It doesn't

matter what sort, any sort. OK, thanks.' Then he got out of bed and went into the bathroom and started the shower. What was Harry up to? But he didn't bother to look for an answer. He'd find out soon enough, so why think about it? He tested the water and got in.

Harry was sitting in the interview room staring into space. It wasn't a new experience and he knew how to deal with it. You waited. He was wearing a loud, short-sleeved shirt with an orange, red, and purple pattern, the sort that got noticed even in Spain. He looked up as Jimmy came in.

'You took your fucking time.'

Jimmy came to the table and sat down opposite him.

'I'd have worn sun-glasses if I'd known you were going to wear the sunset for me. A bit loud isn't it?'

'Was it you who grassed me up?'

'Grassed you up about what?'

'You know what.'

'Harry, they've got you on the porn thing. They can probably make a good try on the Suarez killing. They've got you on supplying that bird Rosa with an illegal firearm which she was going to use to kill Henderson and as we speak she's co-operating like a good 'un in another interview room. They'll probably slip Jarvis's murder in there to tidy the books. Why not? It looks tailor-made for a fit-up. Then there's the tax you haven't paid on the money that's gone through the property business in Gibraltar and if there's any outstanding parking tickets and litter fines anywhere they'll probably add those. Which bit of all that do you think I grassed you up on?' Harry saw his point. 'They were already watching you before Rosa arrived. All they had to do was follow you when you went to get the gun and again when you dropped her off. Harry, you were dead in the water when you missed me the second time. That was when George decided you and Henderson were expendable and he began to wrap things up.'

258

'You know about George?'

'I was stupid. I didn't for a long time, but I do now.'

Harry was silent for a moment.

'What brought you into this? You're not still a copper. Where do you fit in?'

'How come it's you asking the questions, Harry? You're the one being held for questioning, I'm just a visitor. Why should I tell you anything?'

It was a fair question.

'You were always a fucking bastard, but mostly you were a straight fucking bastard, for a copper. You took your money but as I remember, you delivered what you got paid for.'

'Thank you, Harry, I shall treasure that thought. Now stop pissing me about and tell me why I've been dragged out of bed to come and talk to a villain who's too stupid to find a chair when everyone else knows the music stopped a long time ago.'

'Am I stitched up?'

'Tight as an auntie's constipated arsehole.'

'And that's straight up?'

'Rosa's told them everything she knows and Henderson is giving them the Hallelujah chorus with you as the featured soloist. I gave them Jarvis and Leicester, Tate and Wiston –'

'Who are the fuck are Tate and Wiston?'

'Only your publishers, Harry. For Christ's sake, didn't you even read the books you were supposed to have written?'

'I was never a big reader.'

'Anyway I found you weren't making smoking money out of your books so there had to be something else and I came up with the property scam.'

'It wasn't a proper scam. George said it made quite a bit of money even without what we put through it from this end.'

259

'Oh, I am pleased. So glad it was a good investment. Now I don't have to worry what George will do when he retires. He's provided for.' But Harry didn't do satire. 'Look, you're going down and you're going down hard. Rosa has given you to them, Henderson is giving you to them, I've given you to them, all you've got left to deal with is George.'

And that was it. Jimmy could see that was what Harry wanted to talk about.

'I was never a fucking grass.'

'No, you weren't. But you wouldn't be grassing him, he's well in the frame already and he's all you've got. Co-operate, give them the whole porn thing, the production end and the distribution, all of it. Henderson will give them the money side. Tell them George ordered the Suarez killing, he actually did, but they can't prove it unless you give it to them. George is closing down fast, make it easy for them and they can get him before he disappears up his own backside and they lose him. That'll be worth something, not much maybe, but like I say it's all you've got.' Harry looked round. 'Yes, they're listening, they're getting it all, but none of it can count in a court.'

'You sure?'

'I was a copper, of course I'm sure.'

Jimmy took out a small notebook and wrote something then passed it across the table. Harry read it. *Make it worth my while and when I testify my memory will go funny.* Harry pushed it back and Jimmy put it in his pocket. Jimmy started again.

'It was a good thing while it lasted, Harry. You must have been raking in a packet.'

'It was. We made a lot.'

Harry seemed pleased with the compliment. Jimmy gave him a big smile.

'Of course you did. But how can you spend it in a Spanish prison?'

Harry didn't like the smile.

'You don't change do you?'

'I change. I change my underwear every month, even if I don't need to. Well, are you ready to give me what I want?' Then very slowly and deliberately, 'Are you ready to co-operate?'

Things were moving in Harry's head, but slowly.

'How do I know you're on the level about George?'

'Because who do you think fucking sent me here to give you to the coppers while he gets it away on his toes with the money, that's how you know.'

'What?'

'George sent me, you stupid bastard. As soon as you told him I was here he started working out how to pull the plug on the whole thing and get out with the money. And me, Hawkshaw the great detective, goes to London, calmly walks into his boozer and asks for his help. I gave myself to him on a fucking plate. I bet he couldn't believe his luck when I walked into the Hind. He'd put the word out there was money for anyone who ever spotted me if I came back to London but I came in free of charge. It was like winning the lottery. After that he used me. He put the Rosa woman alongside me and just watched how quickly the whole thing surfaced. It was always a house of cards, once one card fell the whole thing had to come down. I did the leg work for him and he sat there and worked out how to do a runner leaving you and Henderson hanging out to dry.'

Harry's brain finally got the message.

'So when Jarvis got done it was really all over.'

'Yes.'

'So who the fucking hell did Jarvis?'

Jimmy threw his hands up.

'For Christ's sake, Harry, forget fucking Jarvis. Why does everyone go on about Jarvis? George is still in London sorting things out and my advice to you, my very strong advice, is to give everyone what they want and see that George gets nailed.' Jimmy's voice changed. 'But it only works if *everyone* gets what they want. You don't want to spend the whole of the rest of your life banged up in some Spanish gaol living on rice do you? And that's what you'll get, life. You'll fucking croak in some shit-hole of a Spanish prison cell. Give yourself a break, Harry, do the smart thing for once in your life, co-operate.'

Harry was weighing up his options. Correction, Harry was weighing up his *one* option. It didn't take him long. He made a sign and Jimmy got out the notebook and pencil and passed them across. Harry wrote something and pushed it back. Jimmy read it, put it in his pocket and nodded.

'OK, Jimmy, tell them I'll co-operate.'

'I think you've made a good choice. You won't come to trial for a while yet so maybe I'll come back and visit you. But I don't know what I'll be doing. I'll only come back it I find we've got more to talk about. If our business is done this should be good-bye.'

'Then you won't be back will you?'

Jimmy smiled and stood up

'That's all right then isn't it?'

Harry looked up at him, a big stupid man who understood violence and not much else.

'He turned out to be a devious bastard, that George. A right fucker.'

'He's clever, Harry, that's what George is and he always was. I should have remembered that. You were just muscle, a hard man, but violence doesn't last like brains. It gets old and it gets arthritis. But arthritis isn't something that affects the brain. George out-thought us both. In your case it wasn't difficult. As for me, I'm getting too old for this and George just pointed it out, that's all. See you, Harry.'

Jimmy left the interview room and the uniformed police officer who had been standing outside went in.

262

Jimmy walked down the corridor. Bloody crime writer! He'd had to print the note he'd written. But then, George hadn't chosen Harry for his handwriting. Or maybe it was the arthritis when he held a pencil. Jimmy knew he should have seen it earlier, George and Harry had always run with the same outfit.

Santos was waiting. Jimmy stopped and looked at him

'You heard?'

'Yes.'

Santos stood there.

'Well what are you waiting for? Go and get him.'

'What else went on. There were a couple of silences I didn't like.'

'I wrote a note to him,' Jimmy pulled out the notebook and handed over his and Harry's notes. Santos read them. 'Harry needed to know I was still bent, still on the take. It was the only way I could get him to trust me. If I'd stayed on the level he'd never have believed me enough to grass up George.'

Santos read the notebook. Jimmy held his hand out.

'Am I supposed to give you these back? It looks to me like you asked for money to lie at the trial and he's handing you twenty thousand to fix your testimony.'

'That's right, he is, and if you think I'm leaving evidence like that in some foreign copper's hands, one I hardly know from Adam, you're stupider than Harry, and Harry's very stupid. Hand it over or my memory will go very funny indeed, just like it says.'

Santos hesitated but the notebook came back and Jimmy pocketed it.

'What do you want it for?'

'What do you think? Harry won't need the money, not where he's going. It doesn't belong to anyone else and it's sitting there doing nothing.'

'But you'll need the key to the deposit box and that will be in his villa.'

'I know. But you can get me that.'

'Me?'

'Get me that key and I'll give you Jarvis's murderer.'

Santos stood silent for a moment.

'You know who it is?'

'I do, and if you get me the key I'll not only give you the killer but I think I can throw in the motive as well.'

Santos didn't like it but if he could get Jarvis's killer with sufficient motive to get a conviction everything would be neatly tied up.

'Will it get me a conviction?'

Jimmy had to think about it.

'Let me put it this way, if I'm right the sentence should be about as bad as it gets.'

'I don't need games. Do I get a conviction?'

'Do I get the key?'

Santos decided.

'OK, if it's there.'

'It'll be there and there'll be a guilty verdict as sure as God made little apples.'

'All right, but I want you gone. Until the trial I don't want you round here or even near until you're needed. But then I want you back with your memory working or –'

'That's OK, I don't want to hang about, I've had enough of this place, it's too bloody hot and too much happens. I'll give you a bell from the airport as soon as I know when I'm flying out. Now clear off into that interview room and listen to Harry sing. And get the fucking Met. to lift George before he disappears up his own –'

'Don't try and tell me how to do my job. Mr Costello.'

Jimmy watched Santos as he walked away to interview Harry. Then he left the police station and walked out into the mid-morning heat. He stopped and said to nobody in particular.

'Why not? Somebody fucking needs to.'

Chapter Thirty-four

Jimmy and Santos were sitting in one of the bars at Santander airport. Both had beers. Santos hadn't wanted to sit and have a drink but Jimmy insisted so he agreed, but he was still impatient.

'You've got your safe deposit key, now give me the killer.'

'I don't need to; you've got her already, or at least you've got her body. You got it yesterday after she blew her brains out.'

'Mrs Henderson?'

'That's right.'

Santos was surprised and it showed.

'Why would she kill Jarvis? If this is just some wild theory you made up to get that key, because if it is –'

'Right, I'll tell you what I think happened and how I think you can prove it. If you don't like it you can have the key back'

If you can break all my fingers to get it out of my hand, thought Jimmy.

Santos sat back in his chair.

'I'm listening, but it better be good.'

'It goes back to something Harry's publisher said. He said the first book was rubbish but they'd got better and the last one had something about it. Jarvis had no employment, nor any hobbies that we know of. What does a man like that do with his time?' Santos shrugged, it was Jimmy's story. 'He wrote the books Harry needed but I think he didn't just write Harry's books. I think he wanted to be a proper writer, that's how he filled his time, writing. I think Jarvis had been working on something of his own and I think it turned out to be worth publishing. If I'm right there'll probably be a copy of it on his computer and if you look through his papers there might even be a letter from a publisher in the UK, a proper publisher, maybe making him an offer or saying they're interested. If Jarvis suddenly saw the chance to be a real writer he'd want to be out of the porn game. As I once said to someone, you can be a hard-porn wholesaler or a successful writer, but not both, not at the same time. Jarvis was frightened of Harry and knew he wouldn't let him leave, not alive anyway. So if he wanted to negotiate his way out he wouldn't have gone to him, which leaves Henderson. He must have decided to try and get out through Henderson, told him that he would keep quiet about everything if they left him alone. He probably wanted Henderson to deliver that message to Harry and he'd arranged to be on his way before Harry could do anything about it. Suarez told me his passport and some money were by his bed and an airline ticket to Paris. He was about to run out on them.'

Santos was interested now.

'But if you're right that would give Henderson the motive, he wouldn't want Jarvis running out on them any more than Mercer and Henderson's no killer.'

'No he's not.'

'So what you're saying is that Henderson went to Mercer and –'

'No. I think when Jarvis went to Henderson and told him what he was going to do they argued. You've seen Henderson, he doesn't take pressure well. Being the one to have to tell Harry that Jarvis had skipped wouldn't appeal. It's easy to see how they'd argue. One way or another Henderson's wife must have found out. Maybe she heard them arguing or maybe Henderson spilled the whole thing to her after Jarvis had gone, either way she decided Jarvis had to be stopped. You've seen her, she liked her lifestyle and wasn't about to have it threatened. She knew if Jarvis skipped anything could happen. She couldn't sit still and risk her comfortable little life falling apart. She took the gun and paid a call on Jarvis. Jarvis wouldn't be afraid of her so when she asked for a cup of coffee or something he walked into the kitchen and she followed, probably talking. When they were in the kitchen she took the gun out of her handbag, put it to the back of his head, pulled the trigger and blew the top of his head off. She had a strong stomach, I'll give her that. Then she went home, put the gun back in the drawer, and waited to see what would happen.'

They sat in silence while Santos went over it.

'No. She wouldn't have risked it.'

'You saw her. You don't think she'd have risked killing Jarvis to save the life she had here? Look what happened when we asked about the gun and she knew it was over. She didn't think twice about topping herself.'

'No, she didn't.'

'Once she knew Jarvis was trying to walk away, why not kill him? He could be replaced. A new writer could be found and her comfortable, respectable life could all gone on. And there was no time to think of anything else.'

Santos thought about Dorothy Henderson. He hadn't seen much of her but what he had bore out Jimmy's description. She was not an ordinary sort of woman. But he still didn't buy into Jimmy's story.

'No, you're wrong. She shot herself because she would lose everything when Henderson went inside.'

'The cow shot herself because I told her I knew she'd done it.'

That really got in among Santos.

'How? How did you tell her that? I was there, I heard everything, you never said anything ...' Then the penny dropped. 'It was when you asked to see the gun.'

'That's right. There was no reason to see the gun, it didn't fit into any of the crimes you were hanging on Henderson. If I asked to see it then it could only be about Jarvis.'

Now Santos bought it.

'God, why didn't she throw it away?'

'Because, unlike Harry, she wasn't a professional. The gun Harry used on Suarez was in the ocean in short order after he'd used it, but she was neat and orderly and probably as mean as sin. She wouldn't throw away a pricey item like that. Anyway, if anyone had heard the shot or seen her and the police came asking questions she had already decided what she would do, and it certainly wasn't going to prison.'

Santos looked a bit shocked.

'You mean you knew she would blow her brains out but you still asked to see the gun?'

'I didn't know for sure, but it was a pretty safe bet.'

'For God's sake, why not wait and tell me and we could have got her and the gun?'

'Because she was an arrogant bitch. When we got there I wasn't going to say anything, I didn't care who shot Jarvis or why. I was only there because you made me go. I was satisfied to let her watch her husband get banged up and her lovely lifestyle melt away round her. But when she looked at me, when she told us to leave, I knew she'd planned something. Somehow, I don't know how, she would have seen to it that Henderson never got to court. She wasn't about to give it all up, she'd already killed to keep it, she'd find a way. So I asked my question and when I did she knew the game was up. Check the gun, ballistics will confirm it.'

'But how did you know, how did you work it out?'

'I used to be a detective, remember.'

'But there was no evidence, no forensics. You couldn't have known Jarvis had an offer from any publisher, you

268

never went near his house. How could you be so sure it was her?'

Now it was Jimmy's turn to shrug.

'Who else was there? There was no theft so it wasn't a break-in. The bullet went in low and came out high so whoever was behind him was shorter than him. She is.'

'And that's it? On that you let Dorothy Henderson blow her brains out?'

Jimmy felt a small knot of anger form against Santos in his guts, but he had the key and was almost on his way so he fought it down. Let Santos play the sanctimonious prick. It didn't matter. He took a drink.

'If it had been my case I would have checked who, among those who might in any way be connected to Jarvis, and that would be all British ex-pats, had gun permits. That would have given me the Hendersons. I would have got the gun, checked it and that would have given me the murder weapon which made it either him or her. I doubt she cleaned it so the prints on the gun would make it her. It's how you catch villains and get convictions. It's called fucking police work.'

Santos had the good grace to look sheepish.

'Maybe I was out of line saying I didn't need you to tell me how do my job. If you're right I needed you quite a lot.'

The knot in Jimmy's guts unwound, he looked at the departure board and saw his flight number had come up as ready for boarding.

'Proceed to gate four. That's me.' He got up. 'Well, do I give you back the key?'

'No, keep it,' Santos got up, 'but one last thing. Mrs Henderson's already dead. Why did you say we'd get a guilty verdict? Why lie?'

'I didn't. She was a practising Catholic. She committed suicide, she was prepared to put herself outside God's mercy. She was guilty as hell and refused to seek

269

forgiveness ,so hell is where she'll be now doing hard time and she'll go on doing it for ever. Happy endings all round.'

Santos obviously didn't see it that way.

'I'm not sorry to see you go, Mr Costello, but as you are going, have a good trip.'

'Thanks, I will.'

Jimmy walked away and Santos watched him go.

Neither had felt the need to shake hands.

Chapter Thirty-five

Jimmy walked into the Hind. He'd arrived in London the previous day but decided to find a hotel and get fully rested before he went to see George. He didn't want to be tired when they met. It was one o'clock and the pub was busy with lunches but George was sitting in his usual place with a cup of tea in front of him, reading his paper. Jimmy went to the table and sat down. George lowered the paper and smiled.

'Hello, Jimmy, nice to see you.'

He waved a hand at one of the bar staff then pointed to Jimmy.

'Will she remember it's Directors?'

'Oh yes, they're good girls, keen and clever with it. Why they come over here to do bar work is a mystery to me. They've probably both got degrees but they come here to do bar work. It's a funny old world.'

'They're not the only ones with degrees who do funny work, remember?'

'I wouldn't know, Jimmy, I just take people as they come.'

'How's things, George? Business still doing well?'

'Oh, so-so, you know. Make a bit, lose a bit. Much as usual. How's it been going with you?' He took a closer look at Jimmy's face. 'You been in the sun? You look a bit red round the edges.'

'I've been in Spain.'

'Oh yes. You went to Gibraltar, didn't you?'

'No, I went to Santander. I met a couple of your friends

271

there, Harry and Rosa.'

George shook his head. The beer arrived but Jimmy let it stand on the table.

'No, sorry, Jimmy, means nothing to me. I don't know any Harry or Rosa. I don't even know anybody called Henderson and I can prove it.' He gave Jimmy a grin. 'Go on, have a drink, there's nothing in the glass but beer.'

Jimmy picked up the glass and took a drink. Still the same old George.

'They both sang and they both used the same song sheet. Have the police been round?'

'The police? They visited and asked a few questions but I told you, I'm legit now. Almost.'

Jimmy watched him. So, he was clean, he'd made sure his end was all tidied up.

'You sorted out that property firm then?'

'Property firm? I think you'll find there is no property firm, not any more. There's nothing, Jimmy, you've wasted your journey if you've come to try and make trouble for me. Harry was never bright and Rosa, whoever she is ... well ,I don't know what she said of course, but I doubt she can back it up with any hard evidence.'

'What if I back her up?'

'Hearsay and circumstantial, nothing a court could do anything serious with. Any half-good brief would get it thrown out. Now if the police had something substantial, some real connection like a mobile phone of mine with a call record. But they haven't, have they?'

'Haven't they?'

'No, I don't own a mobile phone, don't like the things.'

'What was that you gave me in Ebbsfleet?'

'Did I give you anything in Ebbsfleet? I don't even remember going to Ebbsfleet with or without you. In fact I'm pretty sure I've never been to Ebbsfleet in my life.'

'And you can prove it.'

'No, but nobody can prove otherwise can they?'

'The CCTV cameras might help.'

'Think so?' Jimmy nodded. 'Wrong. What they'll show is my Jag with someone in it and you walking away. I doubt they'll have any kind of clear picture if the driver's face, but even if they did it wouldn't do them much good would it? Mind you, I hope I'm wrong. I hope they can identify the driver because the Jag was stolen that night. One of my staff reported it the next day. I was away myself, on business. They found the car a week later, but it was burned out. Pity, it was a nice motor. Still, it was insured, so no real loss.'

'I can say it was you driving.'

'Of course you can. And I can deny it. No, Jimmy, there's nothing solid in that direction.'

'The Spanish police have the mobile, I gave it to them, and inside it will say it's yours.'

'No, now there you're wrong, Jimmy. The inside will say it belongs to my cousin Eamon Doyle, he owned the Hind before me. My mother's older sister married an Irishman called Doyle.He was their son. You know I never even knew I had a cousin until someone told me that the Hind was owned by someone who looked dead like me so I came and had a look and it turned out we were cousins. Funny old world isn't it? I bought the pub off him just after Nat got given wings and a harp.'

Jimmy sat back and laughed out loud. One or two people looked.

'George, that's the biggest load of bollocks I've heard since I was told wanking sent you blind.'

George grinned.

'Of course it is, but you know the game, Jimmy, don't go for black and white in things like this, go for as many shades of grey as you can get. Tie the fuckers in knots and spin it all out. None of it will stand up but none of it can be knocked straight down or shoved out of the way. Not so much lies as endless half-truths. They've got Harry,

273

Henderson and Rosa bang to rights, why drag me in and risk the whole bloody shooting match? I got pulled by the local coppers and told my tales and pretty soon, when they saw what they'd got, what they could actually take into a court of law, we all went home. And that's how it will all pan out in Spain as well, Jimmy, I'll get left out of it and things will carry on pretty much the same as before. I never went inside because I was always careful. You don't …'

'I know, you've told me before, you don't need to be violent if you're clever.'

'And it's still true, not very violent and not often, only when necessary, when someone sticks their noses in where they're not wanted. When people do that they have to take what's coming to them don't they?'

Jimmy picked up the beer and took another drink. It was still good beer.

'I suppose so.'

'I knew you'd be sensible about things, you always knew the score and didn't bear a grudge. So, you staying in London or passing through?'

'Passing through. I thought I'd pop in and say, hello. Maybe ask a favour.'

'Ask away, Jimmy, anything I can do, you know that. Always ready to help a mate.'

'I need to prove I'm Harry.'

George didn't respond for a second.

'You need to prove you're Harry Mercer?'

'That's right.'

'Who to?'

'A bank.'

Jimmy could see he'd got George's interest.

'To do what?'

'Free information, George? That's a novelty. I need to be Harry for a visit to a bank. I can pay if you can make me into Harry for a day.' Jimmy waited a moment. He

didn't want to hurry this, to seem too pushy. He took a
drink. 'How much would it cost to make me Harry?'

George smiled.

'That depends on the money.'

'Who said anything about money?'

'You did, you told me it was about money when you
said you needed to be Harry to visit a bank. Why would
you want to be Harry except for money?' Jimmy said
nothing. 'If I do this I'll do it on a percentage basis, not a
straight fee.'

George waited and let him think. The way George
looked at it, Jimmy was a long time out of it and London
wasn't a place he had any friends. He could try elsewhere
but he doubted he would want to deal with strangers. And
he was probably keen to get the money and get out. It had
to be a fair sum to make Jimmy come all the way back to
get it.

George knew he held the stronger hand so he waited.

Finally Jimmy spoke.

'What per cent?'

'Well, it's got to be a fair sum for you to be here, and I
can guess what you're going to do for Harry, you're going
to fix the evidence and you always put a high price on
doing that. Mind you, it was always something you did
well, I'll give you that, you gave value for money. With
your evidence wobbly Harry might even get off the
murder. It has to be a neat sum doesn't it, you never came
cheap and Harry really needs help on this one. I don't
think you'd do anything for him for less than,' he thought
for a second, 'fifteen grand.'

Jimmy gave him a smile.

'In your dreams, George, try and think with your brain
not your wallet.'

'No, I'm close. I know Harry and I know you. Harry's
in deep shit so you'll have screwed him. Don't try to kid a
kidder, Jimmy, you've been out of touch too long to be

any good at it.'

'Maybe I've been out of touch too long to know the value of things. Ten grand, in a safety deposit box. I need to prove I'm Harry to lift it. Well, what's your end going to be?'

'Only twenty-five per cent. Cheap really, but like I said, always happy to do a good turn for a mate.'

'Two and half grand for a passport? I really must be out of touch. When can you have it?'

'Twenty-four hours after you give me a decent likeness of that ugly boat race of yours.'

Jimmy stood up.

'Where can I get one?'

'There's a booth in the WHSmith down the road. Five minutes' walk.'

'I'll be right back.'

George watched him leave the pub. He got up and went through the door marked 'Staff only'. Just over fifteen minutes later Jimmy came back and George was back at his table. Jimmy came and sat down and pushed a strip of four photos of himself across.

'These OK.'

George left them on the table.

'You won't need them, Jimmy.'

'Oh yes, why not?'

'Because I'm going to do like I said, I'm going to do you a favour. I'm going with you to the bank and I'll collect your money for you.' He put his hand inside his jacket and pulled out a passport and threw it on the table. Jimmy picked it up. The face looking out was George's but the name was Harold Reginald Mercer. 'I sometimes needed to be Harry for business reasons and Harry couldn't always be popping across to London or wherever, so I had that made up a while back. It'll do the job.'

Jimmy put the passport down, George leaned across, picked it up, put it away and sat back. Jimmy picked up the strip of photos and pushed them into his jacket pocket.

'And what if I don't want you to pick it up for me?'

'Then you don't pick it up at all.'

George waited, he still held all the cards.

'No, nothing doing, George. I'll find somebody else.'

He started to get up.

'Sit down, Jimmy, and use your brains. You must have the key to the deposit box and you know which bank. But I've got the ID. If we do it now we both know where we are. Neither of us can pull a fast one. If you walk out of here I'll find you and send a few lads and have them take the key off you and get the name of the bank. Knowing you, you won't co-operate so you'll get hurt, maybe badly hurt. I'll get the key but maybe not the name of the bank; if you get stubborn you might even finish up in a box. All that does is get you dead and me a useless key.' Jimmy sat down again. 'That's better, that's using your brains. So, do we go and get our money.'

Jimmy sat for a minute. George let him think, even though there was nothing to think about.

Jimmy stood up.

'We'll go now and take a cab.'

George stood up and came round the table.

'Sensible man. How much is it really?'

'Twenty.'

That got a big smile.

'Sneaky bugger. But I'll still only take twenty-five per, after all we're mates, aren't we?'

And they left the pub to look for a cab.

The bank was busy, there were queues at all the cashiers' windows and a queue at the information desk. Jimmy stood in the middle of the bank at a sort of table with forms and pens on it. He had a form in front of him and held one of the pens trying to look inconspicuous. Every so often he wrote something on the form. Nobody looked in the least bit interested in him. He looked at his watch. George had been gone ten minutes. He should be back soon. Jimmy watched the door George had gone through with one of the staff. It opened and George came out with a carrier-bag. He walked towards Jimmy, smiling. Two men detached themselves from the information queue and quickly walked to George, two others left the table where Jimmy had been fiddling with his form. They went to George and stood each side of him. George stopped as one of them took hold of his arm. Jimmy put down the pen and joined them. George wasn't smiling any more but Jimmy was. One of the two form filling men took out his warrant card.

'Chief Inspector Hatcher, sir. May I see what you have in the bag?' People in the queues waiting to get to the cashiers began to take notice. George looked round but there was nowhere to go. He held out the carrier bag. DCI Hatcher took it and looked inside. People in the queues waiting to get to the cashiers began to take notice. George looked round but there was nowhere to go. He held out the carrier bag and the man who had shown him the warrant, DCI Hatcher, card took it and looked inside.

'Can you explain how you came by this money?' George didn't reply. His eyes never left Jimmy's face. 'May we see some identification, sir? A passport perhaps.' George took the passport from the inside of his coat and handed it over. Hatcher opened it. 'And are you Mr Harold Reginald Mercer, sir? It says here you are.'

George didn't answer. There was nothing for him to say. But Jimmy felt like talking.

'You're clever, George, but you're a villain which means you're also greedy. Harry believed I'd take his money and it made him trust me because he thought he could buy me. You made the same mistake and it's going to put you away for a long time. You're clever, George, but the trouble is you're too clever.'

'Fuck you.'

278

Now the men beside George had both his arms held firmly.

'No, George, you're the one who's fucked this time.' Jimmy turned to Hatcher. 'I'm off now, Chief Inspector. You've got all you want.' He turned back to George. One of the men had a pair of handcuffs out. 'See you, George, or, on second thoughts, no, I probably won't.'

Jimmy walked towards the exit, George, with his hands handcuffed behind his back and with his police escort, followed. Outside there were two police cars. Jimmy turned left and headed towards the nearest Tube station which was about ten minutes walk away. He didn't look back. He wanted to remember George just as he had last seen him, handcuffed, with a copper on each arm and another holding the evidence.

Chapter Thirty-six

'I'm back.'

'Mr Costello,' her voice, even on the phone, had ice on it, 'I hope you have a very good explanation why you have been away for so long and why you switched your phone off every time I called you.'

'Yes to both.'

'And those explanations would be?'

'First, I was busy doing what you sent me to do, and second, I didn't want to talk to you because you would tell me to come back.'

'I would indeed have insisted on your return. As I remember, I *did* insist on your returning to Rome.'

'See? I told you, and I didn't want to be impolite and have to tell you to go and boil your head so I switched off my phone when you called.'

There was a silence.

'Where are you now?'

'I'm in my apartment.'

'I think you should come and see me.'

'So do I. I'll bring my list of expenses.'

'Hmm. We'll talk about that among other things.'

'When shall I come?'

'Three o' clock this afternoon.'

The phone went dead. Jimmy put it down on the table by his chair. It was eleven o'clock, mid-morning. He had flown in from London the previous evening at seven and come straight home, made himself a small meal and gone to bed. He'd woken half an hour ago, showered and gone down to the café on the street below his apartment to have a light breakfast. Now, sitting in his own apartment, he felt almost human for the first time in over a week. He was glad to be home. He'd slept well but was still tired. He put his hand to his side and pressed gently. He was mending nicely. He had four hours to kill and nothing special to do so he phoned his doctor. He wasn't an especially good doctor but Jimmy hadn't chosen him for his professional skill, he chose him because he spoke good English and Jimmy's brain stubbornly refused to make any serious progress in becoming competent in the Italian language. When the doctor's receptionist put him through he explained that he had been abroad and cut himself badly in his side. It had been stitched and seemed to be healing but he wanted someone to take a look at it. He got an appointment at two o'clock for that day. He'd only been to the doctor twice before but on both occasions had been able to phone up and get an appointment for the same day. That was what made Jimmy think he couldn't be much good as a doctor.

Jimmy stood up, went to the window and looked out into the sunny, tree-lined street below. He felt restless, his mind wasn't like his body, it couldn't just close down and accept the much-needed rest. It needed to wind down more slowly. The day looked like being hot but he decided he wanted a walk, to stroll to some quiet, shady bar and sit down with a beer. After that he'd walk some more and find somewhere to get some pasta for lunch. Then he'd go to the doctor. His mind, still restless, flitted to his coming meeting with McBride.

Six months ago she had pulled him out of Copenhagen. She didn't have to do that, she could have left him to the Danish police and their Intelligence Service. But she had got him out and offered him a sort of job. She had told him he would be her eyes and ears in places where the Catholic Church got into the kind of trouble it didn't want anybody

281

looking into except itself. Like the Santander thing. That had been his first real job and he had the very strong feeling he'd bollixed it up, at least bollixed it up as far as Professor McBride was concerned.

The trouble with her was, you never knew exactly what she wanted and he had used his own judgement. Today, at three, he would find out just how good his own judgement had been. Until then he'd try to settle, to stroll and not think too much.

Jimmy's apartment was in a pleasant part of Rome, the Prata, not far from the Vatican. It suited him, it was quiet, expensive, and dull. Each morning he would get up, breakfast and then go to Mass and after Mass go to a bar near the church for coffee. The church he used was a half-an-hour away. He had chosen it because it gave him a good walk each morning. After he'd had lunch somewhere he liked to come home for a rest and then, in the afternoon, he went out for another walk and a beer. It was a quiet routine and now he wanted to get back to it. The Santander thing served to remind him, if he needed reminding, just how much he didn't want any more excitement in his life.

He looked at his watch and decided that he wouldn't stroll aimlessly, he'd walk to his church, go in and light a candle and say a prayer for Suarez. It wasn't much but he felt he owed her at least that. He collected what he needed and then left the apartment.

It was as he had suspected when he'd looked out of the window, it was indeed hot, but being back on familiar territory made up for it. He put his mind in neutral until he arrived at the big old church and went inside. The interior was dark after the bright sunshine but his eyes quickly got used to it. He lit his candle and said his prayer.

'Dear God, look after her and don't hold anything against her. I think she was trying to help, maybe she saw what I couldn't see, that I needed someone. I don't know how she did, if she did, seeing as I didn't know it myself and you certainly never told me. Anyway, I let her down, I got her involved. Don't you let her down as well.'

And that was that. What else could he do? He left the church and went to a nearby bar, sat inside away from the sun, and had a beer. What had happened between him and Suarez? And why did he care? From what he had been told by others all those years ago in pubs and bars when they were boasting about their exploits, the whole idea seemed to be not to care. So was it just a casual, sexual encounter? A one-night stand. In all the many years of their marriage he had never been unfaithful to Bernie so he had no idea how these things worked. As far as sex was concerned he might as well still be sixteen. Of one thing he was sure, it might be classed by his Church as a sin, but it hadn't been wrong.

Except that it killed her. That bit was wrong.

A man about his own age came in and sat at a table nearby and nodded to him. This was the bar he used for coffee after Mass each day so he knew a few of the regular faces well enough to smile to or nod or occasionally exchange some simple remark. His Italian wasn't good enough for conversation above or beyond the simple things. Not that it mattered, because he didn't want company and he certainly didn't want friends. He sat thinking. It was funny how, once everything was over, you noticed things, things you missed at the time. He should have spotted George as the London end when he was first talking to Rosa. She said George had told her there were already bodies. Plural, bodies. But he hadn't told George about Jarvis or Suarez, only the bloke who come after him with the knife. One body, but George told Rosa bodies. That meant George knew about Jarvis and probably about Suarez. And then she said George told her that Harry had sent a bloke to stick a knife in him. He hadn't told George that Harry sent the bloke yet Rosa had sounded as if George had been very definite. How could George be sure unless he was mixed up in it? But he'd missed it all and it had nearly bloody killed him. He wasn't going to be much good to McBride if he missed things like that too often. Still, better late than never and it was all over now, except meeting with McBride, so he finished his beer, put some coins on the table and left.

Despite the heat he decided to walk, it would take him an hour if he strolled and he could get another cold beer somewhere on the way if he wanted to get out of the sun and fill in the time. He thought best when he was walking and wanted to go over what he would say in the coming interview. He had the very strong feeling she was not going to be a happy bunny when they met. Not at all a happy bunny. He set off trying to keep as much as possible to any shade that was going, heading for the doctor's surgery.

At three Jimmy stopped outside the modern office block. He felt his side. The doctor had said the stitches should come out and had done the job there and then. Now the thing felt a bit sore. Whether this was normal or due to the doctor Jimmy didn't know. He went through the main door, out of the heat into the cool of the air-conditioned reception.

'James Costello to see Professor McBride, Collegio Principe.'

The girl began the same routine as she always did, she checked a screen then picked up a phone.

'Signor Costello to see you, Professore.'

She put the phone down, made a visitor's badge for him and handed it over. Jimmy slipped the cord over his head and put the plastic identification into his shirt pocket.

'You know the way?'

Jimmy knew the way. He went to the lift and when it came headed for the top floor. He arrived at the door and knocked. A voice answered his knock.

'Come in.' Jimmy went in. Professor McBride looked

at him. There was no smile of welcome. 'Please sit down.'
Jimmy pulled a white envelope out of his back pocket and
sat down. He put the envelope on the desk and pushed it to
Professor McBride. 'Your letter of resignation, a written
apology, or a bribe to get you off the hook?'

'My expenses.'

She pushed the envelope to one side.

'We'll get to that, perhaps. Now, why did you stay
away so long, why did you not take any of my calls, and
why did you go to London?'

'You sent me to do a job. I stayed until it was done.
You wouldn't have wanted me to come away with only
half the work done, would you?'

'As I remember it I sent you to talk to a Mr Arthur
Jarvis about a report I received. Mr Jarvis was dead when
you got to Santander. You were told to talk to Fr Perez and
then return. Why did you not return to Rome when you
were instructed to do so?'

'Because that wouldn't have got the job done.'

'Your job was to ascertain whether the story Jarvis told
to Fr Perez about a senior cleric being a member —'

'Of the ETA central whatever it was. I know. But that
was what I was told to do. It wasn't the job I was sent to
do.'

She looked at him for a moment.

'Explain the difference.'

'I was told to go and talk to Jarvis. That was what I was
told to do. The job I was sent to do was help convince
ETA that the senior Catholic cleric who was one of their
inner council was in danger of being blown.'

They both sat in silence.

'I see. Go on.'

'Shall I begin at the beginning?'

'Does this fairy story have a beginning?'

'All good stories have a beginning. They also have a
middle and an end.'

'Then begin at the beginning.'

'Someone finds that a senior Catholic cleric is an inner member of a terrorist group, operating at the very heart of the organisation. I don't know who or how but it doesn't matter. Problem – what do you do? Arrest him? No good unless you've got him absolutely bang to rights. And it's very rare to get the very top people in things like this bang to rights even when you know who they are. He doesn't do any of the actual bombing or shooting so it's not easy to get a conviction. And he can't be picked up and interrogated by men who keep his head under water in between beating the shit out of him and not letting him sleep. And he can't be assassinated because he's a senior Catholic churchman, one of the untouchables, very naughty but one of our own. But nor can he be left in place, nobody wants that. The politicians don't like it, the Church doesn't like it, Spanish Intelligence doesn't like it, nobody likes it. Everybody wants it solved but no one knows how to solve it.' Jimmy stopped. 'That's the beginning.'

'Is that where you come in?'

'No, that's where you come in.'

'Indeed?'

'The problem gets passed on. Everyone turns to someone with experience of sorting out Church-related messes, especially the tricky ones. Someone approaches the Collegio Principe and the thing gets dropped on your desk. How to get him out without everything going public and turning nasty? Now we come to the middle. An insignificant retired priest in Santander gets told to write a letter to the Bishop's secretary. He should say that he has been told that a senior Catholic cleric is an inner member of ETA. But he must create a source for the information which will make it absolutely unbelievable. The story has to come out into the open but it has to be completely discounted as nonsense by anyone who looks into it. Fr

Perez came up with what seemed to him the perfect man, his friend Jarvis. Perez writes his letter. The secretary tells the Bishop and the Bishop puts it in the bin, or forwards it to Rome where it's duly ignored as nonsense, it doesn't matter which. What matters is that you send me to talk to Jarvis. He was supposed to deny all knowledge of the information, which was true, of course. I would then talk to Perez who would stick to his story but have nothing at all to back it up. Just to make sure all this gets properly noticed you tell the police I'm coming and fill them in about my past and suggest I should not be made welcome. When they come and talk to me you say, go on, give your full co-operation, tell them everything and what you end up with is a whole lot of people who have been told that I have come to find out if a senior Catholic cleric is a key man in ETA, but told in such a way that none of them believe a word of it.'

'Doesn't that make it all a bit pointless?'

'Oh no. You see the message wasn't meant for any of them, not the police or the Bishop or Spanish Intelligence and certainly not for Rome. The message was for ETA. They were the only ones who would believe it because they knew it was true. And with so many people knowing about it they would certainly get to hear. Once ETA hears about it they know your churchman is compromised so he has to get out and cut all ties. Job done. Where is he now by the way?'

'In South America. He put in a rather sudden application to be allowed to go on the foreign missions. I believe he was sent to a particularly dangerous part of Colombia. When did you realise what was going on?'

'I think it probably started when Inspector Suarez turned up. It was a good plan, if Jarvis hadn't been murdered it would have worked. It was a pity he was mixed up in Mercer's porn racket.'

'But why did you go on? You were supposed to stay

287

only long enough to make the police aware of Jarvis's supposed information. Why didn't you just do as you were told? '

'Because I was sent to do a job and that's what I did.'

'But it wasn't what I told you to do.'

'I know, you told me what I should do, but you didn't tell me what I was doing. I had to work that out for myself.'

'Good heavens, Mr Costello, can you never leave things alone? Do you always have to work things out for yourself? You nearly got yourself killed. You certainly got Inspector Suarez killed. And for what? Your job was done as soon as you told the police why you were in Santander and certainly after you talked to Fr Perez. There was no need to go on. Why did you?'

That was a good question. Why did I go on? What did I get out of it?

'When I told you about Jarvis you told me to co-operate, to act as an observer. So I stayed on. I was only doing what you told me to do.'

'To observe. I needed to know what was going on. I didn't want you to go out and take on the London underworld single-handed. I just wanted to know what was going on, to be sure enough had been done.'

'I don't like loose ends and neither does anyone else when a copper's been killed. Once Suarez was dead I couldn't leave it alone. If I'd walked away, it would have been someone else doing the digging. Who knows what they might have found? I had to close the whole thing down, get a result on Jarvis and see that it was all finished and tied up. Perez is an old man, a priest, not some ex-villain like Harry Mercer. He would have blown up if anyone had questioned him properly. It had to be me doing the questioning to keep him well out of the frame. He hadn't lied, at least not a lie of his own. All he'd done was tell someone else's lie. He was a frail old man who had only done what he had been told. He'd spill the whole story if anyone put pressure on him. He was your loose end and he could unravel the whole thing. That's what I was doing, looking after Perez, making sure your clever lie worked like it was supposed to.'

McBride thought about it and knew he was right.

'So now do we get to the end of your story?'

Jimmy nodded.

'Now we get to the end. I worked out what was going on, why and how and who was involved. I gave it to the local police all wrapped up. Nobody is looking for anything else. No-one will talk to Fr Perez and he can get on with his retirement. Once it was all finished, properly finished, I came home. The job I was sent to do was done. The end.'

They sat for a moment. Then she picked up the envelope and opened it and read what was inside it.

'Oh no. I can't approve this, it's far too much. My budget for this operation couldn't possibly include all this.'

'It's all legitimate expenses.'

'A candle, five Euros?'

'It couldn't be a cheap candle.'

She read some more.

'Sheets?'

'Blood on them, my blood. I doubt they would have washed clean so I left the money to replace them. They belonged to Suarez's cousin or brother, I forget which. He was doing me a favour.'

And they sat in the office and went through Jimmy's expenses. Jimmy was sure he would get his money, the expenses were all legitimately incurred. He hadn't fiddled anything, not broken faith; he wasn't bent any more, just a bit more broken.

For more information about
Accent Press titles
Please visit

www.accentpress.co.uk

Unholy Ghost
James Green

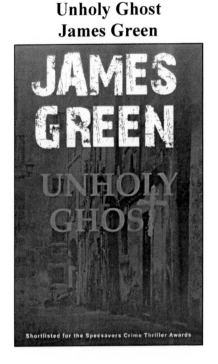

Fourth in the Jimmy Costello crime thriller series
shortlisted for the Specsavers Crime Thriller Awards

Jimmy Costello, corrupt ex-copper and now fixer for
the Catholic Church, always liked Paris, but never got
the chance to spend time there. Now his boss in
Rome wants him to go back. It's a simple job: find
the missing owner of a piece of valuable property.
But Jimmy's not the only one looking.
What is he looking for and who else wants it so
badly? No one seems to have the answers. This time
Jimmy is on his own.

Lightning Source UK Ltd.
Milton Keynes UK
UKOW01f1441011216
288932UK00001B/6/P